PERPETUAL
MOTION

GRAEME
GIBSON

SEAL BOOKS
McClelland and Stewart-Bantam Limited
Toronto

All of the characters in this book are fictitious and any resemblance to actual persons living or dead is purely coincidental.

*This low-priced Seal Book
has been completely reset in a type face
designed for easy reading, and was printed
from new plates. It contains the complete
text of the original hard-cover edition.*
NOT ONE WORD HAS BEEN OMITTED.

PERPETUAL MOTION

*A Seal Book / published by arrangement with
McClelland and Stewart Limited*

PRINTING HISTORY

McClelland and Stewart edition published June 1982.

Seal edition / January 1984

ISBN 0-7704-1842-2

PRINTED IN CANADA

COVER PRINTED IN U.S.A.

U   0 9 8 7 6 5 4 3 2 1

For Peggy and Jess

Acknowledgements

The author would like to thank the Canada Council, the Scottish Arts Council and the Arts Council of Ontario for their invaluable help in buying time for this book.

He would also like to thank, among others, Phoebe Larmore, Dennis Lee, Carolyn Moulton, Peter Pearson and David Young, for their continuing faith and encouragement.

". . . but what I mean is this: you, who took part, could you foresee everything? No, and neither could I, who did not take part. Perhaps engagement and detachment are equally blind and helpless, and in this. . . Although there must be, of course, some difference. In short. . ."

— *The Death of Artemio Cruz*
Carlos Fuentes

PART ONE: 1860

Chapter One

". . .and let me not be ashamed of my hope."
— Psalm 119

I

With the rushing of wings, darkness gathered in the forest behind him. Robert Fraser stretched, rubbed his head with both hands, and cautiously arched his back to ease the pain.

Late that morning when his ploughshare had caught and held fast, he'd cursed the bloody rocks, the tree stumps, the roots and the land. Ned and Smoke had paused, then soothed by his voice leaned back into their harness with the uncertain excitement of animals remembering previous defeats. He'd strained against the handles, coaxing, driving with his legs and bearing down until he felt the obstruction lifting. He watched incredulously as it broke the surface, an enormous yellow bone rising to meet him. It was as long and thicker than his leg and for an instant he heard it like breath escaping the body. "Whoa," he shouted at the horses, recoiling as the bone shuddered against the mouldboard. Smoke was trembling, prancing as if the earth had begun to scorch her feet. Even Ned was agitated. Feeding them strands of tobacco, massaging and pulling their ears, he whispered a confidence he scarcely felt.

After scraping mud in strips from along its length, crouching beside it at last, he cleaned both ends. He worked methodically. Poking at it with his belt knife, he decided it was the leg bone of an elephant, it had to be! He knew about elephants, astonishing creatures with small dark men riding on their heads. Once in Toronto he'd discovered that an elephant had left the previous day for Montreal. After dinner the men had recounted how a handsome young woman in costume had permitted herself to be encircled by the animal's sinuous trunk and then, to the astonishment of the crowd, she'd been lifted high in the air where she gracefully waved her arms and arched her back. Patting his waistcoat smooth with both hands, one had described how the young woman, now supine upon a Moorish carpet, had commanded the beast to rest its foot directly on her face. Nobody had ever seen anything like it and from time to time she comes to Fraser in dreams, a slim and pretty woman, neat in her brilliant costume, a simple tension in her arching back and loins — she postures elegantly, her arms beating the air like wings.

His pipe lit, he'd contemplated the bone for the better part of half an hour, in a welcome drying wind that burst from the treetops, gathered momentum across his field and whipped the smoke away from his mouth almost before he exhaled. With strands of dirty hair slapping his forehead and cheek, his trousers trembling the length of his calves, he crouched in concentration, his body folded down upon a rock. The bone rested across three furrows, with the shadows of clouds rushing on the land. He didn't see the straggle of wild pigeons shoot low over his field, nor hear the querulous shriek of a hawk somewhere in the forest beyond his fence. Fearing an evil omen, as if with spring the earth had cast up a warning, he tried to understand if he should bury it again. . . .

Lifting the bone impulsively, cradling it like an infant or a corpse, he heard it again: a telluric sigh, an infinitely resigned and mournful breath that resisted him as he straightened, weighed him down as he struggled onto the unworked ground at the edge of the bush. Releasing the bone, stepping back as it fell, he waited; nothing more happened. Fetching his shovel he drove it into the earth, to uncover another bone almost immediately. And then a third. One after the other he placed them on the ground by the first, meticulously reconstructing what he'd begun to disinter.

And so the day had progressed with the growing certainty an elephant could not have come to die here beneath his land. The bones he found were too old, too porous; he could have crushed the smaller vertebrae in his hands. Whatever the beast, it had been waiting long before that day six years earlier when Joshua Willow, the half-breed, had stopped and said, "She starts here and runs to the stream." Robert Fraser would never forget that moment. Just twenty-four years old, he'd stood on his land for the first time, and it had been indistinguishable from everything else on the route. The monotony of the bush was overwhelming; it more than diminished, it threatened to absorb him, transform him into a thing, an object like the birds. He'd left Mad River with Joshua just after dawn and for five hours they had walked in the silence of a heart beating without movement or sound: each tree and tangle of bush was like the next, each turn in the path endlessly repeated what he had just seen; it was as if a dark cloth was being dragged across his eyes. Vegetation caught at his clothes, brushed his hands and face as if to hold him, to enclose him with tendrils and take root. While air had moved in sunlight among the treetops, the forest floor was damp and still.

Flat-faced and silent, almost disapproving, Joshua Willow had watched Fraser stand appalled, barely able to hear the water he could not see; and somewhere to the north and west, less than a hundred paces from them, this intricate and marvellous cage of bones had been lying even then just below the surface of a small clearing in the forest.

With the rushing of wings, darkness gathered in the forest behind him. The wind subsided, leaving the earth unnaturally still. The noise of his breath, the fatigue of the body inside his clothes, the sudden rasp of his shovel against another immense bone — these now familiar sounds thundered in his ears like blood. High above him, torn and ragged clouds streamed northward as he dropped once more to his knees on the wet earth. Clearing carefully with his hands and belt knife, following the hard plunging curve of bone, he encountered a ridge that must have been the brow and then the first of two gaping sockets; both of them, indeed the entire skull, were clogged with dirt. After excavating the interior, he rolled it out of the shallow pit and manoeuvred it into place among the disinterred and reconstructed maze of bones spread out on the tangle of last year's growth.

Another clutch of pigeons circled rapidly over the forest, to alight in some beech trees at the other end of his fence. This time he heard the urgent wings and as he turned to watch them land he saw a larger flock away to the south. The birds in the wood had begun to call plaintively; half a dozen flew down to perch on the fence, their voices trilling, echoing curiously in his head.

With the distant sound of a gun from Casey's, he returned to the pit. Dragging an ochre tusk to the skull, he imagined a great beast moving irresistibly, bulling its way in the forest, the angular ribs, each separate vertebra in a line, the empty sockets, those grinding teeth bigger than his fist, all of it clothed again, rising on massive legs. . . .

Finally, climbing to sit on his fence, filling his pipe and immensely weary, feeling the silent flight of bats about his head, he faced the grotesque jumble of yellowed bones. Light convulsed beyond the forest; yellow and orange it swelled to a sombre green, a shaft stabbed brightly up, throwing the tops of trees into relief before vanishing like lightning. Pausing to relight his pipe he heard the winnowing of wings falling above him; and the night wind, setting leaves in random motion, breathed on his face. Reaching for the ground with his foot, gingerly climbing down, pressing both hands into the small of his back, carefully he twisted and stretched, chewing the stem of his pipe until his muscles relaxed, the pain subsided.

"That's it," he said. By Jesus, it can be done. "I'll do it!"

II

Just before noon Annie Birdwood arrived with Joshua to preside at Mary Fraser's childbed. Uncommonly pale, she greeted Robert with a thin smile, an imperceptible squeeze of her hand. "She's not begun yet, has she?" He shook his head. "Relax then," suddenly laughing. "She will soon enough."

A gust of wind moved in the forest as Joshua Willow, gesturing with the hook where his left hand should have been, went to shoot pigeons as if that was his only business. And now the wind shivered young fruit trees and set Robert's wind machines clattering in the yard. Atop a pole by the gate, flapping its wooden wings, a rooster with blue eyes bounced mechanically; while on another, a team of white-washed horses trod without progress, the stridulate wheels of their wagon turning in the air. The models rose and fell; driven by whirring cedar blades they squeaked and clacked, idiotically repeating each gesture as Mary appeared, her belly filling the door. Hens pecked with worn beaks, tapping wood on wood; sows jerked spasmodically from side to side; a donkey (the size of a small dog) dropped its head and kicked repeatedly with hinged legs; and farther from the house a lean creature, it struggled erect, the lower jaw flipped open and a whistling shriek issued from the faded mouth. . . .

Mary's labour began during dinner as if she'd been waiting for her mother. The child gave a cry inside her, a muffled declaration that straightened her in her chair, forcing sweat to her forehead and under her pale eyes. While Annie Birdwood hustled her upstairs, he tried to recall if she'd been different that morning but couldn't remember. As her belly had grown over the months, so had his confusion; he'd watched the skin stretching like an animal's in bloat, like hide drying on a drum, and felt the body convulsing within her body, tentatively at first, then violently so that lumps shifted beneath the skin's violet surface, and he stopped looking at her. He knew how it was done with animals; he'd presided at the birth of pigs. Customarily he tied ropes to the protruding feet of calves and pulled them out; he'd reached up into heifers to seize a slippery foot. Is that what midwives did? He couldn't imagine how it was with women. Cows at a difficult birth lie panting, dumb, their swollen bellies heaving; they grunt in pain and sometimes bellow, their tongues lolling over yellow teeth.

He was splitting wood for the stove when Annie came to him and said, as he knew she would, "I read the waters."

A vein pulsed at her temple and the planes of her skull shone beneath her face. "And they speak of trouble." He sank his axe into the chopping block and turned to her, resigned. She had dashed spring water into the cracked basin so it swirled against the clock, and she stared for signs, for portents, only she could see. "Not right away. She'll be all right, so she will. The baby too. But later. . ." Along the road Dr. Tom Sanderson appeared, a small dark figure on a swayback horse, followed by the Caseys on foot. "They speak of trouble."

"How so?" Shooting by the beaver meadow, Joshua was moving closer to the bones. His hook looped to the barrel with a rawhide thong; he'd scarcely miss a bird.

"Never you mind." Annie's fingers fluttered gently on the back of Robert's hand. "We're best not knowing these things."

"Good day to you both," cried the doctor, still at a distance, his voice reedy, slightly mocking in tone.

"But, Jesus Christ. . ." Robert's voice overlapped. Why have you told me then? Her eyes like egg whites. Why have you told me? She tried to squeeze his hands. It's God's will, she seemed to be saying, be brave, be brave. . . He wrenched free, turning to greet the others, but Annie spoke first.

"You'll not be needed here, Tom Sanderson. So don't think that you are. And you, Robert, bring a load of that wood. We'll be wanting it before morning." Bustling among wind machines that were momentarily still, she called back over her shoulder: "Come along, Missus Casey, we've work to do. . . ."

Drifting like tall ships, thunderclouds gathered in the west. A flock of pigeons darted erratically behind the barn as Barbara Casey, quick as a hen, scurried into the house.

"Well, at least you'll offer us a drink, Robert Fraser, eh? Hah! It's your estate after all." Sliding from the horse,

Dr. Tom dug enthusiastically at his crotch. "Christ, she's bony." Laughing shrilly like a child he added, "Stella here, the nag. . . I didn't mean, oh no sir, not the old woman, you wouldn't catch me riding. . . Eh?" He winked and spat. " 'You won't be needed here, Tom Sanderson!' I'll tell you boys. . ."

"That Joshua I heard shooting?" Strong as an ox, and often angry, Will Casey had the voice of a boy.

"He's a devil with a gun all right." Still rummaging in the crotch of his voluminous trousers, Sanderson showed his yellow teeth. "Myself, as you know. . .I couldn't hit a barn if I was inside it." He grinned fiercely, knowing some believed he'd murdered the corporal, dropping him with a single shot to the back of his head.

Light was fading rapidly, the wind gusting as the storm approached; colours draining out of objects left them flat among pullulating shadows. The men settled themselves by the barn, listening to the clatter of the machines and thunder, full-throated, menacing beyond the enclosing walls of the forest.

"More often than not, a good storm like this'll bring them on." Nodding to the doctor's words, Casey raised the bottle and drank; his armpit and the side of his shirt were black with sweat.

"That's true enough with cattle beasts," he said, putting the bottle in Dr. Tom's outstretched hand.

"You mark my words. . ." The doctor filled his mouth and swallowed quickly. "It won't be long now."

Robert sat with his hands between his knees on an upturned log facing the house. Pairs of swallows clung to the dead branches of trees lining the stream. Chittering crazily, they launched themselves in wild circles against the sky, hurtled low over the barnyard where animals stamped their feet waiting for the storm to break, waiting as Smoke cantered erratically along the fenceline, her breath in low impatient whinnies.

Robert's pipe was out; he tapped it against his boot, blew to clear the stem and casually remarked, "She read the waters, Will. She said they spoke of trouble."

"Well, Jesus, Robbie, she's been wrong before." Crushing one square hand in the other, Casey cracked and pulled each knuckle vigorously, then reversed his grip and began again. "Plenty of times," he whispered. "Plenty times she's wrong." There were only eight or ten heartbeats now between the lightning and its thunder.

Springing suddenly to his feet, the doctor skipped and hopped like a marionette, his oversize suit flapping and cracking as if at some point he'd shrunk inside it. "By Christ," he cried, "it's a terrible thing she does! And her own daughter, too, this time." He had to raise his voice, shout above the gathering din. "None of us know what fate we're born to. Good fortune or ill, they come and go as the Lord decides."

Drops of rain the size of a child's fist were exploding in the dust by the time they reached the porch. Heaving in subsiding light, the forest abandoned itself to the storm as they sheltered by the log wall. They smelled the lightning before it shattered, and even with hands over their ears they heard it like boiling fat hitting a stove.

Shaken by the full diapason of rain and thunder, the house shuddered as they entered; it creaked and twisted in every mortice and joint. Except for the staccato brilliance of lightning, there was neither light nor darkness but gradations of shadow, a penumbral gloom in which two lamps had been lit, one by the stove, another on the long table: two brown pools that trembled violently until Robert closed the door.

On the table between Joshua and Barbara Casey, half submerged in their own shadows, lay two enormous grinding teeth. Fraser knew what they were. Oh, Jesus! He leaned against the log wall and closed his eyes.

"What have we got here?" Rubbing his hands briskly, Dr. Tom approached the table with Casey at his heels.

"Teeth." Robert cleared his throat and said again: "Teeth."

"Teeth, for Chrissakes. . ." He reached past Joshua and cautiously touched one with his index finger. "What sort of bloody tooth is that, eh?" As he bent closer to the lamp, his sharp features appeared to soften, his lips and protuberant eyes glistened like oil. "Crikey!"

"Joshua found them." Pausing, Barbara appealed to Fraser. "Robert, he says there's the skeleton of some monster out there."

"Not too long since she's been dug out either." With flat cheekbones and hair the colour of gun metal, Joshua watched Fraser curiously, then reached to pick at the largest, rocking it with the hook. "Must of been some big animal," he said, "eh?"

Robert pushed himself from the wall, shrugged and put a fresh bottle among them on the table, then went to wash his hands.

"Monster," gargled Casey. "Skeleton of what monster?"

Mimicked by broken shadows, Robert splashed water into the basin and rolled up his sleeves. "How's Mary?"

"She's resting fine," replied Annie from the bottom of the stairs. "She'll be a while yet but she's fine." Her grey hair undone was surprisingly full, a wiry bush shrouding her face and shoulders. "Well, Robert," she said, bringing cups from the shelf, "what was it you found out there?"

"Yes, tell us, man." The doctor was pouring whiskey even before she'd finished arranging the cups. "What kind of an animal has teeth like that?"

"That's a tooth all right." Casey had finally picked one up. "Holy Mother of God."

"No popery." Annie didn't smile. "What was it, Robert?"

"I don't know." He pulled a stool into their circle. "I haven't the faintest notion, but I'll tell you I've never seen anything to match it alive or dead, and I've never heard tell of it either."

Clustering in lamplight they took turns with the teeth; hefting intently, they pursed their lips, nodding as if they perceived the magic planes and shadows, the revealing weight within them. They listened gravely as Robert tried to find the words, some combination of words; but like an inarticulate Adam he found nothing to interpret or contain the mystery, and so he talked of his own wonder and confusion, the dumb conviction he should have reburied the first one, left well enough alone, and that terrible breath, dear God, as he'd clasped it against his body. He lifted his hands, reaching towards his breast; and afterwards they swore they'd heard it too, each of them, and as the days passed, the weeks and months, they became more certain: it was like a body's final breath, so it was, as if you'd thrown your weight on the chest of a corpse, or the sigh of a sleeper entering some dolorous territory of dream. . . .

III

Angus was born after midnight with the guts of the storm well off to the south. Rain was falling steadily; rushing from eavestroughs it overflowed the rain barrels as the men heard a new sound in Mary's labour. Then Robert heard a small voice, a feral cry; it pierced his ears like needles.

When he could wait no longer, he climbed the stairs in his stocking feet. Stooping to peer into the room as if he'd become a stranger, with shadows massed on the side of his face like a birth scar, he had to resist the urge to creep back down to the others waiting by the fire, another bottle between them on the table.

Three women in candlelight at the head of his bed. Annie's high voice in a private song. She stood with her back to him, her head bowed, holding the child against her thin bosom while Barbara Casey helped Mary into the freshly made bed. The rain had passed but water fell crazily onto the roof from leaves and branches. He should have waited to be called.

Had a child really uttered that desolate cry, like something caught in the forest at night?

He spied on the women in the circle of light. Mary's legs, plump scissors, disappeared beneath the covers, the glowing flesh of arms and shoulders as Barbara Casey began to brush out her hair. Holding it from the head with her left hand, she pulled the brush sleepily from the scalp, then back again to the rhythm of Annie's crooning chant. Her lovely hair, it crackled and shone about her face, so distant and serene he had to rest his forehead and cheek against the door jamb.

"It's a boy." Annie's face was empty, her body calm as she held the child up to him, an offering she didn't expect him to take. A small pinched face beneath a cap of damp fur; it wasn't much bigger than a potato. He didn't know what to say. Black hair curled tightly against the scalp like moss; the closed eyes were enormous and set to the side of its head like a fawn's.

The baby shuddered as he leaned to touch the tiny cheek, the jawline exquisite as a fishbone beneath his finger. Heavy drops of water splattered on the roof, a lone frog called from beside the pond as the mouth twisted;

trying to catch his finger it opened to suck, a flash of teeth, a mewling cry struggled in its throat as he jerked his hand away.

"Are they supposed to have teeth?" He hadn't meant to say that. It didn't even sound like his voice. He shifted from one foot to the other and cleared his throat.

Robert was never to mention the teeth again. Because they slipped out of the baby's gums within the week, and Mary found most of them in his cradle, smooth and un-blemished, with no roots at all, Robert was able to con-vince himself he'd been mistaken, they'd never been there; it was a story told by old women recalling dead babies or childbed fever.

"You'd best go now." Mary lay with fingers curled on her flat belly, her eyes closed. "You can tell the others you have a son."

The baby convulsed in Annie's arms and gave a piercing cry before she could speak again. The face was brown and wrinkled as old fruit, the teeth like needles, rat's teeth, and as he fled the room he saw black hair like fur across the shoulders, it clustered down the spine. He saw Mary's face. Two women crouching over the bed, that urgent body wriggling like a ferret beneath their hands.

IV

With eyes the colour of melting snow, the infant stared gravely at Robert. A ruminative gaze that would cease to see him, lose him in the background. It disarmed him with its conviction, its primordial indifference; as when some-times a doe raises her head to contemplate a trio of wolves, receptive but detached, her eyes limpid like his six-month-old son's, her body serene, so that hungry as they are, they turn from her and set upon another. . . .

Visiting women have insisted Angus resembles his father: "Look at the mouth," they enthuse. "Dear gracious, that lower lip! And the shape of his head, isn't that just something?" Emboldened by colour rising in his face, they wave their hands curiously in the air, they clasp them together, their faces slack with pleasure, with hidden laughter. "He's such a lovely child," they sigh. "You should be pleased, Robert Fraser, you should be proud."

He stood beside the cradle dreading what they claim to have seen. During the past ten months, he's found himself inhabited by his own father. Reaching for a tool, a cup of tea, once even to stroke Mary's face, he'd discover his father's hand issuing from his sleeve, the familiar spatulate fingers, the brutal thickness of it mottled with freckles. Or else, without warning, he'd be walking like the old man, his feet striking the ground precisely, a mournful exactitude of heel, then sole, heel and sole; so that sometimes, when ascending the stairs or crossing a room, it was not his body but his father's. So shaken by that unmistakable tread, he'd decided at first it must be his boots. Crouching on the top step he pulled them off; they didn't look like any boots his father had worn but it couldn't be his feet, surely these were his own feet? He examined them carefully, one and then the other, he placed them side by side and wriggled his toes. It simply had to be the boots, so he hid them behind a stack of birch in the summer kitchen.

He finally had to admit that, for reasons unknown, Calum Fraser had decided to intervene in his son's body as if violent death hadn't been enough for him. To be sure the moments passed. His body was released easily, without rancour or fanfare. No clanging of pots or souring of milk, no eldritch gusts of wind or sudden shivers, accompanied his father's departure; even the yellow cat sunning itself against the window failed to notice anything.

Wind machines rattled and whistled in the yard outside; particles of dust danced in sunlight between them as a skein of geese beat noisily over the clearing. It's true that Angus would not soon see his father's gaslit town, the ladies and gentlemen in fine carriages with horses like maidens, their meticulous feet on cobblestones glistening after rain, the sweating castle rock, that coal-black menhir hunched against sea winds. Perhaps he never would, but the urgency of feet running at night, the angry shouts and shadows, Robert had brought him these. His grandparents quarrelling endlessly, a woman staring through polished window glass while her husband, Robert's father, a man invariably between drinks, crossed the courtyard steadily with hands thrust deep into his pockets; he departed without noticing his children in the rain. If it hadn't been for the money he brought, none would have cared that he came back as often as he left. Watching them slyly, his thick hands produced small gifts, gewgaws that glittered briefly and were lost.

Mary draped a shawl over her shoulder before releasing a breast to the child made frantic by the smell of her milk. Decorously arranging the cloth, she sank back in the chair, her eyes closed, the lids trembling as if she had known Robert would speak, would finally say: "I'll tell you what. . ." His voice rang too loud in the room. "By the time that young fellow's, ah, not too much older anyways, before too long, we'll have a brick house here. Yes, we will," he insisted, although she hadn't even opened her eyes. She sat resolutely, the tip of her tongue moving between her lips. "It'll be the first one on the line. Just there on the hill." With his arm flung out behind his shoulder in the low-ceilinged room, he shuffled his feet, swaying from one to the other like a bear. His eyes glistened with an eccentric light while his child, gasping and snorting, suckled with abandon beneath the shawl. "We'll make a straight drive in from the road. It'll be a real road by then and we'll plant maples on either side, or elms. You'd prefer maples, wouldn't you, Mary? Mind now, the elm makes a fine shade tree when it's grown and a fence by Heaven! A white-washed fence beyond the machine. . . ."

Never talking to anyone else like this, indeed seldom to her, with the words tumbling one upon the other, he rattled on and on about the variegation of coloured bricks and stone for the lintels, the porch with fine fretwork, embellishments of all sorts, fluting, moulding, beading, flourishes under the eaves, patterns of coloured glass and arabesques in the shingled roof. He rhapsodized sternly about weathervanes, and his voice, rising in jerking leaps from baritone to tenor, took on a visionary hue, a strident conviction that soon had him galloping clumsily about the room, smashing a fist into his open palm. "Maples it is," he cried, his eyes rolling hopefully. "You're right! And we'll tap them in spring when the weather's right."

Angus left off sucking and began to cry, his shrill voice only partially muffled by the shawl and chest beneath.

"Now look what you've done!" Mary stared into her child's angry red face. "He's crying. . ."

"Give him the other teat," he shouted. "We can't stop now!" Then, as if the house were already built, he launched into a description of the interior: valances and curtains with gimps and galloons, carpets from Buffalo, Edinburgh crystal incised with enough light for the darkest room, mahogany sideboards, serving tables with trays and silver cruets, a tea service, absolutely, and a new bed, an enormous bed with tooled and burnished posts, he'd seen just the one, the very one and. . .

With eyes swollen by the force of his visions, he gulped great quantities of air, his mouth agape. He flung himself about the room and at that moment, with Angus snuffling disconsolately at her fresh breast, Mary leaned deliberately, indifferent now to the consequences.

"Robert," she announced, "that's nothing but foolishness."

He couldn't believe she meant it. Straightening so his head almost touched the ceiling, he gasped for breath. He hadn't begun on the parlour, let alone the kitchen. Surely she couldn't mean it? He clenched and unclenched his thick hands, opened his mouth to continue, to celebrate a fine summer kitchen. . .

"Wind machines," she hissed, and "piles of bones." Jiggling her child she watched him deflate. "Perpetual motion!" By now her voice was matter-of-fact, her triumph complete.

V

When Will Casey arrived with the stranger he found Robert trying to burn the shattered handle out of his axe. Even from a distance they could see something was wrong. There was such tension, indeed such fury, in the arc of his body over the forge that they found themselves approaching on tiptoe. "That's him," muttered Casey as Fraser, desperately juggling the hot axe, howled then hurled it into a rain barrel. "That's your man."

Shading his eyes against his reflection on the water, Robert glared into the barrel because his arm wasn't long enough. Even if he took off his shirt and vest he'd have a job of it. He'd have to climb from the ground and more than likely immerse his head before he could retrieve the axe. The two men watched in silence. "Well," Fraser said methodically, "piss on it."

"Thinking of fishing, are you?" Regretting having said this, Casey changed the subject. "Mr. Hackett here has come to see about that monster of yours. Haven't you, Mr. Hackett?"

"Mr. Fraser. . ." A plump tidy man with expensive boots, he revealed, on removing his hat, a bony protuberance that was conical in shape and perfectly bald, a tonsure swelling out of his otherwise normal head of hair. "My dear Mr. Fraser, if you only knew how pleased I am to finally. . ." Seizing Robert's hand in both of his, holding and shaking, he enthused: "After such travels and with such impatience, Prof. Carruthers showed me your letter, and if you have what you say you have, and Mr. Casey assures me you do, well, my goodness. Oh, my goodness, and here you are! Finally. Such a pleasure, sir, such a pleasure. Hmmn."

Releasing Robert and standing back, rubbing his hands as if washing them, he surveyed the clearing, the log house and barn, the work sheds and nearby fields. "And that must be. . ." Pointing at the mill wheel turning in its sluice, he blinked with one eye and then the other. "That must be your experiment with the perpetual motion. Hmmn," he murmured again. "Marvellous. Yes." He sniffed. "Hackett's my name. Rochefoucault Chesterfield Hackett. But you can call me Ches."

"You're not Prof. Carruthers?" Covertly eyeing the dome which shone in the midday sun like a greasy elbow, Robert didn't know if he wanted the man to replace his hat or not. He'd have been appalled to find it was Carruthers, for how could you respect a man with a head like that? It wasn't brains, it was bone, a solid chunk of bone, yet there he stood blinking and grinning as if he had an everyday head like anyone else. By God, you had to admire him! Robert figured if he had a thing like that, he'd never take his hat off at all, not even in church, not when he crawled into bed with Mary, Christ, no! Still, if he had a mind to, he could give a man a terrible bloody thump. You could say that for it.

"I see you're looking at my head."

"No!" chorused Casey and Robert together. "Well, perhaps. . ."

"People are fascinated by my head, this head of mine." Ches Hackett smiled benignly while rapping on the astonishing growth with his fist. "Solid bone." It sounded like it all right. "I suspect my interest in the pre-Adamite world, the world of antediluvian monsters, springs from this particular bump. It *is* highly developed, wouldn't you say? And situated in the region of. . ." Producing a clean white handkerchief, a gentleman's handkerchief, he carefully unfolded it as he spoke: "It could also indicate, of course, this specific formation placed where it is. . ." He blew his nose violently. "I mean to say, the conical shape is typical, absolutely typical." The smile on his pudgy face deepened as he stuffed the handkerchief inside his coat and leaned conspiratorially. "So it could mean you're in the presence of a *criminal lunatic*, both of you! *Ha!* Are you by any chance familiar with the principles of phrenology?" Balancing on the balls of their feet, they desperately shook their heads. "No? Ah, well," he resumed cheerfully, "never mind, never mind." Replacing his hat, he noisily rubbed his palms together. "Now, where are those bones of yours?"

Since neither Fraser nor Casey was prepared to lose sight of Hackett even for an instant, it would clearly be better, much safer, if he went first. But since the man didn't easily follow directions or felt uncomfortable leading the way when he didn't know where he was going, the trio managed to get moving only after some difficulty. Robert urged them on with cries of "Behind the barn, that's right. No, to the left, the big one, ha-ha, over there," and pointed encouragingly. They stopped and started, veering erratically with Rochefoucault Hackett always in the lead. They paused to admire the wooden animals stuck in the middle of a berserk dance, their hinged joints waiting for wind. Hackett had never seen such a collection, and so ingeniously constructed! After a bit, Casey suggested there was nothing at all like seeing them in a good stiff breeze, and Hackett agreed that must be so.

Eventually they rounded the corner where, sheltered in a lean-to, the skeleton lay.

"Dear gracious," exclaimed Hackett, breaking into a trot, "what have we here?" With hands resting lightly on his rounded hips, he surveyed the bones happily. "How very nice," he cried, cavorting briefly, his shiny boots tip-tapping on the beaten earth. "Oh yes. . ." Pouncing on one of the teeth, he held the familiar shape up to the light, muttering, "Hmmn," and chewed his lip. He squinted through a small glass, frowned briefly, exchanged the tooth for a smaller one and, chuckling, shook his head in admiration. "Ah!" Waving his free arm dramatically, he stuffed the tooth into his pocket. "Imagine it. . . Cast your minds back, ladies and gentlemen. Cast your minds back! What a marvel we have here. . . This great antediluvian beast, this hairy monster shambling through. . ."

"Hairy?" For pity's sake, Robert hadn't considered that. "What do you mean, hairy?"

"Well, it was hairy." Hackett fluttered his hands down his chest, over his comfortable belly and thighs. "You understand my meaning? It had hair. It was hairy."

"All over?"

"*Of course.* . . Yes, of course."

"How do you know?"

"Because it's a *hairy* mammoth." Hackett smiled weakly. "That's why."

"We thought," said Casey mournfully, "we've considered it might be some class of elephant."

"You've got the eel of science by the tail if you're thinking this is an elephant. No, sir, it's a mammoth, *Mammuthus Primigenius*. Yes. Hmmn." Taking out his handkerchief he blew his nose enthusiastically. "And a marvellously complete specimen too, if I'm any judge."

"What about my tooth?" Robert interjected politely enough. "Mr. Hackett, you've. . ."

"Won't you call me Ches? And I'd. . ." For a moment it appeared he might remove his hat. "I'd be privileged to call you Robert."

"You've put it in your pocket."

"Yes. Well, naturally, I thought I'd take a few pieces to show Prof. Carruthers. Just, you know, to whet his appetite a little." Ches Hackett giggled and winked happily. "He's going to be very excited, Robert, I don't mind telling you, very excited indeed."

"Whet his appetite?" Clenching his fists, Robert cleared his throat of phlegm. "Surely you're not thinking to take any of this away with you?" Slamming stiff arms against his sides, he began to growl unintelligibly.

"But, of course. Isn't that. . ." Flustered by this nasty turn of events, sharply apprehensive, Rochefoucault Chesterfield Hackett sidled away from Fraser and towards Casey; while Robert began to shake his head violently as a horse might with a bee in its ear. He towered above them, stamping his feet and groaning.

"Easy, Robbie," Casey soothed. "Easy there, boy. That's all right, Robbie, hoosh, boy, easy now. . ." He was almost about to offer him a chunk of sugar from his pocket; he even had it in his hand but remembered in time.

"Oh no," muttered Robert, breathing through his nose. "Nosireebob! I'll not be hornswoggled, no sir. It stays here." He held his hand out in Hackett's direction, the palm turned up. He waggled his fingers tentatively, then with conviction. The tooth was returned and accepted with thanks. An uneasy calm descended.

The sun was already behind the trees when they hunched by the lean-to, preparing their tobacco. Young robin redbreasts chased each other noisily and a single branch of scarlet maple, winter's oriflamme, the leaves prematurely resplendent, swayed on the forest's darkening wall. Blue smoke from their pipes settled like mist.

"Do you think we should have a drink?" Casey assessed Robert from the corner of his eye. "Should I maybe get us a drink? Right then," he said, getting to his feet. "I'll do that." Tapping Robert on the shoulder, he nodded encouragement to Hackett and set off for the house.

"That's a fine fellow." Hackett nonchalantly broke the silence.

"He is so."

"It's a blessing to have good neighbours, a blessing altogether." Robert nodded into his pipe as if there was something wrong with it. "And he's got a good head of hair on him still."

"Yes, he has. They say if you soak your feet every day in cold water. . ."

"Is that what you do?"

"No." From the dead branch of an elm, a wild pigeon stared at them with its red eye. Believing Fraser had regained his old self, Rochefoucault Hackett recovered his confidence along with his voice. He apologized for any misunderstanding that might have occurred and refused to accept Robert's protestations. He should have made it clear he was authorized to make a fair deal, that's it, yes, a fair deal. He glossed over the fact that some people, certainly not all that many but some, donate certain objects to science (at this point he stood up and marched over to the skeleton), but never when the specimen is so fine as this, no, sir. Be that as it may, he pointed out in his high pedant's voice, Prof. Carruthers had arranged for a most generous sum of money, right enough; there wasn't any thought of gain for nought, of reaping where they hadn't sown. The professor was realistic, but a generous man. Robert would enjoy doing business with him. He was certain of that. As certain as death.

Pleased with his performance, he rubbed his hands briskly and returned to perch on his log. "Do you have any thoughts on a fair price, Robbie?"

Hunched over his knees, Robert Fraser broke pieces of twigs and threw them at an anthill.

"I mean what do you consider it's worth to you after all?"

"It's not for sale, Mr. Hackett. Not to you or anyone else."

By the time Casey appeared with a bottle and three cups, Rochefoucault Hackett was at his wit's end. Tiptoeing between the barn and the forest, folding and refolding a fresh handkerchief, he prepared various arguments, only to have them rejected out of hand.

"For God's sake, man, what will you *do* with it?"

"I'll piece it together. I'll use it, so I will."

"Here?" squealed Hackett, throwing his handkerchief in the air. "In the bloody middle of the bloody bush?"

"I'll do something with it."

"Arrgh..." Staggering suddenly, his bright face gone doughy, flaccid. "But science, man," he tore off his hat and violently rubbed his appalling cranium, "*think of science!* Science *needs* this goddamn thing... don't you see?"

"Then science can come and see it."

"Give me a drink... Oh!" He lurched to take the whiskey from Casey. "Jesus," he said and drank it down. "Holy Jesus... um... more..."

"I didn't know if you took water," Casey whispered while pouring generously, "so I didn't bring any."

"Listen. Listen, both of you." Hackett scuttled back to crouch beside Fraser. "Here, for God's sake," he gulped at his drink, urging Casey with his free hand. "Listen to what I have to say to you." Stiffening his index finger, pointing heavenwards, he took quick sips from his cup and told them of the Great Exhibition of 1851. "What a spectacle that must have been! This is London I'm talking about, London, eh? So when I tell you people came in their thousands, I mean princes and crowned heads, I mean dukes and barons and suchlike. You can imagine that, imagine the money that was there! Money and power, lovely women, rich women with feathers. They've never done a stroke in their lives. They're as delicate, as smooth all over as the inside of your woman's thighs. Begging your pardon," he laughed apologetically. "And common folk, folk like you and me, they came in droves, on foot and in smart carriages. They came in flaming parades! And do you know why? I'll tell you why. . . ." He held his cup out for Casey to pour. "You've heard tell of the Crystal Palace, eh? Maybe you've seen pictures?" They nodded together, glad of the whiskey, for a breeze had come up lending a chill to the air. "Well, they moved the Crystal Palace to Sydenham. Piece by piece, they moved the whole blessed works."

"I read about that," marvelled Robert Fraser. "Wouldn't that be just something? Mind you," he added, brightening, "if you have the willing hands. . ."

"The whole blessed works," crowed Hackett, "piece by piece, and they rebuilt it in Sydenham just for this exhibition, this collection of monsters. They were life size, you understand: huge bloody things with skin. They were made to look real, you see, with glass eyes as big as plates. They got this artist fellow, Hawkins, Benjamin Waterhouse Hawkins, he made them. Must have been a clever bugger that one, eh? And he filled the hall with plants. You got to imagine this now. . ." He leaned intently as if finally reaching his point. "Huge ferns and I don't know what, so it looked like before the flood, like nothing you've ever seen. . .antediluvian. Then he had these terrible animals situated so you'd swear they were real. They had a *Basilosaurus* and some class of flying reptile hanging from the ceiling, way up there, like." He pointed and the three of them stared solemnly at the gently swaying treetops. "And a mammoth. Not so big as yours, Robbie, not so big as that." He smiled without irony. His face had recovered its original brightness, his voice its timbre. "Dear God," he laughed appreciatively, "it must have been something to see."

"You mean to say there was a roomful of these creatures?"

"A palace is more like it, Robbie. The Crystal bloody Palace."

"Dear Jesus," said Casey, "I'd love to have been there. Wouldn't you, Robbie?"

"That's what I'm telling you, lads. That's what the lords and ladies, the soft fancy women, were coming to see." Confident of his audience now, he paused to shake his head as if remembering marvellous details. "And they came from everywhere."

Fraser opened his mouth to speak, then shut it again. They sat in silence for a while before Hackett said, "And that's not the best of it either." He proferred his cup. Casey poured and they all drank, then reloaded their pipes. "You've got to understand, right enough, there's a professor, Richard Owen, who's been collecting these specimens, and this exhibition was his, you see. He's such a famous person he can do that sort of thing just as easy as spit. All sorts of gentry are at his beck and call because, well, I'm telling you, lads, these skeletons, they're what everybody wants. So there you are."

"Robbie's really found himself something."

"No question about that at all." Slumping down on his spine, Hackett whipped out a handkerchief and sneezed wetly. "Bloody hell!" Wiping his nose and upper lip, he sipped his drink and ventured it could change Robert's life altogether. "When you dug that thing out of the ground, you stepped into a class by yourself. Yes, you did. No doubt about it. Look," he exclaimed, winding himself up again, "Albert Koch, you take Albert Koch now: back in the forties he pieced together a *Basilosaurus* or some such and he travelled all over Europe exhibiting it for money. He made a bit too. You won't find that German wanting a bit of change in his pocket when he's got a fancy for something nice."

Contemplating the ponderous skull, a curving tusk in the shelter of his lean-to, Robert listened avidly. If he shivered, it might have been the chill wind, its promise of winter, or it might have been the lurking memory of a taut young body, a brilliant costume, her languorous arms outspread like wings. "Anyway, this Richard Owen. . ."

"To Richard Owen," cried Casey, lifting the bottle by his side. "That's a Welsh name, Owen. There was a family of Owens, so there were, on the boat coming over. Couldn't sing worth a damn, not a one of them."

"This is good whiskey," said Hackett, accepting a little bit more. "Just a small one for me. Hmmn." Rising decisively as if seizing an opportunity, causing a clutch of pigeons to fly off in alarm, he paced back and forth on his small feet. "This is going to be hard to believe," he warned. "Still, it's gospel, yes it is." He'd read reports in various journals, indeed he'd seen an illustration in, what was it? some magazine. An illustration of this very event, and what's more, Prof. Carruthers himself had been present. Yes, he was. So there you are. In order to free both thumbs for his waistcoat pockets, he put his cup on the stump he'd vacated, then resumed his strutting back and forth. His voice full of drama and conviction, he began his tale of the astonishing dinner held to celebrate the triumph of that Great Exhibition.

"There's never been another meal like it," he vowed, "in the history of the world." Even the preparations were legend: gastronomic experts were consulted; the finest of chefs interviewed; each pled his cause, they squabbled among themselves, each had his defenders and detractors. The Queen herself sent a personal note supporting her favourite. Renowned and succulent dishes were submitted, tasted and pondered over; ancient cellars were plundered for their rarest wines, while news of the intended feast spread like wildfire. Who would be invited? Who excluded? London and the counties were agog. Greed, competition and arse-licking were rampant; erstwhile friends vied shamelessly for the Great Man's eye, and then came the announcement! The table would seat twenty-one. After Richard Owen, his patrons and immediate colleagues, there'd be places for fourteen guests and each would be chosen from the academic and scientific fraternities.

"Well, my God, lads, all hell broke loose," marvelled Hackett. "You can't imagine." He paused to gulp from his drink. "The Duke and Duchess of Ord were seen bursting into tears, gangs of students chanting the names of their candidates roistered in the streets, odds were set and changed, restaurants offered versions of the celebrated meal to wealthy customers and, scandalously..." Hackett paused here for effect. Certain doctors of philosophy offered access to their mistresses, yes! Some hint even their wives...in return for a seat at that illustrious table. "Those poor women," he snorted behind his hand.

While Casey insisted he'd heard of such things, and Rochefoucault Hackett quoted the poet, "Thus the worm ambition doth make cuckolds of us all," Robert shook his head in disbelief. He could lift that round bastard and heave him against the barn. What's he going on about? Call me Ches, for Chrissakes! That one would take another man's woman, sure he would, if she was offered. His body clothed in soft white fat, greedy fat, he'd take anything.

Bending forward from the waist and laughing like a drain, Casey began his joke about the newlyweds.

"Waitaminute," Hackett cried good-naturedly. He hadn't come to the main point of his story. He apologized for his prolixity; it was the drink no doubt. He promised to make the rest of it short and sweet, to the point, and then raising his arms like a master of ceremonies, he declared loudly, "The guests, when they arrived at the Crystal Palace, they found the table. . . Oh!" Dropping his hands, rolling his small eyes, he took a dramatic breath. "You see, the table was inside the belly of the *iguanodon*, right inside the monster itself."

"No!" Fraser protested, leaping to his feet.

"Yes, oh yes. . . Set for twenty-one, twenty-one places: all the fine china, the expensive glassware, the glistening candelabra and room for the footmen to serve each course as it came. What a spectacle, eh? What a triumph!" Even Hackett was briefly silent at the prospect: threading through a jagged pre-human landscape, twenty-one dignitaries in evening dress, while above them, far beyond the graceful dome, three-quarters of a moon cast icy shadows through which they must wade; black and white, they file one after another into the reptilian body. Do they jostle each other searching for place cards, or has Owen provided a seating plan? Gratefully sipping sherry, they attack turtle soup, the sound of spoons scraping tureens, the sucking and gulping of twenty-one mouths. And all the while the giant ferns outside, the ancient grasses, are still; no breeze stirs them, no night air moves in the Crystal Palace. Only the footmen whisper in velvet jackets; they shift from one leg to the other, their white stockings and delicate pumps catch the moonlight when they are called.

"That's a corker all right." Standing to stretch, Casey searched his pockets for tobacco. "I've an uncle and auntie in service over home." Finding none, he approached the lean-to and glanced inside. "The three of us couldn't scarcely creep into this bugger for another drink." He stretched again. "Even if we had one." Glancing at the sky and the forest, he thrust his hands deep in his trouser pockets. "Well," he said, "chore time. I'd best be home." He shuffled irresolutely. "I might drop by the house, Robbie, after supper."

"It's not that we don't enjoy your stories," Robert spoke steadily. "We do. . ." He could, my God! Seizing Hackett by his collar, by the slack of his trousers, and before the dandy bastard knew what was happening he'd hurl him *crash* against the barn as hard as he bloody well could. Yes. . . .

"Barbara's going to have my guts for gaiters."

"I can send you the picture." Hackett spoke precisely, as if talking to a child or simpleton. "And Prof. Carruthers, you should hear him on the subject, he was there. . ."

"Yes," agreed Fraser. He stopped to urinate and Casey joined him. "Ah," they said, "uhm." Casey pissed copiously, a dandelion yellow stream that continued long after Fraser had finished and buttoned his fly.

VI

"Have you been to London yourself, Mr. Hackett?" With supper finished, Mary put a fresh pot of tea on the table and joined the men, who were listening to the wall clock.

"Well, Missus. . ." he began tentatively. Reaching into the light with fine hairs golden on her arm, Mary poured the tea. "Thank you." Dropping his head over his cup he slurped loudly. "It's been some time, though."

When he'd first taken off his hat, revealing the brutal lump, she'd felt a thrill of revulsion, as at stories of two-headed calves, bearded ladies, of alligator boys and sisters joined at the belly with only two legs, and other tales of heaven knows what Freaks of Nature travellers brought from the South. When he covered it almost at once with a knitted skullcap, like a snood or tea cosy riding on top of his head, she'd been more disappointed than relieved, and to her alarm she'd found herself wondering what it felt like; was it dry and warm like an egg, or cold as a stone?

"Doesn't appear Will's coming at all."

"If there's company, he'll attend." Examining a shirt for missing buttons, Mary spoke sideways, with a needle between her lips. "Though it's quiet enough here tonight."

"It seems quiet," agreed Fraser.

She couldn't tell what it was with them. The man Hackett had insisted on filling the wood boxes while Robert did chores and then they'd settled in to eat, casting wild glances at each other, sizing each other up as if preparing for combat. She remembered boys like this at home, rivals for her sister's attentions, or her own, unfortunate boys who appeared at the same time. Intense as jays or blackbirds, they shied stones into the forest; they pushed and tripped each other, insistent until one or the other, resigning from battle, tried to rediscover some dignity in self-pity. And so this evening, smiling mercilessly as on those earlier occasions, she'd found herself asking bright questions that elicited surly responses. Yes, it was the skeleton that brought Mr. Hackett; but, no, Robert wasn't interested in selling. Indeed, Prof. Carruthers would be disappointed. And, yes, it was worth some money, real money, but. . .

Showing the whites of his eyes like a cow with its horns caught in a fence, Robert hadn't known whether to answer first or not at all. He'd grunted as if beginning, whereupon Hackett dutifully shut his mouth. Robert then glared at the ceiling as if daring his guest to try again. As a result, Rochefoucault Hackett, his delicate nostrils quivering apprehensively, had come to resemble a rabbit pretending it couldn't be seen.

Apparently there'd been a collection of monsters like the one outside; in fact, a Great Exhibition, and a meal of some sort where famous men had dined inside the body of a giant reptile. "Whoa!" she'd cried. "What?" But that had been the end of it, absolutely. Neither would meet her gaze. Hunching over apple pie with globs of fresh cream, they'd scraped and chewed, moving their jaws vigorously; and because Casey would have told Barbara, she let it go. Her smile was stiff like dry clay, so she abandoned it. "What's it like then?"

"What?"

"London. What's London like?"

"Do you mind?" he ventured, holding his cup for a refill until Mary took it. "I don't recall eating a better pigeon pie."

"Why, thank you, Mr. Hackett, though I fear I was liberal with the salt."

"Not at all, Mrs. Fraser. Not at all. It was ideal." He blew his nose into another clean handkerchief. "There's nothing like fresh meat well cooked."

"We'll be missing it in a few months, right enough."

"Oh yes. . ."

"There's rabbits," said Robert darkly. The wall clock ticktocked and a log collapsed in the firebox. "And venison. Often enough there's venison."

Fortunately Casey arrived with a stamping clatter, throwing open the door. "Aye-aye," he cried, "here we are." Producing a bottle of whiskey, he plumped it on the table. He struggled out of his coat and threw it to the floor by the wall, dragging a chair among them. "Evening, Mary dear."

When they refused, he shrugged and poured himself a glass. "I've been thinking, Robert. Barbara and I've been talking, and it seems to us," saluting with his drink, "it seems to me you've got hold of life by the arse." He took a preliminary mouthful. "Smooth with no bite," he crowed, "it's going down like molasses!" Peering into the glass he wriggled his buttocks, then resting his arms on the table bent forward so the light revealed ordinary detritus caught in his beard, strands of tobacco and bread crumbs, globules of something or other, partially chewed carrot by the look of it, and tangled bits of yarn. They smelled the liquor on him while he marvelled at the way Robert's life would be changed. Change was scarcely the word! Jiggling his right leg, revolving his glass on the table, he extolled the virtue and fascination of travel, the rewards of fame. He begged them to sample the new batch. The thing is, he insisted, there's plenty of money in the States and folk who don't mind spending it; so if Robert got those bones together, by God, that would make some difference, all right. Yes, sir. . . His voice hoarse, melismatic, he conjured hundreds of Americans, thousands gathering like bees in Washington, Buffalo, New York and Boston, the hum of eager voices, a dime a throw. Step-up, step-up, he bounced and jiggled, cracking his knuckles mightily at the prospect. Why himself, he'd ride her for all she was worth and he wouldn't get off, no sir, not until he'd cash and to spare for a place down South without a goddamn tree to be seen, where folk never heard tell of snow and they ate Tories for breakfast. Lurching on his short legs to the stove, he spat into the fire. "I would so," he vowed, as if expecting Robert's response. "Damn right. . ."

"I've no mind to live among Republicans."

"For Gawd's sake, Robbie!" Firelight glowed briefly on his arm as he replaced the lid; the stove back flickered red then collapsed into black. "I'm talking about *money, pails of money*." Then unnecessarily: "I'm talking about getting out of here."

"I reckon you wouldn't mind a few darkies to do the work for you either."

"Well now, that's. . ." Grinding his teeth, he hadn't meant that at all. Re-entering the circle of light, he opened his mouth, then closed it. Resting his fists on the table, leaning forward on his arms, he tried to catch Robert's gaze. Mournfully, he resisted the fiercest impulse to shout, to pound and stamp his feet. A night bird cried sharply from the forest. A mouse tiptoed into the dry sink.

Robert flexed and relaxed his calloused fingers. Breathing through his nose, his face vacant, bony with shadows, he drummed tentatively on his thighs.

Crouching, Rochefoucault Hackett seemed obsessed by Mary's soft mouth, her parted lips as she swayed in her chair, the mending forgotten in her lap. Wind sighed in the chimney. Again the bird called, raucous and insistent. "Missus Fraser," he hissed unexpectedly, "it was hairy, you know, all. . .uhm." Because his small eyes remained fixed on her mouth, he looked like a half-wit. "Covered all over with long hair." He fluttered his free hand and giggled.

"I beg your pardon?"

"The mammoth, it was a woolly mammoth."

"Hairy?" She didn't know what else to say. "Woolly?"

"Abraham Lincoln," blurted Casey as his buttocks hit the chair. "He's got some niggers himself. So he has."

"Mr. Hackett was going to tell us about London." Mary forced a smile. "He's familiar with London."

"Well, I'll tell you what." Leaning back as if he were alone, Robert stared at the ceiling. "You've got it all wrong, Will."

"Oh, I have, have I?"

Robert nodded. Weary beyond words, he closed his eyes and nodded.

"By Jesus!" Casey emptied his glass. His dark protruding tongue licked inside the rim. "There's a sight more theory in it than there is with your blasted machines."

"Galvanism," intoned Robert, his eyes still closed. "Prof. Vernoy's Improved Family Battery." The mouse appeared to be standing on its hind legs watching them.

"Have you by any chance encountered the Voltaic Belt?" Blinking wetly Hackett finally poured himself a drink.

Mary quickly offered her opinion on your "Heaps Patent" dry earth closet, the portable bedroom commode. Agreeing it wasn't really a machine, not in the strictest sense, she asserted it would be a blessing, nevertheless. No doubt about it. Especially in winter.

"But the Voltaic Belt!" Hackett's voice had regained some of its force and timbre. For those suffering from Nervous Debility, Lost Vitality, Lack of Nerve and Vigour, wasting weaknesses and all those diseases of a *personal nature*, resulting from (at this point he fashioned a sly but most engaging smile and begged Mary's pardon) from *abuses* and *other causes*. "What a grand discovery!" Completely restoring Health, Vigour and Manhood, magneto-therapy was the thing, all right.

Mary didn't know anything about that, but the Eagle Steam Washer must be a fine invention. At the same time, Casey wondered if the Voltaic Belt was in the same class as Wilsonian Magnetic Insoles. "And what about the Gorton Boiler?" he demanded.

"It takes a heap of love to make a woman happy in a cold house," grinned Hackett.

"Steam's one thing. Steam's a marvel, but the best of all. . ." Robert clenched his fists over the table. "The man that properly gets hold of perpetual motion, he'll be farther ahead than anyone." The mouse darted among jars on a shelf as he sprang to his feet and loped to the window. "There's a great future in perpetual motion," he cried.

"Ah," breathed Hackett, massaging his lump. "Prof. Carruthers' sentiments exactly."

"Well," Robert pondered without turning, "are they now?"

"Mr. Hackett." Mary leaned forward and frowned. "This professor of yours. . ." Shadows wavered in the room's corners, but she didn't continue.

"It's not a subject I'm familiar with myself." Before hiding his narrow teeth behind a handkerchief, Hackett showed them in a raddled greedy smile, startling in his plump face, the smile of a mountebank or lecher. It burned then vanished like heat lightning. Did Casey catch that glance, fathom its meaning? Slumped on his arms so it appeared he had no neck at all, his head cocked as if listening to nocturnal skittering, that secret gnawing life beneath the floor, he dreamed; while Mary, her face bowed, searched for the needle in her lap.

"Does he suppose. . ." Turning from the window, Robert leaned against the log wall when Mary spoke. "You don't really suppose it has a future?"

"Maybe it has and maybe it hasn't." Blowing his nose he gasped. "The professor." He snorted wetly, wiping and dabbing while his brown eyes shone over a mouth like raw liver. "The professor," he breathed again, "he's convinced. . ."

"Of course he is." Glaring triumphantly, Robert returned to the table. "Tell me," he said, pouring drinks all round, hesitating over his wife's cup and sniffing wryly when she didn't respond. "Tell us about it."

Swirling liquor in his glass, he watched it catch the light before drinking it down. This was what he'd been waiting for. He smiled a private smile while Hackett, gesticulating like a choirmaster, assured them Melville Carruthers was a man of many parts. Knowledge was Power. They'd be surprised. Anxious for knowledge, as all sensible men must be, the professor had arranged his thoughts in ever so many lectures; and so far as he, Rochefoucault Hackett, could understand — and he was a plain man, not too much worried with scientific scruples — he was confident that if Nature was to be truly conquered then Nature's own Force, her Secret Vitality, must be used against her as the hard frozen earth is mellowed by the genial rays of the sun by Nature's means, in harmony with her Fixed Laws. So true, so true. Nodding soberly, the men sighed in agreement. What was Nature after all but an ideograph of Power?

Casey proposed (just for instance) they consider the waterwheel, and Hackett, well pleased with his explanation, admired Robbie's wind animals again, while Robert, smiling modestly, peeking at Mary from the corner of his eye, suggested there was no better or more promising notion than that of machines running on their own energy. Hoo, they breathed harmoniously. Dear gracious!

"He's not a farmer now, is he?" Mary spoke clearly, her voice innocent of intent. "Professors have the time to believe that sort of thing, don't they?"

Robert didn't know what that had to do with anything. Blinking like a bullfrog eating lightning, he demanded to know who wouldn't want to help advance the march of progress; anyway, it was better than staring into a pail of water. So it was. Clearing his throat, he insisted he didn't mean there weren't other ways. His smile was appalling. He didn't mean that. No, sir. It was only. . .

Delving into his pocket, Hackett produced a handkerchief just in time for a wet repulsive sneeze. "Bloody hell!" he gasped almost before the sneeze had finished. "Bloody hell!" he gasped after a second, then a third, each one like water bursting out of a drain. Curiously elated, his small eyes flitted from Mary to her husband as Robert explained it wasn't necessarily better than divination, it was different. That's all. "More, well, more. . ."

With Hackett's face again contorting, Robert suggested they consider Norman's Electro-Curative Baths, for example; those very same principles used in the treatment of fever, of boils, constipation and suchlike.

Mary, her forehead creased with deep furrows, folded the shirt on her lap and tossed it onto an empty rocker by the stove.

"Hey there." Casey tried to smile as Hackett erupted in another paroxysm. "What are you doing, sneezing this time of the night? Behave yourself," he said.

"With practical results," Robert insisted, apparently short of breath. "The radical cure guaranteed." He puffed, licking his lips, while his gaze wandered about the room, considering pots by the stove, the stove itself, then the clock's dim face, pausing absently, resting on the door as if expecting it might open, as if he might open it himself. He managed to dart painful glances at Mary, who appeared to be having trouble with her jaw.

"And you can be sure a man like that will be well enough off." Poised with his hands beneath the table, Hackett sniffed tentatively.

"Who?"

"Norman, your man Norman."

"Yes," agreed Casey. "Oh, yes."

Mary too seemed to be waiting. Deflecting her husband's covert gaze, she manipulated the lower portion of her face, producing muffled insect sounds, odd raspings and clickings that so commanded their attention Robert gnashed his teeth and Hackett, springing from his chair to remove his coat, placed himself entirely at her disposal. He understood better than most the marvellous consanquinity of tendon and cartilage, the intricacy of ball and socket joints, not only in the jaw but the hip as well. He'd have her right in a jiffy. No doubt about it. Taking alarm as agreement, he skipped towards her, his hands opening and closing like spiders. "The body," he soothed, "the body too is a machine." His elegant pitter-pattering shoes seemed to still her protest and his voice was so assured, its studied resonance so compelling, she accepted the heels of his hands against her jawline.

"The key!" Robert shouted as if Mary wasn't staring bemused from between those hands, his fingers light in the hair about her ears. "The perpetual wheel is your key, that's. . ."

"Here," murmured Rochefoucault Hackett, while Casey furiously cracked his knuckles in an attempt to restore order. "Here," and obscuring her face with his terrible cranium, he jerked his shoulders with an odd twisting motion. There was an audible snap, a sigh, and then, absurdly, he giggled while rubbing his hands together happily. "That should do it."

It happened so quickly, his dancing approach and deft manipulation, that pliant sigh, who would have expected it? And there he was, composed in his chair, refolding a sleeve as if he'd just removed his coat. There'd been no chance to object, and what could they have said?

Robert cleared his throat. True, there was a bubble in the corner of Mary's lips, glinting as she opened her mouth, but it popped when she tested her jaw. It was also true that lamplight played on the shifting planes of her face, giving it a sly, vivid expression he scarcely recognized as she brushed loose threads from her belly and thighs, then yawned and stretched herself.

Casey's pipe made a wet sucking noise. The clock ticked and tocked. Upstairs their child protested once and was silent. Mice scampered behind the stove, and inexplicably Robert longed for the empty night outside, for the dark refuge of sleep.

"Tell me." Dissatisfied, Casey said it again. "Tell me," stowing the pipe in his breast pocket, "did you learn that trick from the professor as well?"

Hackett shook his head, confessing it was his mother; she'd been a woman with the gift right enough, no question about it. He'd learned it from her. He flexed his pink fingers by way of demonstration and explained he wasn't very good, not a patch on his mother, why once she. . . His voice melancholy yet precise, he swore she'd removed one patent pailful of dark grumous serum (from a Mrs. O'Hearn) greatly to the patient's bodily comfort and the dismay of the family physician. As a result. . . Well! Oh, he knew what they were thinking, yes, he did. Opening his eyes as wide as possible, he admitted others had thought of it before, that she was a witch, a lamia, but it wasn't true! She had the touch, that's all. Her cattle beasts were fatter, her hens laid more eggs. He appealed to them, especially to Mary, he'd cured her jaw, hadn't he?

Robert didn't acquiesce, although Mary agreed: "If Barbara smells blood on the stairs, you can be sure there's trouble coming."

Casey furrowed his brow, trying to remember a good example. What Mary said was true enough, he could vouch for that all right, he could recall the time. . .but she wasn't finished.

"I sometimes think," Mary whispered, her sinuses clicking in punctuation, "I sometimes think the Lord is better pleased with adverbs than nouns." How true, they nodded, isn't that the truth?

Standing by the window, Robert saw clouds like smoke, brilliant white and silver cloths shredded about the moon. His wind machines and fences, shingles on the barn roof, each separate bush and tree glistened in eccentric light.

In preparation for winter the forest empties itself of birds; springing from treetops they've gathered each evening, swirling anonymous flocks. He's heard their ecstatic flight and occasionally, tonight for instance, pausing in the yard before his darkened house, he's seen urgent bodies, flecks against the moon's cold eye.

At some point after Mary had gone to bed, explaining morning comes early when there's a child in the house, and after Casey had wandered away gruffly singing to himself on the road, Rochefoucault Hackett, waggling his finger under Robert's nose, had insisted he return to his chair, whereupon leaning intimately he'd closed and opened first his left and then his right eye to emphasize the serious nature of what he was about to say. He'd been wanting to speak all evening, eh? but thought it better to wait, did Robert understand that? Some things are best. . . Hmmn. Burning low, the single flame had cast a lugubrious light on the two men as Hackett prepared his argument. Didn't Robert see what a grand opportunity lay within his grasp? Not only money, which was power, and power meant control, but knowledge! He'd rapped heavily on his skull, saying knowledge again, then money. For a hired man, perhaps a team of oxen. To speed things up. Proceeding cautiously, he'd suggested that was Mary's problem, the good wife's problem. You could hardly blame her, a fair man couldn't blame her.

Then seeing Fraser's cheek contained an ominous twitch, he'd insisted a fellow like Robert, a man full of ideas and projects, he should have a chance to exploit them, eh? Perpetual motion, for example, what a difference that would make! Beaming, his smart shoes scuffling earnestly, he repeated the professor would pay generously; and apart from that, apart from paying Good Money, he'd share his very considerable knowledge on the subject of perpetual motion. Yes, he would. What could be better than that?

And while Hackett proposed intimate scenes featuring Robert and Melville Carruthers over dinner perhaps, certainly in the professor's workshop, he could see them strolling together; and while Robert savoured these images, a darkened window reflected the two of them, distorted figures swaying without speech or hearing in a room that didn't exist.

Now crouched by the gate he watched the sky convulse, swell to a violent purple when the moon slipped from view. As clouds faded, the space between them filled with stars, while swaying imperceptibly, its canopy heavy with darkness, the forest gathered about his clearing. Even lying with the earth's curve pressing into his back he could see it, a black circle; it was as if he stared into the night from a collapsing tunnel. Idly stroking the rough cloth of his trousers, he heard the owl: methodically spaced, powerful, each syllable a question and a warning. The stream churned and danced as it should. He closed his eyes. She talks to her sister, she talks to Barbara Casey, contained and reasonable she appeals for understanding, for advice and support. They drink tea, she explains and explains, arranging him in their heads. The trouble with Robert, why doesn't he... What does she tell them?

The earth seemed to creak, grinding on its axis. He tore at wild grass tickling his ear, and scrambled to his feet. She's even spoken to Casey. The trouble with Robert... And given half a chance, she'd consult with Hackett.

With the moon revealed, the patterns of night reversed again. Wavering stars were lost among clouds suffused once more with an eerie light. His fence rails, water in the stream, even the stones in his chimney began to glow. The forest leaped up, each separate branch and twig etched and glistening. The owl spoke again. A chill wind shivered the foliage about his house, and turning convulsively in dream his child revealed its mantle of fur.

PART TWO: 1865

PART TWO. 1881

Chapter Two

"I only know things seem and are not good."
— Thomas Kinsella

VII

On the Wednesday Angus went missing, an unseasonable cold front appeared in the northwest. It had sat there, a hard metallic line of cloud, a smear of darkness above the forest. Soon after they'd admitted the boy was gone, and just as a search party fanned into the bush, a terrible wind rose. It rushed and howled, so men could scarcely hear other voices shouting the child's name. It had blown for three hours; and by the time it subsided, the searchers were thrashing stoically in darkness.

After combing and recombing underbrush about the farm, wading along the stream from the mill wheel to the beaver meadow and back again, poking with long sticks among last year's reeds and bullrushes, tossing the boy's name back and forth with fading conviction, the women had lit the lamps, gathering in the kitchen to decide who must hurry home for chores.

Agatha Bullock insisted she knew the road like the back of her hand. Lean and dark as a whip, she set out on Ned for Mad River even though it was darker than the inside of a goat.

At the time nobody had mentioned frost, the night's still brilliance or savage animals, the wolves, the bears and catamounts. But towards midnight as folk returned to their homes, pausing to investigate odd noises in the underbrush, calling, "Angus, Angus, child, is that you?" they'd murmured to each other, agreeing the cold was too much, a killing frost, and some had reported snow still hard as granite in gullies, packed among the brittle roots.

Gathering after dawn on Thursday with hoar frost crunching beneath their boots, they were soon joined by others — men raised by Agatha Bullock on her ride to town. Thus their number increased by dribs and drabs until the cavalcade arrived from Mad River with Major Birdwood on his white horse, at which point thirty-two men were swallowed up in the search.

Leaping from her trap, clutching Mary by the arm, Annie Birdwood swore the boy was fine, her daughter's firstborn was alive and well. He was in a clearing. She'd read the waters: a clear place in the forest!

All day the forest rang with cries, the roar of guns, sometimes fainter, indistinct, then stronger, more dolorous, as they circled back without success, without a sign of the lost boy. They encountered deer and moose. There were foxes, even bear, and a plague of squirrels. James Burpee, the giant, and the cross-eyed David Barber had seen a herd of feral swine rooting voraciously for beechnuts: ugly brutes they were, and vicious. Neither man mentioned them at first and later they forgot them entirely, for with darkness the frost returned: the earth seemed to wilt and blacken beneath a sky drawn so taut, so callous, the stars resembled flecks of mica.

The townsmen huddled about a bonfire in the yard, recalling the fate of lost children, their speech guarded as if the family could hear through log walls. They had given Angus up for dead. In that bitter cold, even a man would do well to survive two nights without food or shelter, so what chance had a five-year-old in drawers and his singlet? He couldn't have got that far. "Perhaps he's drownded," one suggested, "or taken by some beast." "When fear knocks at your door," another cautioned, "send faith to answer." But even prayers wouldn't take the child through another night like this.

Still, twice an hour, each of them taking his turn, a figure shuffled to the perimeter of light and after listening for some sign, a call for help perhaps, had raised his shotgun to fire a signal into the obdurate sky. Thirteen times from midnight until dawn the alarm had resounded, rolled forlornly, echoing, re-echoing among dark tangles and thickets, tree trunks and hairy branches.

Mary Fraser, her eyes blank as pennies, curled with that sound over distant clearings in the forest, and sleepers had groaned when the boy appeared. His wan face and thin arms, cruelly torn by brambles or soaking wet, his hair matted over his forehead, he beckoned, his mouth opened as if to speak; he told conflicting stories. . .

Friday dawned grey and cold. Shrouded with mist, the bush seemed an impenetrable wall; and the sky, draped over the farm like a circus tent, cast ordinary sounds back into their ears so they scarcely recognized them.

A feathery circle at first, wan as a moon, the sun struggled above the trees. Already soaked to the knees by melting frost, with a vague image of fire in their blood, Robert consented to whiskey all round. As a result, the search didn't resume until after ten.

Occasionally, men straggled back to the house with hope of news, and when that failed, of inspiration. They were given hot food and more whiskey. Pretending to dry their boots, presenting minor ailments for Agatha Bullock's ministrations, they dawdled uncomfortably. Then driven by a sense of duty, of mechanical time to be filled until sunset, they trudged back into the forest. Without realizing it, they ceased calling his name, shouting only to maintain contact with their fellows. Each lost hope, until by dusk, if they'd been looking for anything, it was a corpse.

Woken before dawn on Saturday by a familiar voice, Robert found himself weeping at the foot of their bed with no idea how he got there. Imbued with curious light, the curtains bellied then collapsed. The bureau, his clothing on the straight-backed chair, their bed, and beyond it the new infant's cradle — these familiar objects trembled as if caught in a discreditable act.

It had not disturbed Mary, that voice. Breathing through her mouth, she lay with Alice in the crook of her arm. Again the curtains billowed, tentative wings that failed. If only he could remember who it was, what it said. . . .

Buttoning his trousers he bent to the window where in the pale blood light of dawn he saw bodies like spokes in a wheel, their feet pointing at a dead fire. Was it Angus, his spirit released from that mournful flesh, its decomposition slowed by the ice that took him? Perhaps Angus had come to bid them farewell, to ask advice of his father, discover some trick or clue to speed him on his way. *I have him*. Grinding his teeth so hard he tasted salt, Robert remembered: I have him. Although it was his own voice this time, the intonation struck him as eccentric, as if he repeated something from an unrecognizable language, a phrase once learned from some cruel tongue.

Outside, his wind machines clattered in a breeze, spreading the curtains with aboriginal light; not so much light as an absence of darkness, it was flat as shale, the colour of gruel. . . . I *have* him. What did it mean? I have *him*. Peering close over Mary and the babe, so close their bodies warmed his face, he tried again, underscoring the first word, but it was no better.

Annie Birdwood continued to insist the child was alive, he'd turn up soon. Even as the first small group pushed Isaac Eskey to explain their case, how it was in Mad River, she strode among the men, her shrill voice berating their lack of faith. "Do the women have to go out and find him, is that it?"

Mumbling among themselves, watching Robert covertly, they knew he'd understand their meaning, they'd been talking right enough and well. . . The poor tyke hadn't survived. Oh, there was a chance, there's always that, but the good Lord in his wisdom and three bitter nights. . .

A pair of blue jays flashed in raucous flight from behind the house; another called within the forest. If only the weather had broke, why then things would be different, eh?

Neighbours and townsfolk watched Robert from beneath their brows, the brims of their hats. Shifting uneasily, waiting to see if Mary would finally appear from the house, they peeked at him from the corners of their eyes. "We'd of heard him by now," declared one, "we'd of found him. . ."

A woman at the back began to keen wetly. A Baptist voice was raised in prayer but faltered as Annie Birdwood stormed among them, waving her arms like a windmill, a maenad, her wiry hair unbrushed. She confronted each by name until the crowd milled uncomfortably. Twisting and turning, they strove to avoid her. Voices struggled in argument, several commenced singing of that comfort found in the bosom of the Lord. Moses Stickney, hopping onto a stump, his face bright with emotion, bellowed the child wasn't dead but was just away! There was a scattering of amens and a wailing cry. Some wept openly. They could have had the funeral right then and there, welcoming the certainty, the resignation, as they welcomed the lesson in a cautionary tale.

Mary appeared in the doorway with Alice on her hip. Few had seen her since Thursday night and so they craned eagerly, pushing to catch a glimpse, an image, a memory. Hungrily they scanned her face for tears and who knows what febrile dementia, the madness of sorrow, and at that moment, pity and guilt swept the crowd. Even Isaac Eskey cast injured glances to see who it was that had counselled despair; so when good old Will Casey brandished his hat, leaping onto the stump to shout "We're with you, Mary dear," it was Eskey himself who fought to lead the whole crew back into the forest, as if the child was hiding, as children sometimes do, their faces buried in their hands, crouching excitedly, awaiting discovery.

Having lost touch with his contingent as it circled to the south and home, too spent to shout and running short of powder, Robert slumped on the roots of an oak. A carrier pigeon, scout for some great flight to follow, inspected him with one red eye and dismissed him; mice resumed feeding in a windfall at his feet; and a red squirrel lost interest as the somnolent humming of unseen life resumed.

What finally would he say to Mary? What would she say to him? In the distance faint shouts could be heard and the dull roar of guns, no louder now than a creek gargling somewhere behind him. The wilderness had claimed their son without notice, leaving no sign. Perhaps some day another farmer, driving a mechanical plough, would turn up a wee bone, so delicate, a thigh perhaps. . . .

There were no words. Instead of drawing them together, the tragedy had served to firm the wedge between them, drive it a little deeper. Her empty face, the face of a dead rabbit, scarcely acknowledged him; and when it did, he turned from her, unable to speak, unable even to soothe her or be soothed in the bed where Angus and then Alice were conceived.

Then as he sat staring without seeing, it was as if a window opened in the underbrush, a curtain raised to make visible what had been invisible. Beyond the maze of branches, soft maples red with buds, beyond a rock face beneath that drooping bough of pine, he saw the figure of a man with his back turned. He too squatted on his haunches but his hair was twisted in oily strands over thick shoulders and his back stretched the torn material of his shirt. Robert later swore he'd smelled him first, the black odour of tomcat or mink but somehow more pungent, a dangerous must that caught in his throat. At any rate, he crept from cover to cover, his gun at the ready, placing his feet with such caution, almost reverentially, even the squirrel ignored him; and yet when he paused, the other sprang to his feet, uttering such a shout as he whirled to face him that Robert was suddenly, inexplicably, filled with terror.

Stricken to the heart by that cry, confronting a madman, for that's what he was, his nakedness bursting through rents in his clothing, Robert stared appalled by the eyes. Beneath spikes of hair on a bulging forehead, the eyes threatened to spring from their sockets. The squat flat-nosed face grimaced, twisting as if the body laboured under an intolerable weight; indeed he staggered like a drunkard forcing air between his teeth in a fluting whistle.

It appeared he'd speak. Matted with hair, his chest and belly heaved, the mouth contorted, a terrible rictus. He shuddered; but in that instant, bounding on stick legs, he vanished like a stone in water.

Deeply shaken, breathing through his nose, Robert

waved his gun, an inconclusive gesture, then stood trans-fixed, waiting. . . .

Eventually convincing himself the apparition had truly fled, he found a shallow cave beneath the upturned roots of a fallen pine. Carpeted with cedar, it contained a turtle shell stuffed with feathers, a green sheepskin, probably the beast he'd thought taken by wolves, and a pathetic collection of knick-knacks, beads and clam shells wrapped in deerskin. Rich as cheese, the rutting stench forced him back into the air. So strong he could taste it, permeating his clothing, it stirred an ambiguous, vaguely nauseated excitement in his chest.

Through corridors of trees, beneath a marmoreal sky descending into the bush, circling odd shapes, he wandered as if watching himself from a great distance, until he arrived in a place he'd never seen before. Too far from water, he confronted a grotesque jumble of dead trees on a breast of primal granite swelling from the earth.

Felled by beavers they lay chaotically, a burn heap or log jam, as if the animals had never intended to use them, as if they'd gone berserk. Many more were fatally gnawed; completely girdled, their underbark was brown and softly weathered to his touch.

Uttering small cries, black and white birds darted among shreds of silver bark that flickered, rustled with a sound like flames. They picked and hammered as Fraser scrambled among sculpted stumps, once yellow now fading to grey. He balanced on fallen trees to search among branches scaled with crisp brown leaves, poking in that debris until he found the demented beaver crushed beneath a butt of poplar. Picked over, polished by ground beetles, the skeleton shone within the remnants of its pelt. What wild lunacy had possessed it? Torn open in anger, the mouth still gaped voraciously, and as Fraser knelt to examine the small grim face, to push at the teeth with his finger, a blue jay commenced screaming incessantly.

The tale of Angus' survival was confused and marvellous, subject to unlikely speculations from the moment Joshua Willow, the half-breed, appeared with the child in his arms. Folk accompanied them to the house, firing celebratory shots while shouting into the bush, and set a barrel of whiskey in the yard. Greeting stragglers with a drink as they emerged from the forest, hooting with disbelief, they praised the Lord and Annie Birdwood, for she'd known all along, she'd told them right enough, how had she known?

"The Lord moves in mysterious ways, so He does," suggested Moses Stickney, "His wonders to perform." While some muttered amen to that, their voices overlapping, others insisted it was Annie Birdwood, she'd the gift all right, no doubt about that. He was in a clearing, just as she had predicted. "John said that a man can receive nothing, except it be given from Heaven. . ." Voices from within the crowd muttered in agreement as they struggled, pushing good-naturedly around the barrel. It was Heaven all right that sent the woolly dog, it must have been. He would have froze without it.

"What's this, what's this?" Wrestling for his first drink, Will Casey tried to focus back over his shoulder. "What dog?"

Agatha Bullock, her black eyes like opals, tousled as a gypsy, elbowed to the heart of the crowd. She explained again how the child insisted it had come each night, a big woolly dog.

"By crikey, it must of been a bear!"

"The breed says it was a bear all right. . ."

"It kept him warm." Agatha persisted with one shapely arm in the air. "Kept the poor tyke warm."

A fierce clamour announced Robert's appearance by the barn, so they descended on him with shouts and whistles.

If it were another, they'd heave him to their shoulders, pummel him, throw him in the air. But not Robert. They couldn't imagine laying hands on Robert Fraser, so they reached at him with odd gestures, with words, disjointed phrases. It was a bear, they shouted, he was saved by a bear. Then drawing back so as not to impede his sudden loping run to the house, they beat their hands on their thighs. Such a story, they cried among themselves, what a story! In subsequent, more curious, more fantastic versions, each was present when Joshua Willow, marching unerringly to that swath of uprooted trees, had found young Angus playing in the mouth of a bear's den. Full of wonder, they'd tell it to friends and strangers, recount it in letters home, embellishing it until the story suited them just fine.

Those who hadn't left gathered in the yard after supper, while Joshua prepared the bonfire. As they clustered watching him, his blue smock shirt with a greasy red sash at the waist, his fluid body and cruel hook, his hair black and shiny like an animal's, they nurtured a special sense of kinship, as if each alone shared with Joshua a rare and secret moment of his life.

As Mary came from the house with his mother's plaid shrouding her face and shoulders, Robert shifted to make room for her, but she didn't notice. Settling between her parents, she leaned to hear something her mother said, and drawing the cloth back from her face revealed a luminous smile.

"I was sure as spit he'd drownded." Lighting his pipe, Will Casey began the procedure with satisfaction.

"Or devoured by wild beasts," agreed Tom Bullock, removing his boots with a sigh.

"You mind Bruce Legge?" At the sound of Annie Birdwood's voice, they settled themselves as if it were a signal. "Old Jabez had this dam for his mill, a mighty poor one it was. You know the kind." Taking Major Birdwood's cup, she drank decisively. "Often bursting, it did great damage, but the most terrible disaster of all, young Brucie, such a sweet child, he fell into the flume and stopped the wheel with his body, you mind that?"

Groaning as if they'd never heard the story, they murmured and sighed while sparks winked maliciously, then vanished above their heads. The house and log barn, the fences, the mill wheel and wind machines — these comfortable shapes became tremulous, indistinct, in a night turning so black the forest retreated, and their circle of light became a crowded room. "You see, Jabez went searching to find the obstacle and found his little boy's body, found little Brucie. . . ."

With light from the flames isolated on their faces, their disembodied hands, they coughed and spat, agreeing Jabez was never quite right after that. From that day he's been several bricks short of a load. They'd stories to tell, so they had, silly old bugger. It made you laugh just to think of him.

Scarcely hearing the somnolent chatter, Robert listened for telltale noises, warnings from beyond the verge of light and dark. He'd have gone for his gun above the door except they'd speak to him, laugh at his nervousness. He'd have to explain, describe the shell, the stinking sheepskin, and so he sat as if he'd been promised something, had it thrust before his eyes, then snatched away before he knew what was expected of him.

It was true Angus slept miraculous in his cot: not so disturbed by his adventure as Robert by the wild man, not even particularly hungry. He must have eaten, he must have been fed, although he'd describe no more than the woolly dog, it kept him warm at night. His brown triangular face puzzled while they fussed, apparently indifferent to their enthusiasm, he finally protested, shrugging off their hands, and scampered into his bed under the eaves.

"Just to think of him with a beast like that, it makes me. . ." Resting her head on Annie's shoulder, Mary smiled complacently.

"Who'd ever believe it, eh?" Will Casey squeezed his wife's thigh as if he didn't beat her, as if Angus would now live forever. He bared his teeth unexpectedly. "What do you say, Robbie, your little bugger's blessed by the wild, eh?" Shaking his head until he lost his balance, he fell onto his back with laughter. "He'll do all right, yes, he will." He rolled back and forth helplessly. "Blessed by the wild," he giggled, and the whole crew, sprawled now with drink, began to chuckle among themselves like ravens.

"You needn't worry about that one."

"Not here, not in the bloody bush!"

"Blessed by the wild. . ."

"Oh yes!" cried Agatha Bullock, clapping her hands. Did they ever hear of the young woman by Mansfield who went out after supper to greet her husband on his return from the bush? Well, she saw him rise up in the darkness, you see; and since he was on the other side of the fence, she gave him the baby so she could climb over and join him. She'd brought the baby and just as she handed the child over, she discovered it wasn't her husband, it was a bear, she'd given her child to a bear. . . . Specks of light glistened in her eyes, predators' eyes set close in a swarthy face, and for some reason Robert believed she spoke only to him.

"What happened to the child?"

"I don't know," she whispered, ignoring their clamour, "that's all I ever heard."

"It must of been dark all right."

"It was," she said. "It was."

Partially drunk because of the whiskey, the heat of the fire and its sombre light, Robert shivered when she touched the birthmark, an exquisite wee fish by the corner of her mouth.

Someone spoke of a wolfboy seen north of Smoky Falls, scampering on all fours he was, wild as wild. They'd tried to catch him. . .

"Bears will eat anything."

With their faces subsiding in shadow, they agreed that Major Birdwood was right. Bears would eat anything.

"Like pigs," said David Barber, remembering the wild swine, their vicious little eyes.

"But you'd have heard if the baby was injured." Curled on her side, her hand on the dark weight of her hip, Mary spoke softly but with conviction. "That would be part of the story."

"Perhaps it is." Fingering her birthmark, Agatha shrugged as if it didn't matter. "I don't know."

"What would that do to a child, I wonder?" As the fire died the bush leaned closer. When Robert got to his feet he could see it, massed and jagged with darkness. "Do you suppose it would make him wild?" The barrel was almost empty but by tipping it he managed a few drops. He was convinced the child they'd found was not the one he'd lost. There was someone beside him, he smelled her first, Agatha Bullock; lifting the keg from its trestle, he poured what was left into her cup.

VIII

"I'll wager a dram he don't make it this far, that he stops at the Globe." Jacob Brodie, sitting with Robert Fraser and Major Hod Anderson Birdwood on the porch of the Queen's Hotel, spat over the railing as a young man appeared on the River Road. He was leading two red horses, one speckled with white. "Like as not, that bloody Yankee will dance him in off the road."

The Major, who on formal occasions affected buckskin jackets with porcupine quills decorating the breast and shoulders, grinned and flicked ash from his cigar, then accepted the bet. A company of sweating townsmen, twenty-five or thirty of them, wheeled in line, turned right at a command by Jesse Gorham, and shuffled behind the blacksmith's and out of sight, their rifles bobbing hopelessly out of time.

"It's not as if I'm selling it," Fraser insisted, glancing towards the top-heavy wagon, its clumsy box built with sheets of birchbark lashed to cedar poles. Hidden inside, so folk couldn't see it for nothing, was the skeleton of his mammoth, cunningly reconstructed, supported by posts anchored in the flatbed. It stood as it once might have, except the skull drooped pathetically, suggesting the beast had received a ferocious blow to the side of its neck. "It's still mine," he said, after a pause. "But being in Toronto, the professor, he knows people, the right kind of people, handy people in the States, and now the war is over. . ." He nibbled his lip, then sucking the corner of his moustache repeated he wasn't selling, no sir. "I've a business arrangement," he confided as the Mad River militia reappeared. Stamping their feet they passed the hotel, swinging their free arms, glaring at the trio drinking on the shaded verandah. "Carruthers gets. . .a percentage in return for. . . He's arranging the exhibition, don't you see?"

Flies bumped and circled crazily under the eaves and against the windows. Twirling the empty glass, Fraser stared at his wagon; and Jacob Brodie watched the stranger, red dust puffing about his feet and ankles, his legs swinging from the knee with the easy gait of a pedlar or preacher. But this one kept his eyes to himself: he didn't appear to notice the line of cabins and shanties separated from each other and from the baked road by burned stumps and tangled underbrush.

"Well now, Robbie, I reckon. . ." The Major picked up his glass and, frowning, put it down again. "I reckon you could use some hard cash for that blasted machine of yours." He smiled vaguely as if to deny his irritation, then dug into his ear, searching for wax.

The man with the horses mopped his face and neck, even rubbing under his bonnet with a large handkerchief, and passed by the Globe without glancing at the Yankee proprietor waving and calling from his door. He ignored the yellow hound dancing at the end of its tether, and only stopped when he arrived at the wooden pump in front of Jacob Brodie's Queen's Hotel.

Fraser rose as the stranger, a dark fellow of maybe twenty-five, removed his shirt. They saw the ropy muscles in his neck and shoulders as he watered the horses. "I'm obliged to you, Major, for your help and advice. . ." Conscious of a dull ache behind his eyes, Robert decided there wasn't anywhere to go. It occurred to him he could check the lashings on his wagon but he didn't move. "The machine is my affair."

"Come along, man, I meant no harm." The Major filled his son-in-law's glass.

The man bent to wash at the pump. He huffed and spat, dashing water on his face and breast.

"There's a great future in perpetual motion."

"Of course there is." Carefully examining the tip of his cigar so Fraser could sit down unnoticed, Major Birdwood grimaced when Brodie shifted onto one buttock, breaking wind as if to change the subject.

"It's a poor arse that can't rejoice," chuckled Brodie. He'd made a terrible smell. "That's a fine pair of animals."

Wrinkling his nose, he eyed the red stallion and speckled mare. "I guess he paid enough for them two."

"It's just, I sometimes think. . ." Picking at a grease spot on his sleeve, the Major spoke carefully. "I wonder sometimes if you're not like Wish, planting a feather and expecting chickens. . . Son-of-a-gun, Jacob," he laughed unconvincingly. "It smells as if something's crawled up there and died."

After drying himself with his shirt, the stranger drank some of the sweet water, then turned slowly surveying the town scattered along the riverbank. Shading his eyes against the sun, he seemed impressed by the variety of recent buildings, their unpainted boards shining yellow among the trees. He was on the point of leaving as he was, stripped to the waist, when Birdwood's Mill and Distillery and the sounds of militia training from the lumber yard drew his attention. He turned back to the men on the porch, his hand resting on his brow in an ironical salute, and they saw the brutal cicatrix curving from belly to hip bone, the proud flesh ridged and glowing. He observed them with pale eyes before saying, "I'm looking to find a Major Birdwood."

"You've found me first shot."

"You are Major Birdwood?"

"I am. . ." Tucking in his shirt, the stranger smoothed it with a fastidious gesture before sliding his arms back into his galluses. He sported the sly assurance of a lawyer's clerk, perhaps a magistrate's nephew.

"And that lot is your militia, sir?"

Robert decided he was a smart one, showing the Major his wound like that. He had something up his sleeve all right.

"Such as it is." Smoking his cigar as if no one else could afford them, squinting through the smoke, Birdwood considered how to assert his authority without endangering it. "And who, sir, are you?"

Before answering, the young stranger turned and, delving into a saddle bag on the mare, produced a package tied with cord which he handed over the railing.

"Shantz, sir. Edward Shantz. And I bring this from the garrison in Toronto."

"Ah-ha!" beamed the Major. "Orders," he cried while fumbling with the knots. "Orders," he repeated on the off chance they hadn't understood. "Pour Mr. Shantz that dram, Jacob. You've got yourself a lodger."

Removing the outer wrapping, he found an envelope stamped with an irregular button of scarlet wax, the official nature of which so impressed Fraser and Brodie that they left off eyeing Shantz, edging diplomatically so as not to appear nosy.

"Jacob," the Major insisted, his voice unusually resonant, "give the man a drink. He's done a fine job." Lifting the seal with his pocket knife, happy not to have damaged it, he adjusted his spectacles, clearing his throat. "You don't perhaps have any notion. . ." Tapping the envelope on the back of his thumb, peering at the messenger reaching for his dram, he cleared his throat again. "They didn't by any chance. . ."

Seeing reproval in the narrow, ungenerous features, he coughed, quickly changing course. "Good. . . That's good, eh? Ha! Of course not." Resting a finger along his nose he winked, bobbing his head. "Ha," he muttered. "*Ah-ha!*"

At the end of the street, Jesse Gorham, his face contorted, was haranguing men of all shapes and sizes. Raising his cutlass desperately, he shouted them into lines and bellowed. They fixed bayonets, seizing their rifles in both hands, pointing them from the waist even before he commanded, they bent their knees. "Ready! Lunge!" They staggered forward, stabbing wildly. "Withdraw!" screamed Gorham, even though he must have known the exercise was utterly futile.

The street had filled with children, with derisive women

and old men, while the Yankee's hound appeared to be strangling at the end of its rope.

"Ready!" Again and again they lunged, sweating and cursing, until Edward Shantz removed his horses to the stable. The Major lowered his eyes and the street fell silent.

"Well. . ." Stepping from the porch as their commanding officer, Major Birdwood was at a loss for words. "Mr. Gorham," he said at last, "we'll have to work on that. . ."

Contemplating the men grinning sheepishly at one another, he paraded as if he didn't notice the bottle passing from hand to hand among the ranks. He cleared his throat. He opened his mouth but only managed a whimpering sort of sigh. Nevertheless, on completing the circle and arriving back by the porch, he had no alternative but to address them. Again clearing his throat, brandishing the document, he revealed the gravest of threats to Confederation, the Grand Old Link between England and the Canadas. Toronto had warned him, indeed by special courier. "Armed men," he cried, "gathering by Niagara, the Fenians!" Waving his arms, his voice rising precariously, he set before their eyes the picture of a Catholic army, Republicans all, fanatics swearing secret and terrible oaths, swearing revenge. Stamping up clouds of red dust between the ranks, he appealed to them as patriots, as men and soldiers, as husbands and fathers. They had families at home, they owned property, or soon would. Hard-working men, sober fellows dedicated to improving their lot, they had a stake in the future, in a United Canada.

"You know," said Fraser as the men began to stir like boiling mud, "if the Fenians weren't dogans and Irish to boot, if they were regular Yankees, most folk here'd greet them with a hot dinner."

"They would so," agreed Brodie, gazing from Birdwood to Fraser, then back to the Major who with fierce eyes was announcing how they'd secure the women and children.

"We whipped them in New Brunswick," cried David Barber as Edward Shantz returned to his drink.

"No popery. . ."

"We'll whip them here!" Taking a deep breath, the Major had begun to formulate his plan when Frances Brodie appeared at the door. She struck the dinner gong, her triceps flapping like turkey wattles.

"Eats," she cried.

"Dismiss," howled Gorham as the men broke ranks, stampeding towards the porch.

"It's on the table!" Withdrawing to one side, Frances watched with satisfaction as the men scrambled in through the door just as Humphrey and Moses Stickney reached the porch with shouts of Hurrah! Close on their heels were the giant, James Burpee, already brandishing his belt knife, cross-eyed David Barber, the blacksmith Isaac Eskey, and Rich Pickard. Among the regulars were Dr. Tom Sanderson, Absalom Hyslop, Jesse Gorham and Billy Greene, who waited for the Major.

Frances Brodie was confident that men would eat anything. Hungry men, she was fond of saying, neither knew nor cared what was set before them so long as you didn't tell them what it was. A handsome woman with substantial hips, she waited until the pushing and shoving subsided, and they settled themselves around her table cluttered with bowls of steaming potatoes, turnips and beans swimming in salt pork, hard bread and biscuits and great jugs of beer. She waited for the expectant hush, then she said formally, "Mr. Burpee, will you give thanks this day to the good Lord for His bounteous nature."

"Begging your pardon, wumman," replied the giant, "it's not my turn."

"Well, certainly it is." Frances Brodie could scarcely believe her ears. "Of course it is."

"No, it ain't. It's. . ."

"Come along, James," smiled the Major, his voice smooth with authority and reason, "do the honours before the spuds get cold."

"It's Barber's turn."

"Sweet Jesus," groaned the doctor.

"Here we go," said Absalom Hyslop with a fierce grin. "You're a liar, Burpee."

"Who's calling me a liar?" Burpee's knees struck the table, rattling the dishes as he sprang to his feet. "You calling me a liar, you cross-eyed little dogan?"

"You're a liar," repeated Barber, his voice high and mean, "a great bloody ox and a thief."

The onlookers gasped with appreciation as Burpee shuddered, his eyes rolling completely white in his hairy face.

"Thief," he bellowed, "a thief am I?"

"The knife, put up the knife, Jamie."

But Burpee, towering with rage and trembling, flicking his beard convulsively with his free hand and blowing through his nose, was oblivious.

"You're a...a..." Snorting and puffing, Burpee searched for words. "A foul republican, so you are, a traitorous goddamn... Aaaargh!" Pulling at his beard, pointing his chin at the ceiling, he stamped his feet like a prize horse. "Aaaargh!"

"You're ugly, Burpee, the good Lord made you power-ful ugly," hissed Barber. "I could drive a sow up each of your nostrils."

"Ruffians," screeched Frances Brodie as she burst past the kitchen girls, both of them watching open-mouthed from the door. "Throw them out, Jacob! Do something, oh mercy."

"I'm gonna hurt him," roared the giant, jumping up and down. "I'm gonna hurt him real bad."

"We'll have no knives." Jacob Brodie shuffled hope-lessly.

"No knives," echoed Robert Fraser, as Missus Brodie reappeared, pushing through the crowd with a large black frying pan in her fist.

"James Burpee!" The Major's voice cut everyone to silence as he sprang into the ring. "Put up the knife, man. There's no need for it among friends." Almost elegant in his worn buckskins, he waited confidently, although the giant must have outweighed him by eighty pounds. "Come along now, Jamie."

James Burpee reared back on his heels, propelling flecks of spittle from his mouth. Shouting "Out of the way," he feinted unexpectedly with his shoulders. The crowd surged and Birdwood raised his arms, crouching defensively.

"Mr. Burpee," the Major commanded from under his elbow, "stand where you are." He straightened with as much dignity as he could muster, and the girls, Clara and Nancy, jumped onto the table for a better view.

"I'm gonna hurt him, you *hear me*?" The giant was stamping his feet and bobbing his head like a man meeting a bear on the road. "I'm gonna cut somethin' off him that he *needs*!"

"*A-ten-shun!*"

"What?"

"I'm Birdwood, Major Birdwood."

"Birdwood, eh? Birdwood, *bah!* You don't have no feathers up your arse like a normal birdwood. *Aaaarrgh!*" The knife flashed as he moved and Frances Brodie, leaping right off the ground, struck him a terrible blow on the head with the frying pan. He fell straight and true as the Merry-weather oak, and the impact of him sprang the corner window and rattled cups and saucers from their shelves.

"My God, I've killed him entirely." And in truth he lay motionless, with the frying pan around his neck.

Dr. Tom crouched to examine him. "Doesn't that beat all?" he marvelled. "The bottom popped right out of it."

"Would you look at that!" They clustered around,

squeezing and shoving for a glimpse of the bloody head and neck with the shattered frying pan encircling it, an iron collar; and none of them could remember hearing tell of anything like it, although the girl Clara recalled a sap kettle bursting into flames.

"It must have been faulty." Retrieving the pan's bottom from beneath a chair, Edward Shantz grinned at Clara who slipped past him for hot water and cloths from the kitchen.

"It must of been." Jacob Brodie set out two bottles of whiskey.

There were cries of relief and a smattering of applause as Burpee sat bolt upright with a torrent of blood vanishing into his heard.

"He's alive all right." The doctor held out his glass.

"I'm as partial to surprises as the next man," said Burpee, wearing the pan like a scarf. He watched in fascination as a rivulet of blood started to pour off the handle and splash onto his trouser leg. "But I'd just as soon be prepared for them."

"The scalp's a terrible man for bleeding. A terrible man for bleeding," ventured Clara as she knelt to sponge Burpee's wound. It proved a difficult job since he kept moving his head, trying to peer into the armhole of her blouse.

"The mouth's worse, by Jesus Christ. You get a good crack in the gob and it'll bleed buckets."

"It's nothing at all, Mr. Hyslop, once you've seen a nicked artery. That's something else altogether."

"That's true enough. That's perfectly true, Missus Brodie, but I was talking of superficial wounds."

"Your good health, Jamie." Dr. Tom raised his glass to Burpee who was on his feet now, twisting the pan in an attempt to extricate his head. "It's better it bleeds." The doctor showed his yellow teeth. "You get bruised blood in the system, there'll be a fever every time, and many a man has died of it."

Everyone agreed with that all right. There were murmurs of approval while they drank. Indeed so preoccupied were they, only Robert saw Birdwood and Shantz leave by the side door. He started to move but Shantz forbade it. Blinking his eyes, he left Robert with an unsettling image of his face as he closed the door. There was such authority in that dolose glance that Fraser was shaken by a premonition, a sense of foreboding. He wanted to follow but instead suggested smearing the pan and certain portions of Burpee's head with lard. It was something, an indication he was there. He regretted it immediately though, agreeing when Clara said that'd be no better than the blood, blood's slippery enough. But it wasn't. No matter how he tried, the pan seemed to catch somewhere, either at the corner of his jaw or the back of his head.

"Anyway, good health, Jamie."

"To a speedy recovery."

"I mind the time, it was right here in this room." Missus Brodie stroked her arm fondly as memories crowded back. "A travelling man he was, making his living o'er the brim of the hill, and I knew right off there'd be trouble for there was thirteen at table. He said it himself. He said, 'Do you know, Missus, we've thirteen of us at table?' And it wasn't six hours later he was stone dead, his throat cut in the street for tuppence. He came in the door there, gargling in his own blood, white as a sheet. 'Save me!' he cried. 'I'm dead!' Oh, it was shooting out of him like fountains. You can see the stains yet if you've a mind to, right there by the door. A lovely man he was. . ."

It had become apparent that James Burpee wouldn't get his head out of the frying pan. The force of the blow had got it on all right, but they'd bust his jaw if they tried any harder to get it off.

Refilling his glass, knowing he'd regret it, Robert considered the corner of his wagon, a birchbark panel visible through the window. Bars of light shot through with dust fell on his beast inside, its blunt flat ribs, the columns of its legs, the great aphonic head tilted as if listening. If he left he could lie peacefully beneath it, admire that symmetry, that silence, familiar to him now as his own hands.

"Here then," said Isaac Eskey, "you come into the shop and I'll have it off after dinner." He shuffled his feet decisively. "It's the only way."

Not until everyone was seated did they discover Birdwood and the stranger had left. "Who's that fellow with him? That Shantz." Hunched over his plate, glancing around the table until his eye fell on Robert, Dr. Tom stopped chewing, waiting for an answer.

"He's got a fine pair of horses." He has so, they agreed with Barber, you can say that for him. They'd cost a pretty penny as well. "Where would a young fellow get that sort of money?"

"Up the cow's arse, third shelf," said the doctor, still watching Fraser.

"Give a man like that a bridle. . ." Robert paused, and emptied his glass, grimacing, because the liquor was raw. "Give him a bridle and he'll have a horse soon enough." Rubbing his hand across his eyes, he knew he'd go on drinking until it tasted smooth.

"I think so too."

"I'll tell you what, Jamie. . ." Jacob Brodie burst into sudden laughter. "I thought I'd bust something when you said that about him not having feathers up his arse, the Major. . ."

"By Jesus, that's right." Jesse Gorham smiled cautiously. "He didn't know whether to shit or wind his watch."

"Heugh-heugh." With his head swathed in bandages, the frying pan around his neck, James Burpee snorted modestly so that tiny flecks of potato sprang from between his lips.

80

IX

"When everybody's got cabbages they pay me with cabbages, with pigeons when you can beat them out of the air with a bloody stick." Dr. Tom spat, exactly hitting the wheel turning by his foot, and stretched, bracing himself, while Fraser eased the team over a granite wave in the middle of the way. Not much more than a track in places, the road south from Mad River had scarcely been improved since Robert first travelled it almost ten years before. There were a few clearings now in which families clustered, waving hopefully as the wagon appeared, and new openings in the bush from time to time, dim tunnels cut into the forest, tentative concessions clogged with the violent growths of early summer. It's also true many original stumps had rotted, and occasionally there was a rough bridge where none had been. Nevertheless, horrible quagmires threatened to engulf horses and wagon, black wet soil slowed their progress, and there were windfalls to be manhandled from the path.

In the desolate silence they had been travelling almost three hours without encountering any human sign. Swaying and jerking, lulled by the heat of the day, the movement of the wagon, contemplating the rippling muscles and shining buttocks of the horses, they came to discuss money, pelf, the sinews of war, hard cash, the coin of the realm for more land. You had to have more land and men to clear it. "And better stock," insisted Robert. "A fellow can't get ahead with inferior animals."

"It takes money to make money." Digging automatically in his crotch, Dr. Tom added, "Or friends in high places."

"Them that has gets."

"Bastards." Spitting again as the wagon lurched dangerously, he missed by a foot and a half.

"Still. . ." Faint in the distance a trumpet sounded. "I'd rather be them than not."

"There's no justice." The doctor was gathering phlegm for another try. "And precious little mercy." Robert blinked, nodding in agreement, although it wasn't necessary. "Do you know what they gave Benedict Arnold?" Chewing on his lower lip, Robert heard the familiar complaint without listening. "Five thousand acres. In Gwillumbury, nobody knows that. . . And another eight and a half thousand for his wife in Elmsley."

The cedar and birchbark frame shifted, tilting uncertainly, then righted itself as Robert manoeuvred the team, their smooth haunches rippling with sweat. "His bloody sons each got two thousand acres as well!" He turned towards Robert, presenting his dirty teeth filmed with saliva. "And what's the ordinary man get, eh? What have you got?"

Robert didn't appreciate this turn of events. Even at the worst of times, he managed to avoid thinking of himself as an ordinary man; and driving his *Mammuthus Primigenius* to Toronto like this, to fame perhaps and fortune, especially now with a deal to be made, he scowled at the doctor. His mind full of dreams and complications, he reached inside his jacket and fondled the notice Carruthers had sent from Toronto. If he could afford a contrate wheel, perhaps a lodestone, materials for overbalancing weights. . . Already yellowed and worn from handling, the paper remained in his breast pocket; it was damp to the touch and warm from his body. *Great discovery*, it said, for he knew it by heart. The Perpetual Motion — one of the grandest *pieces of mechanism* that was ever presented to the world, but it was gone, he'd missed it like the elephant girl. If only he could have seen it — her arched body and arms like wings. . . Long sought by the great *Sir Isaac Newton*, and later by men of the very first talents, this Grand Machine had been going ever since it was invented and would continue to work merely by the Power of its own Balance and Pivots, as long as the World stood. . . .

Closer now, half-heartedly the trumpet sounded. His team surged as Robert slapped the reins on their great buttocks. The two silky tails stiffened eagerly, arching to reveal black crinkled flesh as their sweating thighs churned provocatively.

"That makes me think of the saddlebag preacher who came upon this Orkneyman way and hell back there in the bush." Bending forward, Dr. Tom slapped Smoke's crupper so the horse, startled for an instant, lost her rhythm. "He was so far out he hadn't seen anyone for five years, not a soul, no company at all except for his sheep. He had these sheep, you see. He wasn't married, had no neighbours or anything, so the preacher was puzzled to see a little boy. He asked how old he was and when the kid said four the preacher asked how this could be. You haven't seen anyone for five years? Nope, said the man. And you're not married? Nope, said the man. Really puzzled now, the preacher asked the child his name. 'What's your name, little boy?' 'Basil,' he answered. BAAA," bleated the doctor, "Baah-zil!" Snorting happily he spat and hit the wheel. "I like big-arsed women," he said after a few minutes. Leaning to stroke Smoke's rump again, he giggled. "They keep your ballocks out of the sand."

A scrawny roan cropped along the path as they rounded a corner. Pulling a sledge laden with letter bags, it was the Royal Mail. The guard, a bearded wretch gnawing on a piece of, well, it looked like meat, wandered behind with a post-horn in his free hand. Seeing them he exchanged it for whatever he was eating and trumpeted violently. Then wiping grease from his whiskers, he hailed them with a shout, although they'd come abreast of him.

It appeared there was a mighty nesting of pigeons just ahead. "By God," he bellowed, waving a devastated squab before their eyes, "the biggest you ever saw! Not more than a mile, maybe a mile and a half, birds beyond numbering, sweet as molasses they are, and Yankee netters, you oughta see them work!" Opening his mouth to worry loose a bit of meat, he pressed the carcass against his face, the face of a dullard behind his beard. Spongy like a mushroom and as pale, it appeared he never ventured from the forest but he'd of signed on with them, yes, he would, if they'd of had him.

"There's money in it all right." Still eyeing Smoke's arse, Tom Sanderson scratched absently between his legs. "I hear a good crew takes thirty or forty barrels a day. . ."

"Them Yankees are getting fifty, easy."

"Fifty!" Robert would believe that when he saw it. "What's a barrel worth now?"

"Over the border?" The doctor seemed certain. "Twenty-five dollars."

"Fifty cents a dozen live in Toronto." The postman's mouth was full of meat.

"For God's sake! That's. . .twenty-five times fifty. . ." Thinking in numbers, Robert examined his hands. Fifty times twenty-five. "That's over twelve hundred dollars, for God's sake." So it is, they marvelled, but there's costs, eh? There's barrels, the ice and transportation, don't forget. . . Still and all, Jesus! Three hundred per barrel times fifty is fifteen thousand birds a day. That's more than a hundred thousand a week, maybe half a million a month at, say, eight cents a piece. . .

Contemplating each other in the forest path, exhilarated with figures, the elixir of numbers, they considered millions of this or that, tens of thousands of something else, so many gross of barrels, hundredweights of ice, box lunches and beer for the netters, the cost of teams, of one thing and another. . . . But above all, as Fraser reminded them, "the bounty of the Great Author of Nature who'd provide for the wants of his Creatures in such an astonishing fashion." It's true, they agreed, the birds were endless, beyond counting.

"Pests," the postman shouted, "they're pests!"

"I read somewhere. . ." Passing a hand across his eyes to improve concentration, the doctor had forgotten exactly where but someone's figured out and he'd checked it himself, if you take a column of birds to be a mile in breadth, and suppose it passes overhead without interruption for three hours, and that's not a big flock. . . They agreed it wasn't, there was much bigger than that, everybody'd heard of three-*day* flights. . . "You calculate two birds in the square yard. They're flying at sixty miles an hour, and you've got, well, Jesus, if I recall, you've got over one billion, one hundred and fifteen million birds right there!"

"Sweet Jesus," breathed Robert Fraser, wondering how many barrels he'd need and where he'd get them; while the postman, in his eagerness vaguely resembling an unpleasant animal, insisted the roost ahead was bigger than that. Make no mistake, a man could get rich on the guano alone! Suddenly feeling hot, Fraser removed his coat. If only. . . He shook his head violently, almost toppling from the wagon. He seized the reins and declared they must be on their way, whereupon the postman, rolling his eyes, clenched his fist on the wheel as though he would stop it turning. Sniffing hopefully, he stuck out his tongue, inquiring if they mightn't have something in the way of a drink for him before they left, just a dram for strength, for company on his lonely way. But they didn't, at least Robert insisted they didn't. He cracked the reins, forcing the wretch to jump aside when the team lurched forward.

"They gave me a drink." With his features twisting in an

ugly fashion, he grabbed hold of the seat as if to mount. "The netters, they gave me a bloody drink!" But instead he blew a tentative note, then panted, "You'll get no bloody mail from me, I'll tell you. . ." He was running now, his fist white on the seat. "You'll get no bloody mail from me!" After blasting a couple of notes, he managed to scream, "I didn't even have to ask them!"

"Piss off!" Desperately urging the horses, faster and faster, Robert expected everything to collapse, disintegrate behind him at any moment, his mammoth strewn in pieces all over the road. He'd kill the bugger. "*Piss off!*" He'd kill him dead.

"They danced. . ." Exhausted, his doughy face now tinged with purple, he let go of the wagon and disappeared. "*They danced*," he called after them, "when I played my music. . ." Then wild and incomplete, the sound of his trumpet chased the cantering team out of sight; a mechanical jeremiad rather than notes, so loud at first, apparently so close they feared he followed. Perhaps he'd fastened himself to the back of the wagon. They'd teach him a lesson. And so the two men leaped with their sticks to the ground, but the loony wasn't there; still trumpeting crazily he must be where he fell.

Although fading with distance, his noise accompanied them all the way to a clearing beneath a ridge covered with hardwood, mostly beech but some maple, some birch, among which a gang of men scurried purposefully. Twenty or thirty of them descended in a semi-circle to the road with the earth seething before them, convulsing like water caught in a stiff wind. Looking closer, Robert saw they pursued a moving carpet of birds, squabs just out of the nest. Unable to fly, they rolled and scrambled in such numbers the road was soon filled with them, a frenzied stream that was two and sometimes three birds deep. It surged around and past the wagon, with many being crushed by the nervous, dancing feet of his team; and still the pigeon men were a hundred yards away, up a slope that was alive with fledgling pigeons; and still they came, birds without number, flowing past them into the forest again.

Speechless at first, Robert finally managed to point out each squab was worth eight cents, ten worth eighty cents, a thousand worth eighty dollars. . .

"And there's millions of them," said the doctor. "Millions."

Goshawks and falcons, raptors of every kind, wheeled and darted, plummeting into the guano-stained forest. Their skreeing cries accentuated the desperate murmur of fleeing squabs and the men's voices as they came tearing at the pigeons, grunting, their hands endlessly repeating the same gesture. Seizing a bird by the back to imprison the wings, turning it breast up, they caught its head and bursting crop between two fingers. With a dextrous twist, they tore both head and crop from the body and grabbed another almost before its fluttering carcass hit the ground. Automatic, efficient, almost silent, the process was repeated six or seven times a minute.

Astonished by the phenomenal slaughter, by the mass of corpses jerking in a futile imitation of birds still scrabbling in the road, Robert could only think the postman was right, the loony was right, the Yankees knew what they were doing, good Lord, seven or eight squabs a minute worked out at something like forty dollars an hour. Per man.

Behind them came a line of children, or were they midgets? Little people, also crouching, but with sacks and baskets into which they stuffed the headless, cropless birds. No matter how quickly they worked, combing the bloody debris, emptying their containers onto a twitching pile growing by the road, they found it impossible to keep up with the men. Their young voices could be heard complaining, protesting their exhaustion. "Anyway," cried an older boy dumping his pannier, "the wagons are full, they're ram-jam full!" And indeed there were wagons at the far end of the clearing, fifteen or twenty of them, each drawn by a sturdy team. They lurched and bumped, already throwing off dead birds in every direction as they approached. "We can't get no more on there."

The men straightened painfully, one after another, suddenly unconcerned as if the fleeing mass of birds was permanent, a river they could dip into at any time. Directing sly glances at one among them who was wiping muck from his hands with a yellow bandana, they called softly:

"He's right, the kid's right."

"Sloot. . ."

"Hey, Sloot! We been at it all day, that's enough, eh?"

Nearby, one with an enormous straw hat groaned "Jesus!" to nobody in particular. Apparently unable to straighten his back, he leaned in a crouch against the wheel by Robert's boot. "I'm getting old," he muttered, "too old." He released a column of brown tobacco juice from his mouth. "This is shitty work." Seeing Robert and the doctor were strangers he grinned stupidly. "Trapping's all right," he whined, "so's collecting them straight off the bloody nests, but this, Jesus, it's like to bust a man's back." Seizing the spokes, he pushed on his arms, panting, forcing his body until he'd reduced the crouch to a mere stoop. "Mind, it's a good job," he gestured impatiently. "I'm not complaining."

"Where you going, friend?" The man Sloot, his square body on bowed legs, waded through bewildered pigeons, hundreds still cascading after the main flock. "You going to Ardvassar?"

Robert nodded. "And Toronto," he said.

"You got any room in that wagon of yours?" He

motioned at the mountain of squabs, the overladen wagons behind him. "We've had ourselves a pretty good day, haven't we, boys? Yes, sir."

While many had slumped, dark now and motionless, others approached, their boots and leggings stained, their hands encrusted as they shifted, breathing as men do after heavy work.

"What kind of wagon's that, anyhows?" The old man waved his hat as if regretting his earlier weakness. "What you got in there?" He was old all right. On closer inspection, his neck resembled a chicken's ankle.

"What are you selling?"

"Nothing." Robert shook his head. The doctor moved uneasily beside him.

"Nothing? You got a wagon like that, you gotta be selling something." Pulling himself onto the axle-tree arm, the old fart appealed to his companions. "He's gotta be selling something, eh?"

Again Robert shook his head. If their wagons hadn't blocked his way, he'd set the whip to his horses, ride over the buggers!

"What you got in there, friend? You got any room or not?"

It was Sloot he had to handle. He let go of the reins to find his pipe because he couldn't think of anything else to do. The afternoon sun lay indifferent on this open place in the bush, on these men, these horses, the harvest of birds.

"You talking business or what?" Ignoring the others, he'd spoken to Sloot, but the dotard, poking his face at Robert, shifted his chaw and mocked, "You talking business or what?" Spitting copiously onto the dead and dying pigeons beneath the horses' hooves, he grinned and said it again. Robert knew he could snap that scrawny neck like a squab's, kill him before the others. . . .

"I'm a practical man." Sloot's voice silenced them. "So

when I ask a fellah if he's got space in his wagon, I'm talking business, pal, business. I'm not fooling around. I don't have time, you understand me? I don't have time." As if to demonstrate this, he began kicking dead pigeons with one boot then the other while rubbing his hands together. That litter of corpses would soon rot, all right? "From the inside out, pal, and sending empty wagons from Ardvassar costs money, so it's obvious, see?" His eyes were hooded, milky, with a stillness belied by his urgent body. He was about to suggest a deal when an exclamation, an astonished curse, issued from behind the box, and then a ripping sound. The wagon heaved as the hunters clawed at the birchbark, so it wasn't clear if Robert leaped or was thrown to the ground.

"Keep your hands to yourselves!" So violent was he, with such fury in his voice, the men fell back as if physically shoved. For an instant it seemed he would pursue them but instead, because they'd begun picking at the covering, prying it away, he pulled on two cords that lifted a hinged panel, opening the box like a stage. "You may look," he threatened as the five-toed feet, the mighty legs, were revealed. "But you must not touch, you understand that?" He spoke so low, his voice so intense, they strained without taking their eyes from the beast, they strained to hear him as it appeared, a *Mammuthus Primigenius*, a woolly mammoth right enough. Almost quizzical in mottled light, the great head inclined towards them. He described how he'd turned it over with his plough, he'd consulted with experts, men of learning. . . .

"Like a flaming elephant," said one. "It's an elephant."

"You've got the eel of science by the tail," Robert hissed, "if you think that's an elephant."

The doctor remarked that he wouldn't mind a drink, but Robert had launched into a description of the Crystal Palace, the Great Exhibition of 1851. They should have been there. It was, well, it was, antedeluvian. There were flying reptiles, monsters of every description! And the dinner, dear God, this fellow Owen gave a dinner. "There's never been another meal like it in the history of the world!"

He might have been there himself. Striding feverishly between them and his spectacle, his speech clumsy with excitement, Robert set the scene: the gangs of students, the Duchess of Ord, even the Duke bursting into tears and scandalously, "Certain doctors of philosophy, men of the very first talents, they offered access to their mistresses." He paused heavily. "Even their wives, yes! In return for a seat at that table. "Och," he groaned. "Think on it, those poor women!"

"Listen," said Sloot. "There's room in there for plenty of birds." Testing the wagon, he heaved on one corner, then grunting with satisfaction he heaved again. "We could pack them in there, lots of them. You could make thirty, forty dollars, friend, easy. . ."

Robert gestured impatiently. He hadn't finished. He hadn't told them how they dined inside the Iguanodon, right inside the bloody thing! A table set for twenty-one, all that glassware and expensive china, whispering footmen and the moon. He imagined a hunters' moon orange over the palace, and afterwards, after the festivities, the wines, the renown and succulent dishes, those comfortable and advantaged men wading tipsily to their carriages among the shadows and their horses, skittish as maidens, light on the cobblestones, carrying them to women, lovely women with feathers, smooth as thighs they were. . . .

No, he wouldn't take any birds. Like a picket, he resumed pacing with his skeleton on one side, the Yankees on the other. "It's the blood," he apologized with more of a grimace than a smile. Although tempting, no doubt about it, he'd like to help, it was the blood and guts;

they'd soak into the bones, he'd never get them clean, never get his money either. And glaring to see they didn't get too close, he paraded back and forth explaining how Prof. Carruthers had arranged an exhibition, maybe lots of them, all over, like Albert Koch the German; and like the German, Fraser would soon have change enough in his pockets, but not if the beast was spoiled with pigeon muck. They saw that, surely they saw that.

By now the full complement of hunters was pressed close about the wagon. At least forty in all, men and boys of every shape and size, but each hollow-eyed with fatigue, each staring with dumb patience. They struggled to get a better view, while Robert fought to keep them from upsetting, even dismantling, the exhibition. And the children! The blasted kids, like rats, unable to see from the front, they appeared at the back. Hurling clods of earth at small faces poking through rents in the wall, he cried, "Tom," without knowing where his friend had got to, "mind the wagon, Tom!" And still those without a view bulled forward, the crowd of them milling and shifting so their boots pulped scores of birds into gristly meat and feathers. And still he shouted them back. His voice growing hoarse and desperate, he eventually cajoled them into rows, with the kiddies in front. "Let them through. Shortest to the front, tallest to the rear. *Move!* That's the way, hah!" he exulted. "That's it, move, there's room for all. . . Science," he finally puffed in relief, "the world of science *needs* this specimen. Human knowledge," he said in a solemn tone, uncertain how to continue, "human knowledge," he repeated, wondering what would happen if he passed his hat, if the doctor, wherever the hell he was, went among them for contributions. Small change, that's all. They made enough, God knows. Pigeons was the business to be in all right. . . .

If the truth be known, Robert was tempted. He might

have insisted on fifty-five, even sixty dollars, a sixty-forty split if he argued compensation for blood damage, unreasonable wear and tear. Sloot was over a barrel right enough because the harvest would rot where it was, waste into a stinking pool or be devoured by hogs already rooting in that carnage above them on the ridge.

At least you should have passed the hat.

Of course he should. Why didn't he? It was too late now. Most had drifted away before he spied the doctor, a scarecrow dwarfed by Sloot, the two of them marching in animated conversation as Robert, after lowering the panel to conceal the bones, pretended to examine half a dozen tears in its birchbark shelter. Stupid shitbags! Mistrustful and full of complaints, he couldn't imagine why they conversed so intently, with such familiarity, as if he wasn't there. And the hunters, muttering now and picking at their hands like old men, they too were oblivious. Bastards! He'd lost his chance, he wouldn't make a penny on the day. . . .

Grinding his teeth, Robert peered from behind the wagon. It seemed all the scavengers of the forest were descending on this place: skunks and wildcats, wood rats and foxes, the hogs and snarling creatures. Emboldened by greed, paying scant attention to the activity on the road, they'd set to and were feeding angrily.

Chapter Three

> "I believe there is a life after death.
> I know it. Anybody who says there
> isn't, I'll smash his face in."
>
> — Anon

X

Although the doctor muttered and gaped, his hands rummaging hungrily in his pockets, there was too much activity for Robert. After so long, there were too many people: issuing from among brick and clapboard buildings, intent upon thoughts that skulked like small hot-blooded animals, apparently inured to the clangour of metal on metal, the shriek of a steam-driven sawmill and gull-like shouting hucksters, Toronto was full of them. They flowed on either side of his wagon which seemed a ludicrous structure here; a drunkard or gypsy, it bumped and swayed, causing some to turn with jocose winks and leers, while others, holding their hats aloft, waved stupidly as it passed.

The din increased as they approached the rail yards near Queen's wharf, for here wagons rampaged around dangerous corners. Crouching low the teamsters urged their animals with curses and strident cries. Robert imagined them drunk and vainglorious: suspenders hanging from their waists as they pursued women and children with similar oaths, the same cries; or else they sit on straight-back chairs with hands exhausted on their thighs, watching some girl brushing out her hair in rooms across the way. . . .

Strange engines laboured in smoke and fire, hurling carriages into line with such noise, such purpose, the earth trembled; they felt the grim thunder with their fingers, even the palpitant air in their lungs. Occasionally a carriage looking like any other was diverted, left to roll by itself as though it might escape; but this too was part of some pattern, whatever the pattern. Scampering figures among freight cars, townsmen crowding the streets and public clocks in towers or steeples, watches tucked in the waist-coats of men discreetly pursuing the business of property and money. Even Robert, his mammoth and the doctor — each were elements, each gestures playing their part, for this was the centre, the trunk of that tree whose branches were roads, tracks and paths spreading into the colony. And while the sun shone brilliantly in a sky pulled tight as satin over the spacious streets, the rail yards, the lake and commercial buildings, while life resounded violently here, it seemed a reality brittle as new ice, a shout that Robert couldn't interpret.

Before them a pair of double doors: off-centre in a brick wall with the words *Deo Volente* scratched on their lintel. They trembled when Robert beat upon them with his stick.

Small wet eyes and mouth, it was Rochefoucault Hackett who pushed open the door. "Mr. Fraser," he fluted, "Robert, so here you are. Finally, hmmn. . ." He seized Robert's hand and pulled him over the threshold, assuring him they'd begun to worry, there's so much fever about, so much ague. His breath smelled of cloves and he stood so close his body nudged Robert like an animal bumping for sugar, for strands of tobacco. "He's arrived!" Skipping on polished boots, he called over his shoulder. "He's here. . ."

In the cavernous shadows beyond him, Robert now saw Prof. Carruthers' perpetual motion machine. It was breathtaking, a cathedral or banausic forest, so much bigger, cleaner, more accomplished than his own! It sprawled serene and immutable, freed by intelligence from all the woes and joys that burden and exhaust the human body. He could scarcely bring himself to examine it: the flywheels and gears, assorted pendulums, weights and counterweights, push-and-pull rods, rings, springs, plungers and plugs, balances and counterbalances, arms and levers, knobs, rollers, housings, gaskets, washers and shift forks, couplings, bearings and carriers that rose to the rafters in astonishing complexity. The whole of it poised in accordance with Leclanche's reaction and the essential principles of Neeff's hammer. Still as dream it was, tensed and marvellous as the guts of a perfect clock.

Even at rest, the apparatus filled him with envy and dismay. The machine seemed an ideograph of intelligence, a measure of excellence that revealed the futility of his own.

Clustering close, between the wind and the wall, with Hackett nudging him on one side and the doctor grinning at the door, Robert struggled to see his team, his absurd bloody tinker's half-arsed wagon. Discovering there wasn't enough air in his chest, he opened his mouth to seize more but his jaws were locked, the muscles were like iron rods; and before knowing it, he'd flung himself free and was standing in the middle of the warehouse, with Hackett calling the professor by name.

Dwarfed by his creation, so small and slender he could be taken for a child, Prof. Carruthers appeared. His body tilted from side to side as if he'd once been fat. His feet kissed the ground lightly, as fat men's often do, and when he greeted them his words came dry and isolated, following one and then the next like figures in a column. He was pleased, indeed he was. They had much to discuss. He was particularly eager, for example, to examine the skeleton, the mammoth. Had they eaten? He was pleased. Had it been difficult, an onerous journey? Himself, well, if they must know, he despised wilderness, all empty places. He counted the astrolabe, the sextant and the quadrant chief among liberating inventions, for without them Bartholomew Diaz and Columbus, Vespucci, John Cabot and Magellan, where would they have been? Vincente Pinzon; speaking the names like a foreign language, he repeated Vin-chentay Pin-sown with a satisfied smile. "Maps. . ." Whispering, he peered like an owl in an ivy bush. "Maps provide cohesion. Without maps society falls apart. Man's subdual lust," he snickered unexpectedly, "the spread of knowledge. Man's subdual lust."

His mouth scarcely moved enough to reveal it was he who spoke, who now suggested they must have a drink, perhaps see something of the town. But first the mammoth, *Mammuthus Primigenius*. Turning so his profile appeared against the accusing jumble of wheels and levers, weights and balances, he closed his eyes; then opening them as if resigned, as if he were alone, the visible eye bulging suddenly, alarmingly, he became an ancient child rather than a man, a boy transformed into an infirm dotard whose lower lip hung slack, protuberant. "The mammoth," he tried again. "Make no mistake. . ."

Robert had heard of children who die of old age, monkey corpses collapsing from within! His father had described a plague of six-year-old men and women shrinking like dried fruit, octagenarians before they're eight. Propped in warm corners, trying to remember a non-existent life, they responded to no treatment whatsoever and it was impossible to tell how old they were, poor beasties. When it came for them to die, disputes arose among churchmen, with some insisting they remained children. Reason dictated they must be children, albeit eccentrically punished. Nevertheless, they couldn't have accrued more Evil than others their age. But the Reverend Black Angus Maxwell declared they were adults, look upon them! reduced to drivelling anility, they must perforce contain a full life of sin and error, because it's in our body and its appetites, that is to say in Time, with Time, the Devil insinuates himself. Vigilance is temporal, Evil is absolute. . . .

"The mammoth," he tried again. "Make no mistake, if it actually is a mammoth you have out there." Regaining himself, the professor turned from his machinery to where sunlight filled with dust beckoned in the doorway. They would go outside; but instead, apparently unwilling to move, he pinched the bridge of his nose between thumb and forefinger. "It would be remarkable," he whispered.

Robert had expected something else, some authority, certainly not this wan confusion. He knew he could take hold now, get out in sunlight and make the best possible deal, forget the bloody machine, yes, the humiliation. But shame, like jealousy, demands to be scratched until blood comes. "I believe. . ." He coughed unhappily, clearing his throat. "I believe there's a great future in perpetual motion." He knew it, setting the whole into fantastic, effortless, sidereal motion, they'd confound him with theory, chatter on about Fludd's Closed Circuit Water Wheel, clockwork drummers, Vaucanson's Mechanical Duck. His own machine now, how did that compare? Ha! There wasn't anything like this in the bush, eh? But screwing up his face, Prof. Carruthers only pressed childlike fists, velvet paws against his eyes.

"Ah well. . ."

"Professor!" bellowed Hackett, causing a flock of small birds to spring in alarm from the rafters; they circled about the room and vanished.

"Maybe there is." The little man groaned. "And maybe there isn't."

"Robbie, come outside. . . Professor. . ." Desperate on plump legs, Hackett managed to hustle Dr. Tom into the sunlit street while pleading over his shoulder, "Melville, there's no need, you don't have to tell them." But Carruthers paid no attention. He suggested instead that Robert might as well see for himself. He had no secrets, unhappily he had no secrets. He was crumbling before their eyes.

While struggling with the doctor, Rochefoucault Hackett lost his cap. It slipped inexorably over his eyes to reveal the terrible bone swelling out of his head. He began to whimper and pant until he subsided against the jamb and gave up completely, whipping out a handkerchief and blowing his nose.

"What do you mean, no secrets?" Robert seized the professor. "What do you mean?" His hand completely encircled a frail arm. "It doesn't work, does it?" He could scarcely believe the shudder rippling through that little body, the fraud! By Jesus, remembering his own lean and spare machine with a rush of affection, of faith, he wouldn't be denied, no, not by a long sight. He'd show them, by Jesus! "It can be done," he chortled. "It can be done!" Still chuckling and muttering to himself, he released Carruthers to climb excitedly among the machinery as if to convince himself it was a failure.

With as much dignity and gravity as he could muster under the circumstances, the professor wandered back and forth in front of his creation, pedantically insisting how it was that certain drawings of Leonardo had first set up the hue and cry for wheels that turn of themselves. Enthralled by cross sections of contrate wheels, by variations on the Archimedian Screw, even a rudimentary oscillating beam machine, the great Isaac Newton himself, such men as George Stephenson, the Marquess of Worcester and Sir Richard Arkwright, men of genius in every age, all of them had sought the chimerical power, the elixir of motion. And Albertus Magnus, what about Albertus Magnus? After labouring for decades, he'd fashioned a robot, a mechanical servant that could open the door and greet visitors. "Think on that, think on it," he shouted at Fraser, who was scrambling on a beam twenty feet above the floor, "a clockwork organism that talks with strangers! Ahr-ee-ahr, rugga-ruggah," he growled mournfully, then whistled in an exploratory fashion. And what happened to it, did they know? On opening the door one day it was grievously assaulted. History is a gold mine of wretched stories! An astonished Thomas Aquinas smashed it to smithereens with his walking stick, and that was the end of it.

"Don't you sometimes think a man's personal destiny is only fulfilled in his death?" He stared, apparently without seeing Hackett or the doctor. He appeared to be shrinking; his voice was reduced to a sigh. And yet, and yet, at the same time many have made a false step by standing still. He firmly believed that, yes, he did. No gains without pains. Wasn't it Hannibal who said, "I will find a way or make one?" Still and all, sometimes perhaps one wretched thing after another, it was enough. . . .

"It's magnificent." Interrupting with a voice ringing from near the ceiling, Robert was exultant, nimble as a squirrel. "Astonishing! But don't you see?" There was something that sounded like choking laughter. "Bloody

God, it could never work like this!" Then words the men on the floor couldn't hear. . . .

Peering resentfully at Hackett who had begun to sneeze, a series of spongy explosions followed by marine-like snorts and gulps, Tom Sanderson ventured further into the room as if he wouldn't mind seeing the fat bastard choke. He wanted to hear better, to perhaps see what it was that drove Fraser to fling himself from beam to catwalk, from catwalk to strut to entablature, and finally to the ground. Robert was like a madman; his vehement eyes filled the doctor with dismay. "There's something missing!" he crowed.

"Orffyreus," barked the professor, struggling for confidence.

"That's your trouble all right."

"The legendary Orffyreus, the only man with certain knowledge, practical experience of the Grand Machine. . ." He had to raise his voice. "The only man to successfully resolve the problem of perpetual motion, *perpetuum mobile*, oh! oh!" Raising his fist like a politician, he begged Robert to stop talking, to consider, for heaven's sake, the dedication, the perseverance of a man who'd experimented with no fewer than three hundred and fifty different machines before at last succeeding. "Three hundred and fifty! So there is time, eh? There is time all right. . . Closing one eye he shook his head, squinting meanly, but Fraser was oblivious.

Prattling on about the need for an essential core, some class of rejuvenating centre, Robert confessed he didn't yet know what he should be looking for. He'd grown sombre, almost morose. He asked how they supposed a man should start thinking about that kind of thing. But since the professor was now screaming that Orffyreus died a broken man, neglected and bitter, there's no justice and precious little mercy, neither Hackett nor the doctor could interject an opinion, even if they had one. The professor spoke of princes and crowned heads, of landgraves, doctors and other learned men. They'd come from everywhere. They'd all come to wonder at the success of the self-moving wheel, and of course there were sceptics among them, jackeens eager to unmask fraud. "Such is greed even in the mighty." His little eyes fairly popped with scorn. "Such the fear of change, of Progress, in those jealous of their power. Orffyreus was forced to, dear God! he destroyed his invention. . . ."

Although sensing yet another instance of a wet arse with no fish caught, the doctor was impelled to ask, "Why, what was it they did to him?" Even Robert interrupted his ruminations to wait for an explanation.

"The government of Hesse Castle. . ."

"Ah yes," intoned Robert Fraser, "the taxes."

"You know that?" Robert nodded, ducking modestly with a hard grin. He knew all about it, by God! The professor breathed "Aah," casting a worried glance at Hackett who was peering at the trio from behind his handkerchief. "You do, eh?" Suddenly politic, he smiled at Fraser as one might on discovering the larder was full of beetles. Robert nodded again. It had been a self-moving wheel on an eight-inch axle. Fashioned of light pine boards covered with waxed cloth, it was twelve feet in diameter, fourteen inches thick; and once in motion, even when raising water with an Archimedian Screw, it made no less than twenty-five turns in the minute. And if a man grabbed hold of it, he'd be lifted right off the ground. That would have been somewhere around 1715, 1720. The Baron Fischer was convinced, so was Professor s'Grave-sande who, despite the wars and his advanced age, made a perilous journey from Leyden to the castle at Wissenstein. "Of course he did, of course they were convinced." Diminished by this turn of events, appearing even more homuncular, gnomish, the professor pinched the bridge of his nose, whinnying, "Everybody knows that. That's common knowledge."

"What's this about taxes then?" And greed? the doctor might have asked. "The government of Hesse Castle," they said in unison. The professor quickly added that the government imposed such a punitive tax that Orffyreus. . . Again Fraser piped in. "Orffyreus. . .Orffyreus. . ." they said together, he was forced to destroy his machine. "It's always the same."

"A fine is a tax for doing wrong," declared the professor, "and a tax is a fine for doing right."

"Well. . ." Hackett spoke carefully, pushing himself off the door jamb. "That's really something, Robbie. I mean. . . Who'd have thought, dear gracious, where did you manage to get hold of all that?"

"He's a deep one," Darting his eyes from one to another, Tom Sanderson bared his teeth hopefully. The need for a drink had been growing in him. It filled his chest and throat so he could smell it thickening his saliva, gnawing in his belly. He was sick of that little arse-worm and his endless talk. What are they going on about? "A fellah on the road," he spoke quickly, "that man Sloot, you mind him, Robbie? He said there was a hanging Saturday morning, said it would be a good one too. A big bugger, neck on him like a bull."

"Yeas. . ." Visibly brightening, Melville Carruthers rubbed his hands together. "A Finnish sailor."

"Bloody Finns, there's a game they play, it's called yeow. Jesus, they can drink all right." The doctor shivered, grinning with envy. "They sit around in a circle on the floor with a bloody big knife, eh? Then someone blows out the lights. Heugh," he chuckled, "heugh heugh! When it's pitch black in there, the first fellah throws the knife." He made an alarming lunge at the professor's chest. "Whoever gets hit screams *yeow!* Then it's his turn with the knife, eh? Heh!"

"Ha!" Carruthers laughed. "I never heard that. Ha." He liked it all right. "Yeow," he said and giggled.

"What'd he do?" Leaving off his self-reflective muttering, even Robert had become interested.

"Cut up his landlady," said Hackett. "Didn't stab her, just scratched her up, they say. Cut her something fierce so she bled to death."

"They're knifers right enough." And they agreed when the doctor vowed he wouldn't go easy, tough little buggers. But they'd have him dancing on nothing, so they would, in a hempen cravat. "It serves him right. Why would a man do that?"

After a pause in which they shrugged, raising their eyebrows in a puzzled fashion, Robert explained how the introduction of the long drop, the free fall, made it easier, they couldn't deny that. Done properly, with the right theory behind it, and no matter. . . But Carruthers wasn't sure. To begin with, it's messy. They tore the head right offa that fellow in Montreal. Still, clearly it depends on the hangman, if he knows his job or not. Thus having agreed upon a subject, they came to discuss the hangman's art. Was it an art, after all, or a science? Opinions were divided.

"The fact is," Hackett explained, "they don't actually get to weigh their man. They've got to size him up by looking, peek at him through the spy hole, don't you see? It's a matter of judgement and experience, guesswork almost, and that would make it art."

Convinced yet strangely eager for the professor's approval, tip-tapping on his shiny boots, Hackett insisted it could only be scientific if they got to measure him precisely, examine the physiognomy under clinical conditions.

"But Jesus," they laughed heartily at the prospect, "can

you see it? Some great thumping axe murderer, ballocks naked like enough, sitting there while some barge-arse hangman. . ."

"I say," minced Hackett, suddenly licking his lips, "would you mind popping on these scales? Just for a jiffy. That's the ticket." He pursed his wet mouth. "Thenk yew, ha!"

"Or applying callipers to his neck muscles." Reaching up, the doctor made a precise gesture with his thumb and forefinger like the snapping of a small crab. "Or the base of the skull?" he snorted. "Hah!" Like medicine snip-snip his fingers pinched meticulously. "Like medicine it's got to be an art." Snip.

"They say. . ." Stiff-armed, Hackett raised his fist to his nose in demonstration. "They say it makes you proud below the navel."

"What?" They hadn't heard. No, they sniggered incredulously.

"Hard as a poker," he insisted.

"Go on. . ." Robert didn't believe it for a moment. Priapic death, a carnal demise, to what purpose?

"The bowels empty." The doctor knew that, certainly the bowels empty. "But I don't see any connection, and yet. . ." He wrinkled his forehead as if thinking. "Some class of ataxic phenomenon perhaps."

"It's the shock." Jerking his neck in a grimacing twist, again stiffening his forearm, Hackett stuck out his tongue. "The terrible shock," he gargled.

Perhaps remembering the struggles of a man named Evans, Robert had gone with his father and brothers one brilliant morning and clinging to a lamp post, he saw the convulsions reduced to shudders, to a melancholy twitching, then nothing. It revolved mechanically, a sack of shit under the gibbet between Saint Giles and the Castle where Bank Street intersects the High Street, the honeyed freedom. He changed the subject. "Art or science," he shrugged, "even if it does rip your head off, it's better than slow strangulation." He could still hear his father's voice intone, in death the honeyed freedom they have not in their lives. . . .

"Better for who?" The professor stared, his face like a dried apple. "Better for the murderer, right enough. It's revolting, there's altogether too much. . ." He fumbled in his pockets, searching, apparently finding nothing. "An unhealthy spectacle altogether," he warned. 'There'll be little ones present, womenfolk!" His voice lacked conviction. "Tore the head right off," he muttered. Then after a pause: "Why do you suppose death would give you a hard-on?"

"Hanging," the doctor corrected him. "The Tyburn jig." He was about to elaborate, the Paddington Frisk, but Fraser was too quick.

"Death's a man," he said unhappily.

"No no." Carruthers was delighted. "That's where you're. . ." He became agitated again, counting on his fingers. "You're wrong!" he crowed. "*Mors, mortalis, mortalitas*, all feminine, and the French, what do they say? They say *la mort, la*," he repeated without moving his lips, "yes, they do." It was uncanny. Robert wanted to say something about the Grim Reaper, Gentleman Death, but the professor was still gathering momentum, teetering excitedly, growing in strength and enthusiasm. "For the Spaniards it's *la muerta* and the gallows, they're feminine too, *la potence*, she's a woman, death's a woman. . ."

"That's right." Stowing his handkerchief, Hackett observed them without curiosity. "The professor's right." He spoke formally, then with arms flicking at his sides began shepherding them towards a small door beyond the machine.

"On the other hand," he said, pinching the bridge of his

nose, "*le cadavre, el muerto,* do you see? Both masculine. The corpse is masculine, death is feminine."

How could that be? The honeyed freedom. Robert wandered behind them, passing beneath the machine, entering the very guts of it before reaching the little door. And all the while Carruthers counted examples on his delicate fingers and Robert insisted upon Gentleman Death, the Prince of Shadows. Of course he's a man. It's the Horsemen, isn't it? The Four Horsemen of the Apocalypse, the Kingdom of Shadows, Godfather Death with his guttering candles. . . .

Beyond the main room there was another, the mad crookedness of its walls broken by ogival windows, by doors leading into smaller rooms with rooms beyond; not much more than cubicles some of them, resembling store-rooms they contained such clutter it seemed unlikely even Carruthers knew what was in them. On closer inspection, however, it looked like weathercocks and wind machines in one; wheels with wooden cogs, lead weights and broken clockwork pieces in another; while a third, the smallest, was lined with shelves on which were stacked a multitude of boxes, each identical in size and shape, each with a brass letter and a number. Against one wall between two doors, both shut, there was a great panharmonicon, too elaborate for an original Maetzel, crenellated, delicately carved, resting on voluptuous caryatids with breasts like Yankee melons and mother-of-pearl eyes. They received each man with a fixed and confident stare so that each was convinced the eyes followed him alone. Flattered by this, but curiously unsettled, certain they'd gaze with longing when he left the room, each man positioned himself carefully; sucking in his belly or flaring his nostrils, he attempted and rejected numerous facial expressions before finding one that pleased him.

The doctor narrowed his eyes, licking his thin lips in an

appropriate gesture for one reputed to have killed a man, shot him down in cold blood. Hackett, on the other hand, puffed himself up like a banker exhibiting a prize mistress. The professor became as serious as a child. And Robert, his face empty of expression, pretended they weren't there at all.

And it's true, after the bottle was opened and drinks were poured, they did talk of Neeff's hammer, Vaucanson's Mechanical Duck, Leclanche's Reaction, as Robert had feared. They argued the relative merits of quicksilver, of galvanism and overbalancing wheels. They praised without agreement water wheels with an ample supply of iron balls instead of water, clocks that work on atmospheric pressure, oscillating beam machines, wheels driven by pendulums that didn't regulate but produced power, gravity wheels and wind machines. Yet always they came back to Orffyreus, to the Marquess of Worcester's giant wheel that was maintained in motion by the swinging in and out of weights, each fastened by a rope.

Forgetting at last the challenge of those eyes still gazing from an opposite wall, they clustered around an orrery and discussed the professor's failure. "Here," said Robert, tapping the sun with the blade of his pocket knife, "here at the centre we have the sun, at the centre of the universe we have the sun. . ." What is perpetual motion, after all, but that seen in the motion of our own solar system around the sun, the planets themselves and all movement contained within, our moon. Listening to his voice with growing astonishment, savouring his drink, he repeated himself. The words came perfectly formed and regulated, one complimenting the next as if rehearsed, as if he were some panjandrum from the Royal Society. Then raising the knife until his arm trembled above his head, he said, "Our earth, its tides and currents, that's what's missing, a redemptive centre." He outlined his own experiments, his correspondence with Benedict Singer, and with confident modesty admitted his own failure to date. "Ah, yes!" he cried. "It's true, hard work may have bitter roots. Nevertheless. . .it's fruits, some day its fruits will be sweet. . ."

Of course he was right. They dared not contradict this mechanician of forest and stream who by now, winding the clockwork orrery, had permitted himself an aloof smile. The professor, refilling the glasses before they were empty, even the professor was able to nod his little monkey head, for that made sense all right. No doubt about it. "Once we've found it, this essential centre, why then we've got it, haven't we? The problem's solved." With a decisive click he released the mechanism so the earth, its moon and all the various planets on their wires were jerked into delicate motion around a brass sun heavy with verdigree.

XI

By the time they'd exhausted the orrery, the gyrostatic mechanisms and curious physical apparatus, along with the panharmonicon and a commonplace orchestrion that were packed into the professor's workshop, the bottle was empty. And when they finally stepped into the courtyard, twilight was collapsing into darkness. Graceful against mountainous clouds that were alive with lightning over the lake, the masts of sailing ships swayed and twisted, a melancholy dance as Robert pulled on the ropes, raising the doors on his wagon. Beyond the squatting sheds, an engine laboured in solitude and as the men drew near, jostling each other in a familiar fashion, the querulous head, the sombre prison of bones were revealed. "*That's not a mammoth!*" It wasn't a mammoth at all. The professor was delighted as if Robert's error and confusion restored a necessary equilibrium, somehow compensated for his own failure. "It's a mastodon, the nipple-tooth." His face took on strength there in the yard; the muscles in his cheeks and around his mouth recovered their elasticity. "Who said this was a *Mammuthus Primigenius*?" For Chrissake!

Not Hackett, no sir. Robbie must have got it wrong. Certainly Rochefoucault Hackett, removing his cap, rubbing the misshapen skull with confident vigour, he knew the difference all right, a man in his position, with his experience, make no mistake. He grinned and hearing stiff little fingers abrading his polished lump, they'd chuckled knowingly, even the doctor had joined in; and while Robert protested, it was clear none believed him for none had wanted to believe him.

Then a wolfish supper of meat and potatoes with jugs of beer in the Frozen Ocean, a spit-and-sawdust tavern by the harbour where secret handshakes among the patrons, winks and bird-like clicking whistles were exchanged. Eristic conversations were overheard among men whose pockets were stuffed with papers on which they made furious notes concerning the spread of Libertarian Societies dedicated to the Principles of Mechanism, to Life improved by Reason, to Progress and Equality. They planned Great Works, Learned Treatises, Histories and Chronicles, Memoirs, Arguments, Novels or Pamphlets. One read interminably from a manuscript which he carried in a box, a Rogue's Gallery of Imperial and Clerical Villains in verse; while another, speaking the words as he wrote them, celebrated Revolt then Independence, Constitutional Reform, the values of collective common sense and hard work, the Infamy of Corrupt Power, the fraudulent promise of Confederation among the Colonies.

"They insist on nothing less," he cried, stabbing his pen into an inkwell, "and what they mean is nothing more!" He spoke faster than he wrote and frequently had to repeat himself. "The Righteous and the Sinners will be mixed up together, the Righteous and the Sinners. . ." A moth-eaten patriarch, he rambled in a soft but angry voice; yet when he stared about the room, his gaze was morose, exhausted, as if he'd seen too much to believe his own diagnosis, his own ambition.

While many were students, youngsters sporting flambuoyant hats and boutonnieres, most were older. Some were foreigners, Jews and Lebanese; there were Africans, two Negroes who'd fled the States before the war, and Spaniards familiar with the principles of Anarchy; there were Germans and Italians. All with the soft hands of men who on leaving their homes had discovered the land here speaks an unknown tongue, who worked as clerks to lawyers and politicians, as bookkeepers, tutors and music teachers, as printers' devils, traders in specialized goods and booksellers' assistants, those on the fringes of money and power. There were others, professional men recognized by the money they spent, but all of them dreamers of past or future dreams. They gathered each evening, remaining long into the night, because outside in the rutted streets, the alleyways spreading from the lake, ordinary folk, crowded three and four in a bed, slept heavily, apparently dreamless; while privilege rewarded itself with brick mansions on Jarvis and Sherbourne streets, with smarter carriages and all manner of fancy goods, hampers of cheeses and fruit from the West Indies, French wines, Belgian sausages and Cuban tobacco. They sent abroad for shirt collars and lace handkerchiefs, read two-month-old journals from England, and nobody marvelled that crown lands were miraculously bestowed upon one another by judges, servants of the Crown and politicos, for land was not only the musculature of power but its plaything to boot.

Still, in the Frozen Ocean you were among friends or congenial enemies, free-thinkers, republicans, syndicalists, nationalists who envied or didn't envy the States, passionate fellows who honoured the memory of Sam Lount and Peter Matthews, martyrs and revolutionaries, those two good men destroyed by the times. There was even talk of raising money by public subscription to rebury them under a suitable monument in a suitable spot. And here too the beer was cool from the cellar, so cool it frosted the jugs before they reached your table. There were women who didn't complain when you stroked their thighs or pinched their buttocks; and as a result, from time to time, it was possible to believe life here in the Canadas might some day be different.

Suddenly keen to hear first-hand about Richard Owen's dinner inside the *Iguanodon*, about the Crystal Palace, prehistoric vegetation and the moon, Robert asked if it was true, did they, well, did they offer their women in return for a seat at that table? He banged his glass for more beer. Did it happen as Hackett had said? Carruthers nodded, his eyes half closed like a sheep, pulling on his ear. He'd as soon not discuss it here, eh? Waving his hand, he closed his eyes altogether. His ancient child's face went slack, fruit-like; but the appearance of another jug, accompanied by wee nips all round, restored his vital spirits. Indeed it happened as Ches had said, Ches's an expert, a connoisseur where women are concerned.

"But the dinner. . ." His voice shrill, Robert said it again and asked about the learned men, the fine wines. He wanted to know if Carruthers had really been there. "Tell me," he said, "tell me more. . ." But an argument about Fenian incursions had erupted between two tables, with one stoutly supporting them as patriots, the scalpel of Yankee anger, a cleansing blade; while at the other, men were springing to their feet with veins bulging in throats and foreheads. One in particular — they called him Donkey Ben — he jumped and skipped, beating himself as if his clothes were full of stinging ants. He'd have thrashed the lot but for his friends whose cooler heads prevailed. One, a clean-shaven bookbinder called Meintz, in the same orange suede gloves he wore summer and winter, cried liberty, equality, fraternity. Whereupon a perspiring, gesticulating order was restored, for despite high feelings there was room for theory on both sides. It was to punish England the Fenians came, to liberate rather than invade. Everyone had to agree with that. There was wealth for all, but the principles of Reason, of Libertarianism, must supplant that mean oligarchy, that exhausted paternalism fed by English rule. They recalled barns ablaze after Mackenzie's rebellion, animals gratuitously seized, crops destroyed, and they knew the names of men transported to Van Dieman's Land. Whether Jacobins or Radical Monarchists, Masons, embittered Jacobites or Anarchists, it was as if in the rancour of distant cells, the indifferent cruelty of those reprisals, they might find some vocabulary for change, a shared conviction. And yet . . . how was it common folk who'd fled tyranny in their homelands submitted here, embracing it at that moment when like their American cousins they might have driven it yelping from the land? And how the swine who celebrated the hangings of Lount and Matthews, Scots whose grand-fathers died at Culloden, whose families were harried from the glens, and Irish too, men and women who should have known better, how they were then rewarded, advancing in leaps and bounds until now, not thirty years later, they minced and postured everywhere, comfortable arse-lickers, bum-faced servants of the Crown.

Certainly not a revolutionist, in fact maintaining the

world was as it appeared to be, the professor was nevertheless acknowledged with a respect verging on deference. Perching like a child, frail in that rough camaraderie, he watched from hooded eyes. Greeting those that made pilgrimages to his table, he uttered low words of introduction from a mouth that didn't move at all, while gesturing sleepily to others, all manner and shapes of men who signalled as they entered or left. It was as if he were the host, perhaps a senior officer one had to honour, for there was no friendship in the greetings, and little warmth. It wasn't until the Watchmaker appeared, a precise translucent man with the unhealthy colour of a frog's belly, that Robert saw Carruthers had been waiting for him.

His name was Victor Burnel. Gracious but severe, he combed long fingers through straight black hair while ordering supper. Blue-black as a native's, gun-metal blue, it fell into place as if he hadn't touched it. Introduced to Robert, to another student of perpetual motion, a student of modernity? Good. He inquired if Fraser had an exact timepiece, then produced a pocket watch the size of an apple, palping the closed face while quoting Huygens and Hevelius, praising Galileo's studies of falling bodies, pointing out that Rousseau was both a Calvinist and a watchmaker's son. He whispered that the Intelligence of Man and the Necessity of Nature, those thorny opposites, are finally reconciled in mechanical time. "Clock time. . ."

Exchanging smiles with Carruthers, Victor Burnel filled their glasses, pouring whiskey to the brim. "Clock time emancipates human intelligence from all transcendentals. For every tick," his voice rose like a last exhalation, "a tock." Then opening the lid to reveal an enamelled fascia with glyptic figures behind not only the hour, minute and second hands, but a stopwatch as well, with smaller dials for setting alarms, he proferred the watch.

114

Robert held it firmly. Tick, it said, tock. While Hevelius-Huygens churned in his breast and throat, Orffyreus and Galileo, Albertus Magnus! He felt the whole order of modern civilization pulsing within that membrance of hammered gold, the tyranny of the unit. Overcome by drunken thoughts and fierce ambition, he longed to put it in his pocket.

Absently clawing at his hair, Burnel separated stewed meat and vegetables into bite-size portions and kept an eye on their whiskey glasses. He explained how there'd be no automatons without the rigour of mechanical time, no progress, no technocracy without timepieces, exact timepieces.

Robert recognized what he'd never heard before. Why hadn't he said this himself? Clocks as a precondition to the discoveries and inventions of the exact natural sciences, he knew that. Why did it take some dandy bloody watchmaker to say it for him? Scientific exactness and mechanical time are inseparable. "What about railroads?" cried Robert to show he understood. "Are not railroads. . ." But at that moment the turnip chimed eleven in his fist, a deliberate and nostalgic sound. Ah, yes! they hushed, would you listen to that, so sweetly modulated it astonished and delighted them all. Finally returning his empty glass, Robert crouched over the watch in his hand. "The railroad itself, isn't that a clockwork?"

"Like the metronome." Rat-like, the doctor grinned hopefully. "That's a kind of clock, eh?" But Victor Burnel would have none of it, no sir. "Not blessed music and the metronome?" Any fool can regulate the metronome, it's nothing but a drill sergeant, a hired bully. . .

"Now the music box," soothed Carruthers, "you've another thing altogether with your music box." But Victor Burnel, his forehead liverish with irritation, wasn't sure about that either. The problem was the music itself.

"Music," he said, "music doesn't bring the soul closer to Reason. Rather, it lulls and enslaves it to the world."

"Well, now. . ." The professor pushed his glass towards the bottle. "I'm not so sure about that."

"Goddamn it, Melville, you know it. Music can make a dog howl but I never did hear tell of it persuading him to give up stealing chickens." Ha! they laughed. Hoh! He had a point there all right. They drank to that, although Burnel didn't seem to find it amusing. "Look you. . ." Leaning into brown light, adjusting the lamp as it flared, he retrieved his watch and placed it somewhere within his jacket. Returning to his plate, he hid bits of meat under cabbage leaves and solemnly mashed the spuds before raising a lump to his mouth. "We've got to be vigilant. Are you familiar with the work of Alexander Bain?" They weren't, dear God! Catching the renewed light, his spectacles shone like mirrors while the fork scattered its contents back onto the plate. Robert was from Edinburgh, was he not? And he hadn't heard of Bain? He lifted his glass, staring at his fingers while trying to control disdain. "That's the trouble with this hole, nobody knows anything." Awh now, unfair, squealed Hackett, as the doctor, resembling some mean animal surprised in a woodshed, bared his teeth. But the Watchmaker only released a thin smile. "Alexander Bain," if they'd listen for a minute, "the man's a saint." He would explain if they'd just listen. "You see, Bain's devised a method of running clocks on the natural power of Mother Earth, this earth!" He rapped his knuckles on the table. Didn't they see? "By burying electrodes in moist earth, two of them, he's tapped a galvanic current that drives his clocks."

Dear Heaven! One after another, first Carruthers and then Robert, they began to see implications in it all right. For example, the professor had always figured it was no coincidence that Calvin's triumph in Geneva occurred at the exact same time the watchmaking industry was establishing itself there. "That's absolutely right." Victor smiled benignly. "And Rousseau, a watchmaker's son, you recall, when he returned to Calvinism he dedicated his *Discours sur l'inégalité* to the Great Council of Geneva." Whereupon they all wanted to speak at once. The Intelligence of Man and the Necessity of Nature, *Memento mori*. Jumping their chairs closer to the table, opening and closing their mouths like fish, they began to consider Universal Time, exactly repeatable time that's the same for wild beasts of the forest as it is for us, for the forest itself, for cannibals and Hottentots as if they were civilized men. Look you! Before clocks, time was an empty box; before chronometers, it was only in the sublime machinery of the Heavens that man could apprehend his Maker, in the relentless probity of constellations, the precision of planets, our sun and moon in their constant, scrupulous workings. . .

"Navigation, celestial navigation, the astrolabe, maps," barked Carruthers, while Hackett explained that in ancient China sidereal matters were so hallowed that astronomers who failed to predict some eclipse or other were executed. "Did you ever hear that?"

But clocks running on the power of the earth itself. "Holy old bald-headed blue-eyed Jesus," whispered Burnel, "that's something!" Seeing their conversation threatened to fly apart here, impatient as each struggled to get in edgewise, he shushed them by waving his long arms in a sinuous, irritable fashion. "The brain," he demanded, "while the brain is a complicated bit of biological machinery — one at a time, for pity's sake — it has its limits." Inevitably, since maundering passionate thought was in them, they came to discuss God the Great Watchmaker, the fundamental form of His intelligence (and therefore man's) made manifest in the workings of exquisite clocks, in the resultant forms of practical knowledge, all higher machines, not to mention the infinitely complex yet banausic Heavens in whose implacable course, as Robert reminded them, was a harsh reality that pardoned neither man nor woman.

Later, with a girl playing Annie Laurie on the pianoforte, Hackett inquired about Mary. Startling Fraser, he assured the professor she was a good one, Robbie's got himself a good wife, hmmn, a bonnie woman. Did she send her regards? In the yellow light his appalling head glistened with sweat. Moistening his red mouth, he gestured at the piano player, for she reminded him of Mary, goddamn right. So they all gazed at abundant hair falling over narrow shoulders, her trim waist, the whole flowing down to spreading buttocks, wide and secure, fleshy beneath the cloth drawn taut by her weight; all of her like quicksilver poured into a bag. He'd fixed her jaw, did Fraser recall that? Bending over her, taking her face in his hands, his fingers in the hair above her ears.

Robert drank carefully as Dr. Tom yelped she'd have his balls for bookends, his guts for garters, if he didn't get good money for that monster! She'd been in a proper fury when they left, by Jesus. Shaking his head, he mimicked her berating Fraser for a no-good dreamer. What about the farm? They didn't have enough land cleared. Even Casey had more. If he didn't spend so much time on perpetual motion. . . .

Everything became confused. Robert knew he shouldn't drink so much. How often had he promised himself? With fists like rocks, the muscles pulsing from his neck into his shoulders, he wasn't responsible, it wouldn't be his fault.

Producing an odd smile, Rochefoucault Hackett at some point revealed a collection of pornographic postcards, astonishing tableaux, scenes that resembled an immense crowd of people tumbling naked into a hole and, more specific, detailed couplings, encounters, tastings, licking and sniffing. Robert was fascinated and appalled by the long eye empty or stretching to receive some eccentric tool or organ, by a Noah's Ark of bestiality (some scenes were hand tinted), startling reproductions, prints of awesome male genitalia preserved in jars. So enormous and threatening were they that the men flicked on to females partially clad in Oriental attire, for here was something to remind them of home, a neighbour's wife perhaps, a neighbour's daughter. By Jesus, would you look at the bubbies on that one! Heh heh. More drinks were ordered, heh, they chuckled quietly and remembering one card or another, the lewd promise in a plump knee or painted mouth, some rubbed their thighs while Tom Sanderson, crouching low over the table, rummaged in the pockets of his baggy pants.

Then finally into empty streets, unfamiliar as dream, lurching to a boarding house with valanced curtains drawn against the night, their gimps and galloons, the steady hiss of gas lamps throwing shadows hard as knives against the wall, hard and steady among the women's ankles. It was a parlour, yes, a public room with too many chairs, another piano, a vase of felt flowers beneath a picture of the Circus. It looked like the Circus with Romans encircling what must have been a nude woman tied to a dead bull. He'd have examined it close up but was embarrassed and so he remained sipping whiskey by the door.

At first he thought it Carruthers' house or Victor Burnel's, for despite the hour and their condition, they were welcomed as if expected. Mrs. Horner had seemed so pleased. Did they want coffee, perhaps French brandy? Her hand was strong and cool when she greeted him. He found himself guided into the parlour, a reassuring hand that only increased his shame and confusion. He couldn't afford to stay here, Jesus Christ, what were they thinking of? Reaching into his breast pocket to check again the wad of notes over his heart, he tried to focus on Carruthers, to send him a message. The little man had ensconced himself in a chair so large his feet scarcely touched the floor.

She lay on her left side against the dead animal's chest, almost beneath its monstrous head. Thrown back, revealing a hairless armpit and flattening the breast, her right arm was still tied at the wrist while her legs, strewn with flowers, entangled in a cloth that swathed her groin, her legs were drawn over the belly to its flank. The ropes were still taut, so her bare feet pointed at Nero's disdainful figure in the centre of a small group, both men and women who had descended, entering the arena for a closer look. Nobody moved. Just above her hip a rough spear stood out from between its ribs, and garlands of blood were scattered in the sand. Stragglers watched impassive from the now almost empty stands as Fraser was drawn to that sombre chiaroscuro by the pale blob of her body and the Emperor's soft, dolose face, by melancholy figures along the wall, Nubian attendants waiting with his palanquin and gladiators at a respectful distance. Shifting to avoid flaring light and his own reflection on the glass, he saw she too was dead, her open mouth revealed a line of animal teeth. Try as he might, he could see no sign, no mark on her flawless body, to show how she had died.

A peal of contralto laughter sounded from the stairwell and a woman, pink and white as an enormous baby, burst into the room. "Just passing through," she cried, drifting towards the kitchen with the curious agility and lightness of step characteristic of some fat people.

"You're just passing through." Hackett began to sneeze explosively. "Bloody hell!" he gasped, then muttered, "My God, but you're a huge lady." And so she was, with enough arse on her for two or three big women.

"The universe lies under order and we can understand it." Undoing the buttons on his vest, Victor Burnel showed his teeth and watch to Mrs. Horner and Miss Laycock, a fine creature whose white bosom, expansive as an unmade bed, moved with a life of its own.

"Mrs. Horner, Sadie. . ." Carruthers swung his legs excitedly. "The doctor here wants to know if we ever heard of Eddie Shantz."

"Our Eddie?" Turning from Burnel, easy as a dancer, she laughed: "I should say."

"He's turned up their way. By Mad River."

"Well, I guess it's best some folk don't know that."

"Best for Eddie, all right, hah!" He convulsed into his handkerchief. "Bloody hell. . ."

"I always did figure. . ." Miss Laycock's bosom appeared to be nestling itself on Burnel's shoulder. "I've always figured Eddie'd end up like the Finn."

"The Finn?"

"Valin, the one on Saturday."

"Ah," said Carruthers, "the hanging. Ah, yes. He may do so yet, of course, although. . ." A man like Eddie, they all agreed, a saucy man like Eddie. The ladies smiled ferociously, for he was a lovely man all right, cunning as a dead pigeon, but a lovely man. It's more like to be a jealous husband, some dupe, some cuckold. They had stories right enough, Jesus! They slapped their thighs.

To Robert's astonishment, the fat woman — Jane Shore — lifted Carruthers right out of his chair as if he were a pillow and inserted herself into it with the little man still enveloped in her arms. "You wouldn't believe," she said, arranging the professor crossways on her lap, "you wouldn't believe the scrapes that little growl biter's got hisself into."

"Stiff and stout. . ." Mrs. Horner smiled prettily at Robert Fraser. "He was always stiff and stout."

"A wolf in the groin," suggested Miss Laycock. Good God, was she massaging Burnel's neck with her chest?

"That little bleeder has wolves in the groin, if I ever saw it. . ."

Suddenly exhausted as if after tears, as if recognizing his own coronach, Robert discovered where he was. The notes in his breast pocket would purchase these women, manoeuvre their flesh, if that's what he wanted. All his life he'd wondered what would draw him to this place, free him to follow gentle wheedling voices into the dark.

"A gentleman of the three ins." Jane Shore smiled as the doctor, stroking her bicep (pale it was, substantial as a thigh), glared at Carruthers who appeared to be having some sort of fit in her lap. "In debt," they chorused happily, not for the first time, "in debt, in trouble and in danger of remaining there for life." Scratching intently and stretching, indulging what splinters of memory? bored fragments like as not, they'd offer the upright grin beneath those skirts, mewling, whispering they'd play the hot-arse for money, their practiced hands, expecting nothing perhaps she'd hold him, soothing, an unfamiliar body. . .

"Lock up your daughters!" Springing to his feet, Victor Burnel, his waistcoat flapping and with several shirt buttons undone, executed a lurching jig that revealed his hairless belly. "Eddie Shantz," he piped, "has come to Mad River. . ." Whereupon Miss Laycock pirouetted from the room and darted upstairs, with Burnel in clumsy but enthusiastic pursuit.

One of the postcards: an urgent girl leering over a naked shoulder, the smooth column of her back plunging to soft buttocks. She had something about her, resisting the comparison, his groin stirred, Agatha Bullock with predator's eyes set close in her swarthy face.

Abruptly his mouth snapped shut, no sir! His eyes bulged uncomfortably as though he'd seen something the others were not privy to. After pulsing like birds, his hands were stilled, awkward. It wouldn't work, for he had no ease, only a small talent for intimacy even with those he loved. What would he say to Mrs. Horner approaching him now with the assurance of a favourite aunt? "I can see," her voice was like honey, like someone selling shoes, "you're not like the others," who were leaving the room with Jane Shore, both Carruthers and Dr. Tom, clinging to her, pulling at her, insisting she's mine, me first. One on either side, they scratched and poked around the bulk of her, three wrestlers in such a tangle they stuck briefly, pushing finally through the doorway. They scuffled in the vestibule before proceeding with knocks and thumps up the stairs.

"They both like a bit of fat." Mischievously she shook her head and winked, a conspirator. She didn't squeeze and pinch her bubbies, shake them at him, for he wasn't like the others, a real gent. "What do you fancy, Mr. Fraser? Robert, may I call you that? There must be something. . ." Half closing her eyes, bedroom eyes, moistening her full lips, she said, "The professor. . ." jerking her head towards the thumps and squeals beyond the ceiling, "the professor tells me you're, well. . ." baring her teeth, "you understand my meaning? He says you're interested in machines. *Mr. Fraser!*" But he was gone. "Robert. . ." Like blazes through the kitchen and into the alley. There was no use even looking for him, and so she made herself a cup of tea.

XII

"Without Jesus I'm surely. . ." Almost Gaelic, a solitary woman's voice with long pauses between the lines, heavy pauses, a high clear voice, "without Him I'm surely driftin'. . ." She wrestled and scrubbed, the dead wet sound of work clothes slapping on a board, and when another, passing in the lane, picked up the song, her voice was almost identical. "Without Jesus. . ."

Then, as the professor led them to the tenement through a back yard overgrown by underbrush, ground sparrows sprang from twining nightshade and milkweed, from vipers bugloss, bullock's lungwort in chaos with big Joe dandelion and bushy growths resembling poverty grass.

> Without Jesus I'm surely
> Without Him I'm surely driftin'
> Like a ship
> Without a sail.

Ascending in the stairwell they were joined by others, comfortable men who in their dress and demeanour were alien here, respectable men made foolish by the occasion, by the smell of cabbage, a hysterical mongrel yapping on the first floor. They shuffled on the stairs and their feet made a sound like the wind among leaves, a relentless monody, as drifting formally, one after the other, they slipped behind yellow varnished doors that, on briefly opening to accept them, revealed poor rooms vacated for the occasion. All of their tenants except for one, the agent perhaps, the collector of money, were milling in the street below.

Carruthers had purchased a window in a small flat, cluttered and dark, a pinched and smelly room beneath the eaves, and while it was cheap enough it would be crowded. He and the doctor would have to kneel so the others could see over their heads. Nevertheless, it afforded a fine view of the sky over the lake, the crowded street with a fairground beyond, and finally, glistening in a cul-de-sac against the wall, black as sin in a roped-off clearing by the prison door — the gallows. A curiously awkward structure built as a sledge, it had been dragged so often into the yard its platform was twisted, its beams so askew the rope and familiar noose appeared to be pointing at an angle towards the drop.

Down the street at the corner, whole families were disgorged from horse-drawn trams. They scampered and hopped, ignoring folk that cried "Seats to let" from every doorstep, "A good view of the execution!" They hurried towards the cross-beam jutting above the crowd. There everyone jostled, pushing the better to see. Shouts of encouragement drifted with pipe smoke from windows overlooking the scene as fights broke out, random stupid affairs, for while keeping an eye on the empty flag pole, waiting for the black flag, the flag of death, men had already begun to drink.

All the while more vehicles, more people on foot, were arriving from every direction, countrymen and those from the town in surreys, buckboards and cabriolets drawn by fine nervous animals; phaetons and buggies narrowly avoided collision with farm carts and lumbering wains; but all of them were soon abandoned in the fairground by drivers who, after only the most cursory gestures of concern for their animals, ran after their compatriots, searching for them in a worried and awkward fashion.

"Smashing good gingerpop, smashing good!"

Whistle and ribbon sellers, costermongers of every sort, called their wares, while hungry-eyed preachers, hard as nails, like blackbirds in spring they challenged with practiced voices, each insisting upon his territory, his turf. Repent or be damned, insisted one, for He is an angry God; while another, throwing his hat in the air for attention, bellowed that the wages of sin is death, the agony of death; and a third, leaning dangerously from an upper window across the street, his voice clear and penetrating, explained the land cannot be cleansed of the blood that is shed therein but by the blood of him that shed it — but even he was largely ignored.

While Hackett and the doctor settled in for a game of cribbage, the professor, still gazing into the street, remarked soberly that nothing, clearly nothing but a hanging, not a grand fair or exhibition, not J. B. Lent's travelling Hippozoonamadon or the Athleolympiman-theum, not the promise of Confederation, not even an invasion, could have brought such a mix of citizens together. True. Yes, how true, they agreed, for it appeared all sections of the Colony had sent representatives, it did so. There was even a bunch of Indians and what looked like several ladies travelling from England.

Perhaps thinking of the Frozen Ocean, Robert suggested a revolution, perhaps a revolution, but the others disagreed; not in the Canadas. They'll skin a flea for the sake of its hide, they'll fight at the drop of a hat, but they don't give much of a shit here for anything new, no sir, not if it'll cause trouble.

"Tell me," said Robert unexpectedly, "was there an elephant?"

"A what?" Carruthers peered from beside the window. Hackett and Dr. Tom glanced up from their cards.

"An elephant. . ." Blinking unhappily, Robert shrugged. "You know, in that Hippozoona. . .that, you know, that circus. . . ."

"An elephant, by Jesus, man!" Carruthers slapped his small hands together. "There was an *exhibition* of elephants, a herd of the bloody things."

"And a hippopotamus. . ." Hackett grinned at his sudden memory of it.

"There was everything." He began counting on child-like fingers. "A troop of acting bears, an educated Sacred Indian bull, there were leaping buffaloes, talking horses and performing dogs. There were monkeys dressed up like the Wild West."

"I reckon I'll never forget that hippopotamus and the fellow putting his head, you mind that?" Demonstrating, opening his arms like jaws, Hackett pressed his ear against his armpit. "He put his head right into the damned thing's mouth."

"Well," suggested the doctor, "I understand they don't have much in the way of teeth, now do they?"

"Maybe, maybe not. Still . . . he could give your head a terrible suck all the same."

"And Mademoiselle Ariane. . ." The professor's mouth went soft, useless, as if the words came from somewhere else. "Mademoiselle Ariane Felecia." Methodically blinking, he shook his head. "From Paris, if I recollect."

"Was she the woman with the elephant?"

"She was. . ." Carruthers sighed, closing his eyes as if remembering a marvellous song, "the most beautiful, graceful, daring and dashing equestrienne in the world. I'll tell you. You should have seen. . ." He opened them. "Yes," he said, "and a real lady to boot."

"You'd never have thought by the look of her, just a slip of a girl she was and lovely, lovely. . ." Hackett's little eyes and mouth were wet as entrails. "You'd never believe what she did on that horse."

"She must of had thighs on her like iron."

"Like the neck of God," agreed Hackett, his head nodding, heavy as a sunflower. The professor closed his eyes again as if to hear beyond the rising babble in the street.

"The most beautiful," murmured Carruthers, "graceful, daring and dashing. . ."

"Didn't she have something to do with the elephant?"

"Elephants?" They examined Robert curiously. "With an elephant? No. . ." Exchanging glances, they shrugged.

They didn't think so. Still, there's no accounting for taste. "I reckon not. She was a horsewoman, you see, an equestrienne of the first water."

"I once heard tell of a handsome young woman. . ." A slim and pretty woman, neat in her brilliant costume, a simple tension in her arching back and loins, "she lay down, so they tell me, she lay on a Moorish carpet and commanded the elephant to rest its foot on her face, and the beast did it too, gentle as a cat." Enclosed by the sinuous trunk, lifted above the crowd, she'd postured, smiling, her arms beating the air like wings. . . .

"There's a piece in Cornwall that snuffles up sovereigns with her quim."

"Jesus," said Dr. Tom. It wasn't clear if he believed Hackett or not, but he liked the idea all right. "With her quim?" Making a soft fish-like motion with his lips, he nuzzled the back of his hand. "Jesus. . .eh?" That was something all right. He wanted to know if Ches'd ever had her, what else she could do. "By Jesus, there's some odd things going on, especially with women, foreign women coming in here and all." Then fooling with the cards, he told of one, near Barrie it was, in a tent after the show. He'd have stayed away if he'd known, it must of been the drink, yes, it makes you do some shameful things. . . Well, anyway, here was this crowd of men with just one lantern and the woman, she had the lantern, see, and the men held back in the dark, pressed against the canvass with the woman in the middle, eh? And Jesus, what a sight she was! "Here's me head," he grinned fiercely, "me arse is coming. You know the kind." And by God, they did. At least they nodded, grunting as if they did, and despite an urgent sound, its distracting promise rising in the street (perhaps the hanging was about to begin?), they were caught by this slattern, her lantern revealing men in the tent. What did she do, for Chrissakes? Picking at their fingernails, fiddling with their pipes, the familiar cloth on their thighs, they spat into handkerchiefs, watching the doctor. For God's sake, would he tell them or not? That's a good one, me arse is coming, but the moment had passed, was lost in the gathering clamour, hats off! Voices were crying outside, hats off, and the doctor clapped his hands decisively. "Ah," he said, "that sounds promising all right." Whereupon the four of them scampered to their positions in the window, but it was only the hangman's under-strapper come to check the equipment. With a slight nod to the crowd, the suggestion of a bow, he released a bolt and the drop fell with a boom and echo. Relieved, presenting a small smile, he seized the rope above its noose and lifted himself from the platform to swing, idly at first but with increasing vigour, an ill-looking creature twisting before that ribald crowd pressing closer, so close now it had become a jeering undifferentiated mass but he was oblivious. Dropping lightly to the ground and resetting the trap, he sauntered to the prison door without a pause or glance over his shoulder and stepped inside as it opened from within.

From their vantage beneath the eaves, they saw almost immediately, and before those in the street, a black flag fluttering on its halyard, and at that moment the prison bell began to toll, a flat and mournful sound that emptied the people, leaving them white and ghastly looking in the morning sun.

Suddenly packed in the street and forcing in from alley-ways, clinging to the corners of buildings, swarming on barrows and gaffs, steps and balustrades, along rooftops and balconies, there must have been six thousand if there was a dozen. They fell silent as if underwater, poised and expectant, for the ceremony had begun. Indeed within heartbeats the prison door opened again. The official party appeared to a startling roar, a multitude of shouts, *"Hats off,"* and *"Die like a man!"* Hats off, not out of respect but a lust to see. Die-yeh like a man! It was Hackett shouting with the others as the mob trembled, suddenly pulsing, a single organism. Like-a-man, like-a-man, they bellowed, straining on tiptoe for a glimpse of Valin, the killer, by Jesus. "He's shrunk, can't you see? There, in the middle, look! With the county kerchief. . ."

Teetering ceremoniously at a safe distance, the chaplain and prison doctor led the Finn who was almost hidden by turnkeys, burly men languorous on the balls of their feet. Behind them, curiously ragged in bright sunlight, came the hangman. An awkward figure, black-robed and hooded, he was accompanied by his assistant swinging leather belts and pinions like censers. Finally the warden, a step and a half in front of his deputies, all of them soberly dressed, shuffling courteously, keeping time with the prison bell, with the prisoner himself. Almost gently they came to the foot of the gallows where the doctor halted. The turnkeys parted slightly so the hangman could make his move. Darting among them quicker than hell would scorch a feather, he pulled the white hood over Valin's face and took his arm. Surely he'd resist? The hangman leaned so close, conspiratorially, the two of them coming together like dancers, his black hood resting briefly on the white until the tension in them escaped into the crowd. So it was Valin, cocking his head as if listening, who rested his hand on the hangman's shoulder like a blind beggar as they mounted the steps. So calm, almost intimate, were they that many in the audience felt excluded, deprived. There was some suggestion the Finn had been drugged, even beaten into submission, for how else could the turnkeys remain at the foot of the scaffold? Lulled by the tolling bell, by the two figures, for they even looked alike — two small hard men, one in a white hood and the other in black — the spectators fell silent. The chaplain, who'd taken his place beside the drop, cleared his throat while preparing to recite the beautiful prayers read for the dying.

Meanwhile, the doctor, the warden and his officers, and the turnkeys shifted from one foot to the other, and those privileged to view the scene from windows and roofs stared intently. It seemed to them the air had never been so flat or empty, nor had the sky fallen so heavily on the town. Meanwhile, ordinary folk, crammed in the street, had to press this way and that in order to see the hooded figures. Under the beam on the drop, one raised his arms and the other fastened a broad leather body-belt about his waist. Anticipating each step, he lowered them, waiting while his elbows were strapped to buckles above his hips, his hands to others at his belly. What threat or eccentric alliance subdued them so? He drew his legs together; and the hangman, adjusting his black hood which had slipped over his eyes as if it were too big, as if perhaps it wasn't his own, the hangman worked quickly; he touched the Finn almost lovingly, soothing, and then he pinioned him below the knees.

He straightened to take the rope, opening the noose, and dropped it onto the Finn's shoulders. Pulling tight, he revealed the marvellous contours of a face beneath the blank white hood. It was at that moment, seeing the gaping mouth, the eyes bulging wildly against the cloth, that a rumbling of dismay gathered in thousands of throats until it filled the stone defile of the street, overwhelmed the chaplain's voice, the dolorous bell. For the crowd now realized it was to be denied the Finn's last words. It swelled to an incredulous roar and as some found words it fractured into shouts, leather-lunged cries of "Shame!" "Confess!" A forest of arms was raised in anger. "Confess and be hanged!" They'd come to accept he was in cahoots, goddamn right, with the hangman. "Jesus, Jesus!" Red faces shouted at one another, the bastards. "Bastards!"

At the first bellow, Valin started jerking his head from side to side as if trying to hear, to understand; and those in the first rows saw his mouth, behind the shroud, begin to convulse. It was snapping open and shut, open and shut, like an injured fish. Pinioned as he was, he began to spring, to lunge, as if dancing to the fury of his audience, then quick as lightning he plummeted through the trap! The crowd gasped. Curling his body with astonishing strength, he rested a foot on the drop. Nobody had ever seen anything like it. For Chrissakes, he was scrabbling his way back up through the hole! Men and women fought among themselves, pushing, even striking out in order to see and later boast they'd been there when the Finn, my Gawd, you should of seen the way he lifted himself up, you wouldn't believe, and he'd have got out too except the chaplain rushed forward to kick him off with his boot but the Finn again managed to get a foothold and still the hangman, ragged in his ill-fitting robe and hood, ragged as a crow in winter, he just stood there twisting his hands together so it was the chaplain who had to push him once more to dangle on the rope. "Reprieve," shouted a voice so others joined in. "Reprieve," they bellowed, "reprieve!" because the little bugger had got his foot back up there again. He wasn't going to be hanged, you could tell, and just as the crowd began to cheer, to throw their hats in the air with fierce halloos, the executioner hurled himself on top of the condemned man. By Jesus, the devil must have limped over hell to hear the shrieks of anger, the odious laughter of relief that seized the crowd as it watched two men corkscrewing beneath that scaffold until finally by his own weight the hangman managed to strangle Valin. . . .

"I'll tell you what," said the doctor afterwards as they stepped into the street, "that was a helluva thing all right."

Releasing themselves into the throng — part of which pressed forward to view the rotating corpse, perhaps touch its hand with the hope of curing skin lesions, miasmas or the bloody flux — agreeing each one that it was indeed a helluva thing, they nevertheless found themselves exhausted, shouldering angrily to the fairground in search of something, perhaps a drink, certainly a drink, and maybe the crowd itself would coalesce in some appropriate, some diverting, fashion.

There'd be fights, God knows, and later, after the ritual hour, his corpse would be taken down, then carried with twisted head on a wooden bier into the prison, and maybe the hangman would raffle off pieces of the rope. It was Italian hemp, you see, made especially for the work and had hung fifteen men now and three women. But a dangerous melancholy had seized the crowd. Hot-arsed, teased to a pitch then denied release, streaming to the fairground where among musicians and fire-breathers, a bear perhaps dancing with a ring in his nose, they'd be entertained by Astonishing Freaks of Nature, by drinking competitions and small lewd scenes, by buskers and the turbulent figure of a Spring-heeled Jack.

Knowing he should leave the field, indeed the city, that he shouldn't delay his return another minute, Robert wandered in search of his mastodon. "Our beast," the professor had giggled, "we'll make good money from our beast today." And yet in paying more than necessary for the wagon, insisting on paying for Robert's time, his meticulous reconstruction, Carruthers had proved himself generous, no doubt of it, more than generous, and yet. . . "It's been all spiffed up with mill-cut lumber instead of birchbark. I've a first-rate man to run the joint, make no mistake." Grinning like a monkey, you could tell he had plans, make no mistake.

All about him, men roistered arm in arm. In the distance

a whistle screamed, then the sudden fury of a steam thresher displayed for prospective buyers. There were bottles everywhere, empty underfoot, half filled from hand to hand, it tasted like water. And a drunk old man, his face pinched, desolate beneath his whiskers, was pissing himself unawares. His left boot glistened, his trousers were plastered against skinny legs, and he snarled vehemently, his body shivering in a private rage. Until finally there it was — cunningly situated, you could say that for Carruthers, its open side facing a blank wall so only those who'd paid could see. He was a businessman all right. Festooned with streamers, with freshly painted banners announcing an Atavistic Wonder direct from Buffalo, for the First Time in any of the Canadas, a Prehistoric Monster, a Genuine Dragon from beyond the Dark Ages. Packing them in like that, he scarcely recognized it. Jesus, but there was an awful lot of them at a quarter a throw! He'd go home with real money, so he would, to show for his pains, and she couldn't complain about that, she mustn't complain. He should have felt vindicated, but he couldn't bring himself to push among them, press between the wagon and the wall, because he feared seeing it again, his long-suffering cage of bones, that attentive skull. . . .

Resisting, he was nevertheless carried by the crowd close into the barker's voice, an exultant Yankee voice, right into the shadow of his wagon where folk struggled to congratulate the professor because there's so much Truth, by God, they'd heard such music in those bones, *memento mori*, such pullulating silence. Could he tell them anything about the class of beast, would it eat meat, for example? Imagine the size of its stool! Never having seen anything like it, they nodded their heads. They raised their voices against the din, opening and closing their mouths hungrily for attention, and leaned to Carruthers, touched him for luck perhaps because they knew him, you see, Prof. Carruthers? Melville Carruthers? Ah yes, then they'd smile as if smoking a fine cigar.

Faces and bodies convulsed. Something was happening, what's happening? Not wanting to miss anything, they pushed, crying What! Where? The professor was gesticulating with childlike impatience and it seemed to be a warning. But Robert, as his father might have done, only tipped his hat and smiled wanly. Unable to approach or depart, he relinquished himself to red faces like fists, red the colour of night on every side. By sliding into the flow then paddling with his elbows, he soon arrived to find Sloot, the Yankee pigeon netter, drumming his feet on the earth, his enormous body compressed and furious. He spied in Robert a face he recognized; and even though he shouted so hard, sweat shooting from his face like hail and his eyes threatening to spring from their sockets, the sound was lost even before it left his mouth. Grimacing in a terrible fashion, his body trembled as if labouring under an intolerable weight. What was he trying to say?

"Easy now. . ." Reaching out, Robert stepped towards those bulging eyes, blank as pennies. "Hey, Sloot!" Approaching the Yankee who'd become aware of him again. "What is it, fellah?" He couldn't have heard. In an instant he hurled himself at Fraser, striking him with a powerful blow, then another. Voices yelped in appreciation because he moved quickly, a powerful bugger all right and a fighter, you could see that, but he'd picked the wrong man. Although startled, staggered by the onslaught, Robert feinted once, then hammered Sloot in the ribs, on the side of the head, the body again, then the face. He smashed the squat nose like a flask of wine. Holy shit, this is what they'd come for! The crowd went wild, for suddenly he was all over the man, pounding him blow upon blow until Sloot fell like a tree that had got its last cut, and it was over. . . .

All about him men roistered, sharing bottles, beating fists on their thighs. They whistled and stamped, finally straggling to the edge of the field where owners massaged pit-bulls and mastiffs or teased them to fury while odds were being determined. They marvelled at Robert Fraser's strength, his silent fury, while cursing the banks and politicians, the weather and privileged bastards who hoarded land, for what chance did a fellah have, what chance at all? Maybe the Fenians were right, there's money south of the border. A hard-working man, a God-fearing man, can get ahead, fashion a life down there; but others, well-gone in drink with no intention of stopping now, appealing to loyalty, to patriotism, they'd howl Orange slogans and charge at those who invoked Sam Lount and Peter Matthews, threatening them with mighty buffets like the stranger gave that Yankee, for there wasn't a man on either side this day who wouldn't argue the leg off an iron pot.

PART THREE: 1876

Chapter Four

> "Moreover, flowers are available only
> for a short time, and whole seasons
> may pass without any developing at all.
> For these reasons, they are not of so
> much practical value in tree
> identification as are other features."
> — William M. Harlow

XIII

Imperious as it was, poised over his ill-conceived sheds, a
dark fist above the forest, the tree had insinuated itself
into Mary's life. The trunk rose more than sixty feet to a
splendid dome, to limbs formidable in their weight and
angularity, to a hawk's nest of ragged sticks abandoned
since the man shot its tenants three summers in a row.
Bare of leaves in winter, the maze of branches pulsed and
swayed, as if the rhythm of her own body breathed there
against the sky. It beckoned, whispering so esoterically
she'd come to hear it even in the darkness of her bed.
Rising to stand by the window in the dead light preceding
dawn, she knew her brain was transparent like that, a restless zig-zag pattern branching into twigs and shoots, into
side shoots, whorls and buds. . . .

For half her life she'd seen the man come and go in its shadow until now, at a distance of more than twenty paces, he'd become once more a stranger; sombre yet urgent, abandoning one task for another only to find something was lost, it might have been an awl, perhaps a buckle. He appeared in doorways and at the corners of buildings; he could be seen rummaging among trunks and boxes, searching in long grass or among familiar objects. He'd laugh stentoriously, as if in some pile of junk he recognized a private joke, a conspiratorial game. Then, bounding to his workshop, abruptly changing his mind and accosting the children instead, demanding to know where Angus had left the axe, his wire-cutters, a piece of harness or whatever, he'd suddenly lose interest and change the subject. Grinning fiercely he'd remark the breachy cow had torn a hole in the south fence again, the cattle beasts were in the forest! "There's a cure for that, though." Screwing up his face, forcing an explosion in his throat, he'd shout, "A bullet between the eyes!" Or porcupines, they'd eaten the pump handle, he'd kill porcupines with a stick, a rock, with the axe, if he could find it. . . Deserted by that train of thought, perhaps remembering he'd been on his way to the machine, he'd spring to the door, pausing only to admonish his family: "If our shirts knew our design, then we should burn them, eh?" Winking, chuckling to himself, he'd slip outside, leaping like an insect, all elbows and knees as he crossed the yard, growing smaller, even stranger with distance.

So filled with a longing to do good was he, to accomplish some grand purpose, that his hair stuck out above his ears, his voice rasped like a briny pickle and, as a result, as if unable to drive himself from the clearing, he'd long ceased going into the forest. Moving between the house and barn, the barn and his machine, precise and impatient as a fence-viewer, an assessor, his gaze on the ground as if he might rediscover some of the tools, he seemed unable even to look at it.

While other men, Eddie Shantz, for example, and Tom Bullock, even Casey, slashed and burned each winter, grimly enlarging their workable acres, Robert, staring disconsolately at his feet, retreated into his workshop. And so it was that Mary and her children had to search out the lost cattle, inveigle them back with a trail of oats and barley, while Robert watched through the glass, his face blurred as if under water.

Built piecemeal to accommodate each addition to the machinery below, the various roofs and risers sloped and dropped like one of those Old Testament cities built into the side of a hill. Churning violently, the mill wheel rattled the sheds; they trembled beneath her while the noise of it subdued even the sounds inside her head as Mary, making certain the coast was clear, scrambled over the central ridge-pole and eased herself from one plateau to the next until she arrived at the hidden corner where two generations of walls met beneath an original eave. Inching forward with her chin resting on folded arms, she could see his worktable; and by shifting ever so slightly to the right or left, she was able to observe everything that occurred in the main room. Sunlight from cracks and knotholes slashed the gloomy air, two bars of it intersected, glimmering gently on the wall above him where he calculated, scribbling numbers in vertical lines. From time to time, almost as if releasing a spring, he straightened, pushing deep into his lower back with his fists before swivelling in the chair, twisting and stretching. Each strand of lank dark hair sprang with startling clarity around his bald spot, the ropy muscles fell into his shoulders and the veins were like worms on the backs of his hands. It was as if he were at the bottom of a magnifying pool with columns of light descending among motionless wheels and plungers, the crazed logic of his machine jumbled like an avalanche between the roof-tree and the floor. Suddenly jumping to his feet, raising both arms, the knuckles standing pink and white in his fists, he broke into a little jig. Slapping his hands together and kicking up his heels, he twirled like a flea on a hot griddle, then punched a fist into the palm of his hand and sat down. As he filled a pipe, she wondered if he suspected she spied on him like this, for he'd hammered the pegs projecting against her fingers, he'd cut and placed these boards, how could he not know the hole was there? But he never looked up, never gave the slightest sign.

Not knowing what to expect, she waited tremulous and open as a hunter. Watching him working and reworking the calculations, his gaunt figure crouched and intense, she resented his dance, the awkward pleasure of it, the surprise still curving in his body when he rose again to stretch greedily. For while each year the children grew noisier, more complicated, their games collapsing almost before they'd begun, while the willows along the stream flushed orange as the mornings advanced once more towards the solstice, in that lengthening dusk where lamps aren't lit until after supper and even then they cast tremulous, useless shadows, she would pick the skin about her fingernails and dream. She dreamed of Jacob Rymal grown to a man, changing as they all had changed; so when she met him in Mad River his expression was clear and uncomplicated as if he'd never loved her. Looking into her face, he'd ask after Robert, after his inventions. "And the children, how are the children?" He hoped they fared well in the bush. His hands were large and soft as she remembered. Mad River was booming. Didn't she miss the town?

Then Eddie Shantz, his children if he had them would marry well, they'd inherit a real farm with elms shading a graceful drive. And once, greedy as a child, he'd taken her arm to help her; and despite herself his hand returned in waves, like the ocean, like his voice, a skeletal promise, a hopeless gesture that she didn't want, she wanted none of it.

Ralph Cruickshank had loved her too. A disconsolate boy with bad skin, he'd mooned outside her house until the Major loosed his dogs and then one night, just last year it was, or the year before? playing cards with Black Ramsay Cameron he'd got up suddenly and without a word of explanation took a razor to his own throat, he slashed it terribly and so he died.

Sitting with Robert in the hurly-burly of mealtimes or watching him smoke and rock in the gathering dark, pretending to read she'd search intently, trying to find some movement or gesture that would distinguish him from the other, the man failing among his machines. Shadows and reflections: the unprotected line of a forehead or cheek, a raised hand in sunlight, one of them and then the other so that waking abruptly from dreams, finding herself sitting bolt upright with the muffled breath of sleepers in the house, she couldn't tell if she wept because of a sound or its echo.

Sometimes a brilliant winter morning: crystals of powdered snow like stars, a wind lifts them from sculpted drifts around fences, by bushes resolute as fists; dead weeds cast shadows blue as the night sky; and self-contained, strangely oblivious, the cat sits on a fence post; while caught in the branches of a young apple tree, the red cloth shreds itself bitterly as it has for as long as she can recall.

Then as the days lengthen, each year the birds retreat and others take their place. The sun burns at her window over the sink. Halfway between the barn and house, perhaps emptying slops in her desolate garden or traipsing to the outhouse, she's stopped in her tracks, for beneath her feet, still secret below its empty surface, the snow is melting, miniature forms, hidden castles and bridges are collapsing into rivulets of sound.

Do the dead have dreams? White as tubers shrieking on the porch or where woodpiles trap the sun, venturing further from the house, her children shedding winter clothing piece by piece and the birds! shouting amongst themselves, returning skeins of geese, the buoyant raptors, blackbirds sleek as lawyers and occasionally swans, their quavering three-note chorus falling like glass into the clearing, like shards of reflected light so liver-leaf and dog-toothed violets spring beneath her feet. The sky darkens: violets and pussy willows, open windows and the mill wheel churning, rattling dangerously as winter cascades in its flume with such violence she'd hear it all night, imagine it torn loose, flying off like the head of an axe, its primal power demolishing his clockwork, berserk among the gears and wheels, the struts and pulleys, until there was nothing left, just kindling, bits of machinery, twisted bones. . . .

There'd been a time she wanted to put her arms around him, press her face into his throat. Resting a hand on his sleeping hip or flank, she'd learned to feel such love, such fascination, that tracing the hurt curve of his belly as it rose and fell, cautiously discovering hunger with her finger-tips, she'd longed for him to waken, for the full weight and strength of him. But no longer. The smell of his soiled clothing beside the bed, the acrid must of him, his pale and ropy body writhing with dreams, what did any of this have to do with her? She picks flowers for herself, for the girls perhaps, but not her husband, never their life together.

Sometimes he still insists, moving with the dumb precision of a metronome, his clenched jawbone against her temple. She tries not to hear his breath, his wind machines clattering in the yard, the rooster's wooden wings, sows jerking spasmodically from side to side, the donkey kicking its hinged legs. For the inside of his head must be like that, crammed with interlocking wheels and pendulums, weights and counterweights, full of restless hunger, each bit locked into the next with the whole being driven by a heresiarchal need. And so he persists, labouring grimly on her body until sometimes released but often not, he groans as if dying or else he whimpers. Eventually he clears his throat and speaks of familiar things, of memories and ambitions. "Do you suppose," he might say, "that story of their dinner inside the beast is true?"

"I reckon it probably is. It's the kind of thing they'd do."

"Imagine that. . ."

The great tree bursts into leaf, muddy tracks harden, will bake into dust to explode about her children playing in the yard, while Robert wrestles equipment among burnt-out stumps, casting desolate glances at the road where every day with increasing need he expects news from Toronto, from Carruthers, for the skeleton's back on the road, there'll be cash soon enough. But gradually spending more time in his workshop, scarcely coming out except for meals, he'll stop talking about it, let the idea go as he does, and they'll do with the little they've got unless she persuades him to sell a lamb or two, perhaps a calf. She insists there's nothing to fear until predictably, in the rising and falling of lamps being lit, the night resounds more violently, a skull grins in his face, he cracks his knuckles one after the other. And she's stuck, lost in some littoral zone between high and low tide with everywhere the frenzy of his machines, the bush seeping back, darting like shadows; and she has nothing more to give, five children, another collecting itself in her womb, with the good Lord knows how many more stacked there like yolks in a prize hen.

Imagination being a weapon, she dreamed of clothes well fashioned, hands smooth and cool as pebbles, but she never looked into his face. Who was it? A landscape with new-fallen snow, perhaps the edge of a lake, the marsh by Mad River with ghostly figures, an androgynous couple drifting towards the forest. She knew it was shameful, she'd regret it if she could, but instead at some point she began to eat and drink, to help herself to third and fourth portions. Piles of vegetables vanished into her mouth, along with pigeon stew, bread and pickles. She speared wedges of pie, begging on her children's plates. But there was no satisfying her. She'd devour whole turnips while preparing dinner, loaves of bread and last night's biscuits, jugs of beer, cold beans. Even congealed soups and the carcasses of birds and small animals no longer made it from one meal to the next. And because she lived in horror of Barbara Casey's angry, red little hands, she spent hours massaging her own with oil, with goose grease and lard, as if that somehow might assuage her hunger. She became renowned, precious as the Mad River town band, so that neighbours travelling to other regions, finding themselves among strangers, they celebrated her long stomach. "Here's this woman at home, she's a wolf in her belly, has Mary Fraser." "A champion eater," men bellowed, "by Jingo." And women rolled their eyes. "She's just a wee bit of a thing, quite pretty to look at. . ." Still, they all had stories of what she'd devoured, how many grouse, hens, trout, collops of mutton (complaining all the while about the taste of wool), the beans swimming in salt pork, meat pies or tatties bashed with eggs, minced parsley and salt. "And she drinks like a man, like a funnel!" Banging on the table, they spoke of Great Eaters in History — what's-his-name, the Russian giant, or that fellah by Kingston, and Sir Robert Fowler, Lord Mayor of London, men who took food as time takes life. But they were fat.

Vaudin now, she weighed four hundred pounds before she was sixteen, and Elmer Prinney, huge he was. "But not our Mary, no siree, not Mary Fraser. . ."

She must have worms.

Yeas.

They'll keep you eating, they will so. You'll end up a skinned rabbit with a bellyful of reptiles. .

Thick as your wrist, they are, and twice as ugly.

Fearing she'd be eaten up from within, she purged herself all one summer with anthelmintics such as the inner bark of odd trees mixed with blood bitters and epsom salts or the stomachs of small birds dried then pulverized and mixed with whiskey. She stewed pigeon gizzards in milk, their powdered dung in senna tea, but with no better results than a foul temper.

Neither cathartics nor drastics revealed any sign of the worm, nor did they diminish her appetite. And so she abandoned all treatment and began to stare at Robert, pointing her chin without blinking as he rocked by the stove.

Stupidly cracking his knuckles, he had no more land cleared than ten years ago. The porch step was unmended and treacherous, while burdock crowded shoulder high about the barn. Muttering as if billeted at her house, some stranger, a sergeant from somewhere, he crooned, for the drink was in him. His ugly boots inside the door. That noise vibrating in his throat, growing louder, more insistent as the chair protested his weight. Each sound separate and distinct, and then a rushing like the wind at night or the lakeshore by Mad River in a storm. A man singing, oblivious, rocking by the stove while upstairs children slept their mysterious sleep. The wooden clock ticked and whirred. Logs shifted in the firebox. Some day soon, with a sensation like whispering, Death would come and take one, then another of them by the throat — herself perhaps (that would be easiest), or Rose, maybe Angus with his body too small for the space it had to fill; she feared more for him than the others.

Earlier the night was full of thunder, full of rain. It had crashed against the windows and shaken the door. Now the man sang while her body performed its usual chores. A dipper was hung by the window, the rinsed cloth spread on a wire from the stovepipe. He poured more whiskey into their cups. The windows rattled urgently then stopped.

"Oh, the Dutchmen. . ." Replacing the bottle, his spiky hair almost touching the ceiling, raising his drink as if to salute her, staring vaguely at Mary, at his wife, he tried again in a better key. "Oh, the Dutchmen. . . Oh, the. . ." Slumping into his chair with darkness lurching in the room's corners, extending his long legs, he closed his eyes:

> Oh, the Dutchmen have their Holland
> And the Spaniards have their Spain
> So the Yankees to the south of us
> Will south of us remain. . .

Grateful the rain had stopped, moving brusquely to conceal the noise of her heart, she opened the door and stepped onto the porch where distant lightning flashed deep in the forest. She smelled the muddy yard, saw beyond it their barn, the outbuildings squatting darkly, familiar yet ominous like the bush itself — the whole of it poised somehow and trembling; his wretched machine and the giant tree.

She sensed Angus before seeing him by the fence. Muffled by the rushing wheel, by peepers calling from the pond and a mustard sky flung over the clearing, his approach was endless. Hugging her breasts she retreated against the jamb, watching that feral body approach the step where his triangular face demanded she speak first.

And when she hesitated, the thin mouth opened in a grimace then quick and fluid he was past her and into the house, leaving a smell of damp wool.

"Where you been." Not a question but a rough command. The sound of him then leaping from his chair. "Tell me that, huh? Where you been?"

Cautious as strange dogs, two of them not six feet apart: Angus gazing at his father without expression while Robert, opening and closing his hands, shuffled to block the stairway.

"In the barn," she called. "Were you in the barn?" Angus barely shook his head and that without a glance.

"Where then, where you been, eh?" His neck swelling with anger, he fumbled at his belt buckle. Swaying almost gracefully, Robert seemed to be grinning. "Well," he demanded, "well, young fellah-me-lad, you gonna answer me or not?"

"Angus. . ." Reaching, her hands and voice in the room. "Your father. . ." Undoing his buckle now, thick fingers picking clumsily. No! Gnashing her teeth, she skipped from one foot to the other.

"The boy can speak for himself."

"No. . ."

"He's old and ugly enough to speak for himself, aren't you, boy?" Pulling the belt from around his middle, his pants sagging at the crotch. "Eh?" He grabbed them with his free hand, shifting on the balls of his feet, while his mouth opened and closed furiously. "What do you do out there?"

"Angus. . ." Mary leaned, reaching in air grown heavy as water.

"You neither hunt," his voice cold, manufacturing anger, "nor forage."

"You been to Casey's?" But she might not have spoken. His face blank, expectant, he'd been playing his whistle.

"You been using Casey's fiddle?" Her voice was too high, too shrill for the room, its dead air. Her words were lost among shadows, absorbed in laundry drying by the stove.

"A wild man. . ." Half-heartedly clattering the wind machines, bringing an odour of spent lightning, of broken earth, night swelled in the open door and candles danced suddenly, then guttered, so the boy's face, its ancient stillness flamed before their eyes. "No son of mine." Breathing heavily, the belt swinging from his fist in time with the wooden clock, keeping an eye on Mary now, her shadow violent on the wall, indeed it might have been the shadow he addressed. "The wild man," he recalled uncertainly. "I won't have it. . ."

Convinced it would never end, it would go on and on, she'd find herself doing something else and then one day. . . "Angus!" And the noise of her voice filled the house like smoke. Why do you hate us so?

XIV

He woke abruptly in predawn light because it had been too late to check the machine the night before. Drinking whiskey at the table, with darkness wavering in the room's corners, the shadows of moths fluttering on the walls, he had drawn up a chair for his legs to ease the pain in his back from the day's work.

He had told Mary again how the back field was ready, a good field it was, with the wild pigeons back, he'd seen a flock. . . Crouching over a plate of scraps, selecting pieces of congealed mutton, of potato, she examined pale fiddleheads and limp boiled greens before tossing them into her mouth. "And about time too. We'd have twice the acreage if it weren't for your foolishness with that contraption. Even Casey. . ."

Now lying beside him on her back in the silent house, her black hair like a horse's mane, she snored imperceptibly, her dry lips forcing the air in tiny bursts. His head ached slightly as he raised the covers. Her nightgown twisted above her waist revealed the mass of pulpy thighs, her belly's curve heavily into wispy hair. His children had emerged from that body. In some inconceivable way they'd fought or been dragged out from between her legs. He reached tentatively, putting his hand on hers. Sighing, she moved as if towards him; he paused with fingers aware of the resilient flesh beneath the cloth, he felt the warmth of her against his palm and lowered the bedcovers. Wild Angus was first, the curious and distant heir he'd sired but did not understand. And after him, Alice with her agate hunter's eyes. Then Rose. Calum came next, so much like his father they could hardly speak to each other. And finally Helen. A succession of strangers, it sometimes appeared, all of them except Alice ranged against him with their mother.

Gathering his clothes and tiptoeing into the kitchen, he didn't see that her eyes were open, that she was watching him.

The sun had begun to show itself somewhere beyond the trees, but Fraser, urinating against a stump, could only see a band of ochre light to the east. Buttoning his trousers, with the rooster answering some imagined challenge from the forest, he went directly to the ramshackle building, the pile of connected sheds like an immense and precarious cardhouse jumbled over the stream. A score of wild pigeons were roosting on the other side, but he paid them no attention. The waterwheel clumped and squealed above him as he threw open the double doors and stepped inside. Sprawling everywhere into shadow, stretching from addition to addition, the machinery filled all available space. Threading among the silent mechanism, he followed the machine's logic. Mounting ladders, he balanced on catwalks, randomly inspecting nuts and bolts, gears, struts and pulleys, resting his hand on this component or that. His hours at the forge returned, the meticulous concern for accuracy as he constructed or adapted each piece. Indeed he marked the passage of the years not by the seasons, the growth of his children or the inevitable decay in his own body, as other men, but by the discovery and acquisition of essential components and, more sombrely, for the past three years, by the crushing disappointments when late in September, confident that the sun and its eight planets had fallen into the most harmonic configuration and with the immense and complicated machinery settled into pounding motion, he'd banished everyone from the vicinity, heaved on the lever that disconnected it from the driving power of the mill wheel and tremulously waited, expecting it to run forever. So far it never had.

But the touchstone, his core of faith, was the discovery — and the memory still set his ears ringing — the discovery, back in '68 it was, on a towering night of apogees and aphelions, *his* discovery, by Jesus! He'd known all along the redemptive centre, what sort of rejuvenating core was necessary to entrap the elixir of motion. He'd known it that drunken evening over the professor's orrery... "Here," he'd said, tapping the sun with the blade of his knife, "here at the centre we have the sun... What is Perpetual Motion after all but that seen in the motion of our own solar system around the sun? The planets themselves and all movement contained therein, our moon..."

Finishing his tour, he arrived where the culminating drive shaft passed through the wall by a locked door. Above the door, in his own hand, was written: *Quidquid fit necessario fit.* Beside it and in a corner now, abandoned, untouched for almost a decade but still elegant in a vaguely wretched way, there stood his version of the Great Wheel devised by Orffyreus. Fashioned of light pine covered with waxed cloth, twelve feet in diameter and fourteen inches thick, it rested forlornly on an eight-inch axle.

He slipped the concealed bolts, releasing various latches, and stepped through the door into a white-washed room. Suspended in perfect harmony from tracks and pulleys on the ceiling, criss-crossed by bars of watery light from the morning outside, nine globes hung in eerie silence. It was a perfect model of the solar system with the eight planets exact in their relative sizes and weights, positioned around the sun in such a way that when set in motion by the waterwheel, everything moved in miniature grandeur, their orbits mirrors of the originals.

He had constructed the system after years of research, holding the increasingly splendid design together in his head. Twice he'd made dangerous pilgrimages in the dead of winter to consult with men wise and curious in their understanding of heavenly bodies and their influence on the world of men. Still, he couldn't contemplate his model without a spasm of awe. These globes, waiting to be set in motion by him, shining fitfully in an equilibrium so complete he could sometimes hear it, they'd been transmuted into the solar system. He was viewing the planets themselves through the wrong end of a fantastic telescope.

XV

With the wheel thumping and clanking behind him as he

emerged, he couldn't hear them at first, but he saw them, hundreds of blue-grey birds streaming in over the forest. Some dropped from sight among the beech trees as he went for his gun, while others landed along the fenceline searching for food. He could hear them now, fluttering about and calling impatiently. The woods were full of them as he called urgently for Mary, for the children, loading his guns with number six shot. It was Alice who appeared first, almost before he'd called her name.

Coiled with excitement, the birds gathering like a storm, she had already topped up the powder and shot flasks and was tying empty grain bags into bundles by the time Mary and Calum came hurrying from the barn. Gunshots sounded from the direction of Casey's, and others boomed sporadically along the road to town. Impatient to be at it, he organized his family into teams. While Mary and the two young girls prepared for the cleaning and salting, Alice would join him and Angus in the shoot, and Calum would hitch Ned to the small wagon. After gathering the kill, and it would be a good one, make no mistake, they'd bring it back in the two-wheeled cart. The womenfolk would skin the birds and remove the breasts. He had to raise his voice above the children's and repeat himself as they clamoured. "There's another flock, look! They're like bees." And Mary, shading her eyes with her hand, watched the flights uneasily as they rose to the southeast; while Angus, sighting along his weatherbeaten gun, fired random imaginary shots in the air. "Like bees. . . Oh, look!" They all joined in, chanting as Alice began to sing:

> When I can sight my shotgun clear,
>   To pigeons in the sky,
> I'll bid farewell to salted pork,
>   And feed on pigeon pie.

Heading north, another flock glinted majestically in

sunlight above them as they left the yard. It swooped down suddenly all together over the beaver meadow, the sheen of their plumage fading to grey as they landed in shadow. Exploding in panic as a chicken hawk plummeted among them, they were again caught by the morning sun. They re-grouped like fish and in a flash of brilliant colour vanished into the trees.

As if for the very joy of flight, other flocks flew hither and thither above them, as Robert positioned his two children along the zig-zag fence running beside the woods. The multitude of hurtling bodies filled the air. It was like a sudden violent wind that speaks of storm, or thunderheads ballooning on a yellow sky. Alice's face, as she crouched by the fence, was pale and out of focus. She raised her arm and pointed. Turning, he saw thousands of birds flying at the height of a man across his field; they were coming straight at him. The leaders were within thirty feet before they made a quick turn, some to the left, others to the right, a swift most graceful turn, and then they were streaming past him on either side. He was never to forget that riot of colour, the wonderful whirr of their wings as they passed within a few yards of him. He could have beaten them out of the air with the butt of his gun but he didn't. Swivelling, so the shot wouldn't glance off the thickly feathered breasts, he fired both barrels into their retreating bodies. Reloading feverishly, he heard Angus and Alice shooting along the line. He fired again. The pigeons came on in such numbers behind him that thousands were passing between the discharge of his gun and its reloading. He fired volley after volley as the flock diminished, then turning caught another one crossing at an angle. They flew so close to the ground they had to rise before clearing the fence, and as they cleared it, so he fired into wave upon wave until he'd exhausted his powder and shot.

Engrossed in his battue, he didn't realize that Alice

then Angus, running out of ammunition, had left him alone. Crouched behind the fence, Alice had watched her father and brother. She could see the pigeons, some fifteen to twenty at a shot, hurtling to the ground as the guns roared. Seeing that Angus had finished, she went to join him, but he waved her away. Motioning for her to take his gun back to the house, he left the shelter of the fence and entered the forest.

After laying his empty gun on the ground, Robert hid behind the fence. He selected a slender cedar rail and commenced to batter down many more as they came over. Finally exhausted, overwhelmed by those millions filling the air with wings, contemplating dead and injured birds littered between him and the forest, he stretched his legs along the ground and filled his pipe. Whole branches were shattering under their weight and somewhere to his left he heard an attenuated crash that must have been an entire tree. Even his fences were threatened. How would he seed? And the hunters, hard professional Yankees, perhaps the same he'd met by Ardvassar, perhaps Sloot, would appear on the road, his eyes like melting snow.

Pigeons darted or tumbled before his eyes in such numbers he was at first unable to focus on individuals; it was as if the giant flight was itself indivisible, a single dark and sinuous body roiled from beyond the horizon, eclipsing the sun; so a gloom, pervasive and mournful, settled on him. His hands, convulsive on his thighs, had become foolish, as if he'd seized hold of water or smoke, as if he'd reached into darkness.

Just beyond his feet, a large male stared from one empty red eye. The beast had been pierced by striking a twig while in rapid flight; and since it was an old bird, and the stick much worn, it had survived its wound, carrying that skewer for God knows how many seasons, only to be killed here at the end by Robert's club.

Crawling among them, ringing the necks of those not dead, gathering his kill into a manageable pile, he was astonished and filled with admiration at the old injuries and hurts, the broken legs, deformed bills and healed breast wounds, for these scars attested to the tenacious nature of its species. More numerous than all the trees of the forest, and more beautiful, singing their sweet and plaintive calls, they were survivors, they were life itself. Marvelling at a God who'd provide for the wants of His creatures in such an extravagant fashion, he saw something he'd never forget: a slender rock elm, completely covered with birds, it was bending inexorably to the east. Surely it would snap as more and more birds descended from that immense flock that now seemed a permanent darkness, a hurtling river across the sky. Here and there, having gorged themselves on the soft mast of last year's beech and oak, resplendent males were crashing to the earth, hurtling into one another with stabbing beaks. Or puffing themselves up for their hens, expanding their fiery breasts until their heads, glaring into the sky, were forced against their backs as they strutted absurdly, cooing, trembling. Everywhere they fought or wooed, until, as the ritual progressed, some began snapping their wings faster and faster. An incredible noise rose up in the forest as millions of pinions cracked against one another, against the branches on which the males were perched.

Fraser couldn't believe it at first. Like locusts, a plague of rats, they'd devour everything, he'd be ruined. . . . Leaping to his feet, with pigeons veering away from him, crouching from the rushing wings, he began to run. And by the time he reached his family sheltering by the barn, he didn't appear to recognize them. They stared, waiting for him to speak, to tell them what to do; but he stalked past them with such anger, they could only follow apprehensively as he returned to the house. He paused on the porch.

"There is a wrath gone out from the Lord," he said to no one in particular. "The plague is begun."

He ladled a jug of hot water from the stove, collected his shaving gear and set the small mirror up by the window where he could see; and leaving Mary standing inside the door, he proceeded to strop his razor. He worked ostentatiously, slapping and drawing the blade back and forth, raising it to the light to peer at it before setting it on the windowsill. After working up a furious lather, he splashed water onto his face and began to apply the soap.

When it became apparent he wasn't going to say anything, Mary began to lay the table for dinner. The familiar utensils, the plates and cutlery, had become strange in her hands, somehow distant, like objects rediscovered after many years. And the insistent rushing of wings filled her with wonder as when a child near her father's house she dropped pebbles into a fissure in the ancient rock and heard them rattling and bouncing down towards the earth's centre and she knew they continued to fall long after the sound was gone.

Staring at half his face in the mirror, Robert Fraser shaved carefully, stretching the skin with one hand and scraping with the razor. Glancing out the window, he saw millions of birds. The air was black with them. They shadowed the sun like clouds, and the roar of their wings resembled thunder. It would go on all afternoon and evening; it would continue tomorrow. There'd be no seeding this year, no crops. His fences were collapsing under their weight. They were enveloping his land like flies on rotting meat.

XVI

"Sweet Jesus, would you mind where you're putting your foot!" As the men struggled to throw her father off his feet, Alice hugged her young breasts, accepting the side-long glances, their bold stares. Trying to hold one of his legs from the ground as they'd do with a horse, their moans and curses mixing with her mother's odd cries, they collided one with another and stumbled back from his blows as he hobbled and leaped. They wiped sleeves across their mouths, then clawed themselves back onto the pile.

"'Twasn't my foot, you noisy bugger."

"Whose was it then?"

"His arm," screeched Casey. "Would someone grab his bloody arm before he kills me!"

Robert's bony face was made unrecognizable by fury and exertion. His eyes, blank as pennies, appeared briefly among the tangled bodies. He seemed to be staring at the column of birds still pouring in over the trees. His mouth was open as if shouting, but he made no sound.

Later they'd remember it all as a dream. The great flight continuing from daylight to dusk for three days. And Fraser, increasingly wild-eyed, dementia swelling his body, his shirts splitting down the back as he stormed the edge of the forest firing guns as rapidly as his weeping family could reload them. By the second day he was detonating furious charges among the trees, only to see clouds of uninjured birds swirl into the air before settling back to constructing their ragged nests. Then finally, on this third day, driven completely beyond reason, he'd decided to set fire to the forest.

Mary darted about the perimeter, looking for an opening as the belligerent mass lunged along the fenceline to the barnyard with muffled shouts and blows. It surged through the open gate, splattering mud like some animal in pain, with the dogs, Casey's ill-tempered pack and the pedlar's cringing hound, all adding to the din. Snapping and howling, quarrelling among themselves, they postured stiff-legged just beyond the reach of their masters.

And while they'd jumped her father to stop him from setting the forest ablaze, it seemed to Alice this strangely exhilarating mess rolling past her towards the mill wheel, with various pairs of eyes, one and then another staring at her for approval, that it had no memory any more, no need or expectations, it would roll tortuously onwards, each clutching hold more hopeless and dutiful, more like affection than battle, struggling almost in slow motion now, teetering at the edge of the mill race; with the squat figure of her mother unmoving in the clatter of the giant wheel, hands on her full hips she watches, waiting for them to collapse, fall ever so slowly into the dark rushing waters.

Eventually they succeeded in wrestling him to the ground. The whole group subsided in a pulsing heap so that only Robert's head was visible. The eyes in his muddy face rolled in alarm as Mary, seizing her opportunity, stumbled in and sat on it. Squatting down as she might on a thunder bucket, she arranged her skirts and, apparently unmoved by his muffled protests, raised her eyes to gaze past the barns to the forest seething with birds. Slowly she lifted her arms, opening them in front of her body, offering her uncurling fingers, her palms to the sky. "Are you the first man that was born, eh? Tell me that!" Bouncing lightly for emphasis, she bent to peer at her husband's head pressed beneath her spreading buttocks. "Or were you made before the hills?" Voices from within the pile muttered appreciatively as the men struggled for more comfortable positions. "Do you mind that, Robert Fraser? Do you mind that from the Good Book? If you'd come to your senses, you'd see what a sorry pass you've brought us to this morning."

Imprisoned between part of a leg and someone's shoulder, half the pedlar's face appeared, his visible eye glaring at Alice like a pistol; and despite the lightness of her rising heart, she stared back into that unblinking eye as if it was Casey's billygoat confronting her in the road. Increasingly she'd known it would leap in front of her like this, stiff-legged, trembling with supplication and challenge, its shallow eyes speckled with promise and fury. What startled her was the weakness. It was as if that eye glaring at her were somehow ill-prepared, for try as it might it couldn't hold her gaze. Flicking upwards to her face as she lowered her arms to her side, it darted into her eyes, only to fall wildly away before anything could take shape. Pressing her palms furiously against her thighs, Alice discovered the lightness in her throat was laughter.

Beneath her mother's voice, as she mocked and scolded, they heard a weary curse, then: "Missus!" At the sound of Robert's voice, the pedlar's eye convulsed as if suddenly becoming aware of pain. "If you don't get up right smartly, I'll give you such a thundering bite as you won't sit down until harvest."

"Robert, now you wouldn't. . ." But she was on her feet like a shot, smoothing her skirts and slapping foolishly at her haunches as the pile began to twist within itself.

"Easy, lad, easy. . ."

"All right then, carefully."

"Oh Jesus, my legs! They're paralyzed." Robert Fraser rose because he'd had enough. He cast them off like pieces of clothing, so they all must have wondered why he'd waited so long and how it was they'd managed to hold him down in the first place.

"My good sir, are you injured?" It was the pedlar's voice, charming and absurd. He might have been addressing himself, grinning at nobody in particular, but keeping out of Fraser's reach as he extricated his lean young body from the mud. Manoeuvring nervously in the harsh sound of their collective breathing, they tried to make certain Fraser wasn't encircled, that he wouldn't feel trapped. They didn't for a moment trust the innocent languor in his body, the smile like a knife in his muddy face. "The smile of a dog or wolf," said Casey later, "just before it tears your Christly leg off."

Remembering the times he'd lifted wagons off shattered wheels, they desperately wondered if they were between Fraser and wherever it was he intended to go. He'd almost killed them Yankee slave hunters, you mind that? And they were mean buggers, make no mistake, with knives and pistols. "But he just threw them against the wall, so help me God, *crash!* Then hammered them senseless with his bare hands. . ."

Then there's the case of old man Simpson's poor bloody horse. Everybody knows that one. In fact, Casey's boy Sam almost saw it happen. He did see the horse in the road, dead as a post it was, and soon enough he'll believe he was there, crossing in front of the draught horse on a cruel day in November with a wind straight off the Frozen Ocean. He won't recall what Fraser was saying, maybe nothing at all. He was always a quiet one, so he was, a deep one, nobody got so as to know him much. "But, by Jesus, he's a powerful brute of a man, I can tell you that. I reckon he thought the beast was laughing at him. It made one of them little whinnying sounds with the mouth and lips. It's a bit like a laugh, I suppose, although it's never bothered me none. . ." But Fraser, Jesus, he reared back and gave it this terrible blow to the side of the head. Killed it outright, so he did; the bloody horse went down like a bag of shit.

As young Sam started to beat his jacket, with a dead flat sound, against the side of the barn, the wind was rising, a hollow rushing wind that shook the forest, its empty song ringing in their ears as men brushed and scraped at their encrusted bodies. Darting surreptitious glances at Robert Fraser, they longed for something to be said, good-natured remarks about the weather, or you're too much of a man for us, ha ha, you old bull pizzle. Some words, any words at all against this silence; then the slap of young Casey's coat like an axe into dead meat; and the wind, the deep sucking noise of their boots as they straggled onto dry ground.

Fraser spoke first, his voice struggling up out of his throat to thank them for saving him from error. "No, no," they cried. "We understand. There's no need. . ."

"But there is," he insisted, "from grievous error." He stood so mournfully contrite, they'd have clustered around him if they dared, punched his biceps manfully, shaken the large hand. They'd have reassured him with neighbourly good humour, except for the possibility he might yet go berserk and break their spines. "Indeed there is," Fraser repeated, "for wrath killeth the foolish man, and envy slayeth the silly one." With that he turned and walked towards the sheds housing his machine.

Generous in victory, each of them wanted to speak his name, to call him back among them, but their words collapsed in mouths that gaped like fish. It was unfair of him to leave them like this, with birds in raggle-taggle groups, fragments of that terrible flight chasing each other on an emptying sky. They stared after him. Even the pedlar leaned expectantly. He might have called good sir in his clear voice as Mary raised her arm, an inconclusive and unfathomable gesture; but silence, that familiar vertigo, emptied their throats as they tried to speak. What shall we do, Robert? I wouldn't mind a neighbourly drink, not on your life on a morning like this, we've got to stick together in this desperate bloody land. . . But the words sank like stones within the earth, like shadows that strip the flesh from the bone. As the waterwheel rushed and thumped, in that pause between heartbeats, they saw his face poised in the doorway. And then he was gone.

"Well, by Jesus, what do you figure he'll do now?" At the sound of the stranger's voice, the younger children perched along the fence jumped to the ground with sharp cries, and Sam Casey slapped his jacket twice against the barn as if he hadn't intended to stop.

"He'll be no bother. No, he won't." Mary shook out her skirts and scraped mud from the sole of her boot by dragging it along an edge of rock. "Not after he's gone in there, you understand me? He's. . ." The voice faltered as she scraped her other foot, leaving a second glistening smear beside the first. Clumps of dead grass whispered in the wind that fluttered Mary's skirts and teased the hair about Alice's face as she leaned against the barn.

There was a faint ringing, a high nervous sound. At first Alice thought it came from the wheel or maybe the cluster of flies bumping stupidly beneath the eaves; but as it increased in intensity, she recognized it was her own sound ringing in her ears. She felt the warmth of the trapped sun in the boards against her back. Light crackled in her mother's hair and cascaded over her shoulders; it sprang back from the pedlar's forehead and cheekbones as if it had singled them out.

"He makes inventions. . ." Alice hadn't known she was going to speak; she certainly hadn't meant to. "That's where he. . ." They were all looking at her now. As a hawk drifted over the near field, she glimpsed the red tail. She wondered vaguely if they could hear what she heard. "He does his thinking in there."

"Brooding, if you ask me. It's more like brooding." Mary shook herself suddenly as if someone had walked on her grave. "Well, anyway. . . Don't just stand there gaping. Come inside. There's fresh bread and cheese."

XVII

"Ah now," said Casey, rubbing his hands briskly, "that's the spirit!"

Alice felt the men, drying themselves by the stove in their stocking feet, as they watched her set out the bottle of whiskey. She heard a light shivering from the tumblers, clunk as the bottle hit the scrubbed surface, and the pedlar entered from the porch. He paused, then shut the door, eclipsing the fierce wedge of sunlight slicing his lower body. Still buttoning a dry shirt, presumably dug from his pack in the barn, he brushed past Alice.

"She's growed since last fall, Missus Fraser, that's right enough."

"You mind yourself, William Casey."

"Hoity-toity Mary, I mean no offence, so you needn't take any." Grinning sharply, Casey pushed the pedlar off balance with his forearm. Mary had her back to them now, cutting thick chunks of bread, so she didn't see. "All I mean to say is she went into winter a girl child and has come out this other end a woman. Now isn't that the simple truth?" Alice felt their eyes catching in her clothing like burs. "Now isn't that the simple truth?"

"Then you'd best be treating her as one." Sam Casey, his pinched face snapping shut like a fox, he doubled up behind his father so that for a moment the girl wondered if he was injured. The pedlar, his face in shadow by the window, leaned against the heavy wall and closed his eyes.

Mary set bread among the cold pies and cheese. The black kettle rocked and thumped to a boil. With wind blustering outside the house, it sucked air hoarsely in the chimney. Robert and even Calum gave off that sour bristling odour, while Angus smelled of snow and the thawing earth.

Finally sitting between the pedlar and her sister Rose,

Alice waited, listening to the high thin ringing in her ears as the men poured from the whiskey bottle and passed it on. Does his leg brush hers intentionally? His hands are long and slender with such fine bones in the wrist. Yesterday he'd lifted astonishing silk kerchiefs to the window light and caressed them with the tips of those fingers. Conjuring each treasure from his pack, shaking out lengths of brilliant ribbons, he'd wooed with a voice like spring water running over tiny stones. But her mother had remained unmoved, unwilling even to touch the silk stuffs whispering in his hands. She'd only permitted herself the purchase of a short length of crimson ribbon. So the pedlar, changing his tack, trotted out bread-and-butter necessities — needles and pins, hooks, threads and uplifting pamphlets, drawers and camisoles for Missus herself, for the young ladies. "Do you see, Missus, see what we have here? You couldn't make this for the price I'm offering today." As he held up the simple cotton undergarment, extolling the common sense value of it, Alice perceived with a rush that it would fit her, he hadn't selected it by accident. And so now, in the clatter of cutlery, the wet chewing sounds, the drinking and distant talk, she waited as he emptied his tumbler and motioned again for the bottle. She waited for him to say: Would it be out of place, Missus Fraser, to offer a small and respectful toast to your eldest daughter? She could scarcely break the bread and lift it to her mouth; it was as if her hands had gone to sleep, they floated stupidly above the table as the men devoured cold pigeon pie.

"As I was saying. . ." Mary wiped the back of her hand across her mouth, while Casey grabbed the bottle, dancing it seductively in the air with fingers like sausages, like entrails, until even Mary consented to a wee nip more. "It's the terrible smell of them."

"Ah but think," the pedlar shook his head, "think how

much worse it's going to be two weeks from now, just imagine. Three weeks. . ." No one remarked that Alice had taken the tumbler Casey slid imperceptibly towards her. "They're filthy dirty creatures, so they are."

"We were warned, oh yes. . ." Drumming her fingers lightly on the table, Mary cleared phlegm from her throat. "We were forewarned, make no mistake on that." They shifted uncomfortably, frowning, when Casey recalled Barbara had smelled blood on the stairs. "And you mind the owl?" Alice saw the lost child in her mother's face; it blinked uncomprehendingly, not knowing why it had been summoned or where it was. And just as Alice recognized the elusive girl none of them could know, at just this moment the pedlar spoke. Leaning forward to take the bottle, he gazed at Mary.

"The owl," he said, "what owl is that?"

"Why the owl, of course." It was Calum wriggling, indignant because the pedlar didn't know.

"A white owl. . ." They mouthed it with their mother as if, for heaven's sake, the Bird of Death! The boy Calum, at seven, had already acquired his father's scornful eyes. He became still, his nut-brown hands twitching as Mary described how the bird of ill-fortune had drifted among empty branches out there for over a week. Contemplating the pedlar mournfully, she waved her arm in a slow extended circle. Last month it was, the beginning of March.

Impressed by their mother's conviction, forgetting their father hidden away in his workshop, the children stared eagerly. The Bird of Death. Always at the edge of seeing, its silent bulk dissolving like smoke whenever they approached, a spook until that day Robert led his family by the stream, pleading for protection from the horrible thing to be committed in the land. Mary had looked up and there it was, hunched, its ghostly body low in the Great Tree, its yellow eyes piercing right into her heart.

"I can't help thinking of all them bird lice," said Casey, scratching energetically.

"They're filthy dirty creatures, make no mistake. Oh, I've seen flights all right, but never another to match this." There were footfalls on the porch and a pause as the pedlar drank. "Mercy me," he said as the door opened and the sunlight was full of dust. Seeing it was only Angus, he continued. "The shit'll be piled three foot high before they're done."

"Makes me right itchy just to think on it."

"Did you hear about the fellah?" Angus stood blinking at them hunched around the table. "Said his dog was so smart, he had the seven-year itch, this fellah's dog did." More slender than his father and elusive, his expression always on the verge of collapse, he began to laugh uncomfortably, as if wishing he hadn't started to speak. "And he said he was so smart he scratched it off in three." Laughter buzzed and whistled as he shut the door and came to reach over his mother's shoulder, taking a handful of bread and cheese. Still laughing to himself, the sound of dragonflies caught in his throat, he mounted the stairs and disappeared through the trapdoor. They heard the boards creaking, the pad of his stocking feet as he crossed to the dormer window in the south wall.

When she slipped out of the house, Alice left her mother entangled in a shared inevitability that this tragedy of the birds, as the pedlar had begun to call it, this bloody cruel and hopeless situation, it warranted another glass of whiskey. And although Casey had not yet broken into argument or song, he had stood briefly on his chair, thumping with a bottle on the boards above his head, calling insistently to Angus, "C'mon down, you black son-of-a-bitch! Sweet Jesus, but he can make the fiddle sing, so he can." Then raising his voice again, he shouted, "Why don't you get down here and play us a tune!"

Outside, Alice stood silently on the porch. Male pigeons,

startled by her appearance, leaped into the air with twigs in their ebony bills. Some had sticks the thickness of her little finger as they darted back into the forest. After the heat and smoke inside, she welcomed the afternoon air, acrid as it was. Her nostrils and mouth trembled as she swung her head from side to side breathing lightly, almost tentatively. Flat and indistinct, as if punched from wispy clouds, three-quarters of a moon floated in the south-eastern sky. She knew Angus filled the small window above, that he'd hide as soon as she stepped into view, and she'd have to pretend she was going somewhere else, to the stable perhaps or the privy. And once from sight, only then could she circle back to the red willow brushing her father's sheds, only then was it safe to dart and clamber onto the roof.

Tailing off, the flight was reduced to wispy bands of smoke curling over the forest, stragglers searching in vain for unclaimed branches or twigs among the multitude that now possessed the bush thick as swarming bees, as ants in a rotting log. The roistering babble and the stench of their guano, the noise of splitting limbs, of bursting flight, the palpitant thrum of hearts and lungs, all this clawed at the girl as she ran from cover to cover. Birds leaped into the air, circled about her head, then returned to the task at hand.

Two years ago when first she'd crawled into this cave-like entrance, knowing somehow that the walls at the far end had parted, that her father had left the space for ventilation, she'd been able to move freely. Only occasion-ally had she scraped against the sides, when she was care-less or in a hurry. But she'd grown since then, so now she had to wriggle on her belly with her cheek almost sliding along the rough-hewn boards and only by an act of will did she not panic, convinced she'd be stuck if she advanced another inch.

Pulling with her elbows and forearms like flippers, she

manoeuvred expertly, her head and shoulders, then her torso twisting out of sight.

One by one the pigeons returned. They settled thickly on the roof poles and jostling for position they soon filled all available space so that one could see the whole trembling mass of them begin to sway back and forth. Wedged secretively, unaware of the birds, the girl watched her father thirty feet below. Late that first September, with the rest of the family banished to the beaver meadow, she'd scampered over the roofs and wriggled into place just as her father engaged the main gear to the waterwheel. There'd been a shuddering groan deep in the guts of the machinery as massive cogs bit into one another. The great wheel had seized in a fury of cascading water, a wild protesting howl as it began to move again. And Alice had expected her end was upon her as the skeleton of the building heaved, wrenching against itself. Countless smaller wheels joined in the din. Levers and shuttlecocks, weights and counterweights, protested as slowly the immense and complicated machinery settled into relentless motion, with the figure of her father at the centre. . . .

Projecting from beneath the eaves, her legs and buttocks absorbed the sun's heat. Searching and unfamiliar it soothed and loosened muscles and tendons. Rotating her hips in rhythm, she pressed and released, so the cotton drawers caught and bound. Sensing the pedlar moving cautiously to join her, she turned to greet him. . . .

XVIII

When Will Casey drank, the muscles in his right eye loosened and stretched, permitting the eyeball to roll

170

wildly in its socket. After glancing at the ceiling, for example, it might fall crazily to examine cooking pots on the stove, the carved edges of a kindling box, swoop up to stare at lanterns stored above the window, then slide abruptly, so the pupil would vanish beneath his lower lid, revealing warm ice, a dead man's eye. Even when he held it shut with the fleshy part of his hand, he could feel it, searching restlessly, darting and rolling with a need of its own. On one occasion, recognizing the futility of trying to assert control, he tried to keep his dutiful eye aligned with the renegade one, get it to ride herd, as it were, in much the same way familiar cattle beasts are used to lead a new one into the yard. But it hadn't worked. The results had been alarming, to say the least. His two eyes had swivelled, darted and bounced inside his head in a frantic chase, with the good one just a fraction of a second behind the other. They were like mice, crazed mice, and he became convinced they'd both abandoned him for good. Cascading images stuttered into his head as he leaned to thump his skull on the table; while his drinking companions, trying to ignore the hollow methodical sound of his head on the wood, sauntered to the door, nervously clutching their glasses. "I should feed that horse of mine. . ." And Black Ramsay Cameron, hiding the ironwood staff beneath his bar, his eyes bright and expectant, balanced lightly on the balls of his feet. "By Jesus, it was a terrible sight." Pouring house drinks for them all, he said, "I thought that was you gone for sure, Will Casey, I surely did." They all agreed he'd just have to learn to live with it. "No use complaining, no sir. Nobody listens if you do." Either that or he could give up the grog. "Sweet Jesus, that would be something, wouldn't it?" They laughed uproariously, slapping him on the back and holding their glasses out for more.

Now the pedlar didn't know about Casey's eye, so the first wild glance as they were pulling on their boots took him by surprise. Blaming the good strong whiskey — the wave of dizziness he'd encountered on standing up was proof of that — he followed Casey from the porch, both of them walking with exaggerated care past the outhouse to a burnheap piled high with brush where, concealed from the house, they proceeded to relieve themselves. "Aaah!" sighed Casey with obvious pleasure as he released an intimidating golden rush, and there it was again! To his horror, the pedlar discovered the eyeball had rolled unbelievably to the side of Casey's head. It was glaring at him balefully, half hidden in the corner. His bladder seized shut, his penis struggled to escape back into his trousers, and it was all he could do to keep his balance.

Meanwhile, Casey, peeing with the power of a horse and manipulating his tool with a flourish, began to inscribe elaborate patterns on the burnheap. "Did you ever hear the one about the wife shakin' her husband awake in the middle of the night?" Mercifully the eyeball appeared to slip back into position as Casey turned to look at him. " 'Tom, Tom,' she says, that fellah, whatever his name was, it don't matter, that fellah Abner has pee'd our Sally's name in the snow under our window.' And the husband who was wantin' to sleep said, 'Well. . .so, just means he's in love, I guess.' And the wife screamed, 'But it's in her handwriting! Her handwriting, eh?' " Casey wiggled his tool in demonstration and asthmatic laughter burst in his chest as the glistening stream shivered and broke on its way to the ground. "Can you write your full name?" The laughter wheezed to a stop and his smile was suddenly like a wound.

"What?"

"Your name, can you piss your whole name? Like this, for Chrissakes. . ." Staring helplessly as the stream rose and fell, rose and fell, the pedlar could only shake his head, tucking his dry member back inside his pants. "I can. In fact, once I peed the whole of the twenty-third psalm, but you got to write real quick for that, so you do."

"Yeh?"

"Yeh. I can piss more than anyone around here." The pedlar discovered he was dizzy again and the wonky eye, trembling out of alignment, was peering intently as if expecting a challenge. "I can piss more than any of the animals on this goddamn farm, so I can. Anybody can tell you that."

"Well, ah. . ." Staring at the forest full of birds, he heard a wet slapping sound as Casey finally shook himself dry. "I have to say, I never seen anything like that." He jerked his head towards the enormous puddle. It was almost a pool shining at Casey's feet. "There many good pissers around here?"

"Some." Apparently losing interest, Will Casey folded his flesh out of sight and his thick fingers fumbled at his buttons. But the eye wasn't satisfied. It followed the pedlar, insisting darkly, demanding something as he sidled away from the burnheap.

"Well, I can tell you honestly." His clear voice had risen, sounding shrill even in his own ears as he tried to appease that eye. "I've travelled lots and not just in Canada either, and I've never, oh I've seen my share of sights all right. . ."

"Well, that's a handsome enough woman in there, wouldn't you say?" Casey spoke nonchalantly, concentrating on his pipe. "Mary. . .the missus in there." Both eyes glanced at the pedlar and magically both of them fell away.

"Maybe she is, maybe she ain't." Standing between Casey and the house, the pedlar clenched his fists in his pockets to stop them trembling with relief and excitement. "I reckon she is for her age and size, but I'm kinda partial to that filly of hers."

"Alice?" Keeping his face empty, the pedlar watched as

the older man rubbed his head with both hands, running his tongue over dry lips as if he had daughters or maybe the old pisser's got his eye on her as well. Unsteady on his feet, with the hint of pain deep behind his forehead, the pedlar hopped on his left foot three times, then on his right. "Anyways. . ." Maybe another drink, see what they were up to inside, and then he'd skin out and find where she'd got to. "She'll have to go some to catch that mother of hers. I've always figured. . ." The voice trailed off. It wasn't clear whether Casey was unwilling to continue or had lost the thread of what he wanted to say.

"What have you figured?"

"Nothin'." Casey smiled weakly, shaking himself like a bear with a sore head. They contemplated each other on the path by the outhouse between the burnheap and the yard. Oblivious to the mill wheel, the sharp cries of pigeons massed among the trees, they swayed expectantly, and even from a distance one could have seen muscles working in the young man's face as he tried to speak.

When Casey moved decisively, surprisingly agile for a man of his bulk, and rested his arm across the pedlar's shoulders, the latter cringed, although he made no move to escape. "Tell me, you must. . .being a travelling man and all, you must. . ." Casey's vague smile became more confident as he spoke. "Going in and out of all them houses, with the men, like as not the men are away working somewheres, you grasp my meaning?" The pedlar felt a rush of nausea as heavy sausage fingers kneaded and patted his shoulder, and acrid sweat, the smell of whiskey, assailed him. "You get much of a chance with the women?" Pat-pat and squeeze as they started to walk towards the house with a shambling gait. It was impossible to tell if Casey was leaning on his companion or holding him up. "I'm not saying, no sir, most of the womenfolk in these parts are decent God-fearing souls, make no mistake on that, but there's widows, eh? And all them hired girls. I reckon a young buck like yourself'd do all right for yourself, eh?"

"Yeas," he nodded bravely. "Oh, yeas." Certain the eye had broken loose again, he stared fixedly along the path, through the gate to the steps beyond. The hand on his shoulder had stopped its massaging and patting. It clutched urgently with fingertips biting into his flesh.

"Some of them hired girls are awful young, so they are, younger than, say, even younger than our Alice, eh?" An uncommon amount of white appeared in the pedlar's eye as he nodded again. "Twelve, some of them, and right off the boats, fresh young things. Don't it bother you none, fooling around with them at that age?"

"What I say. . ." A small muscle had started to twitch at the corner of his mouth and the sound of his voice came from a far distance. "If they're old enough to bleed, they're old enough to butcher is what I say."

"Women in towns, that's a different class altogether, you, ah. . .you spend a lot of time in towns, eh?" The pedlar smiled uncertainly, vaguely wishing that he did. Maybe he'd get the shirt off the likes of Alice Fraser; and there were darkie women, young ones that would do it for money, he'd seen them. Rolling his eyes like a calf, he scarcely heard the insinuating voice continue. "I guess you'd be considered what we call a ladies' man. You'd admit that now, wouldn't you? You wouldn't mind admitting that?" The pedlar shrugged, half in answer but mostly to squirm, shift from the painful pressure on his shoulder. "Hey! Are you listening to me at all?" The pedlar nodded again. Twisting, pulling to free himself from the fingers imbedded in his flesh like roots, he discovered the farmer had grabbed him by the other shoulder and was lifting him from the ground. "So you're a ladies' man, is that so?" Contorted by the strain, Casey's face swam before the pedlar's gaze, with the crazy eye frantic in its socket.

"Well, you're pissing into the wind around here, Mr. Ladies' Man. There's fellahs around here that'd feed you to the pigs, you understand my meaning?" Suddenly exhausted, he released his hold, flinging the young man to the ground, and almost in the same motion he sprang onto his left foot and kicked with his right one, driving it between the pedlar's legs. Then pressing the heel of his thumb against his bad eye, he stared at the writhing body with vomit on its chin. "Seems to me you ain't got much of a riding whip on you anyhows."

XIX

Projecting from beneath the eaves, her legs and buttocks absorbed the sun's heat. Searching and familiar, it soothed and loosened muscles and tendons. Alternately extending one leg and then the other, she felt winter's chill besieged in her marrow as he returned to his desk with sunlight from cracks and knotholes slashing the gloomy air between them. It was as if she were seeing him at the bottom of a pool with columns of light descending through the machine's chill silences. She wriggled her elbows and hips until she was comfortable, and then lying with her chin on her folded hands she settled in to watch and wait.

Thirty-four years later, as an old man in a new century with vestiges of past strengths hanging on him in tatters, he'd still be telling how the birds descended on them like a plague. His voice cavernous with satisfaction, he'd embellish their dismay at the astonishing bounty of the Great Author of Nature until on the third day he'd perceived how to turn what might have been a disaster into a blessing for the whole Fraser clan. And as he'd reach towards the ceiling, waving the yellowed paper in his hand, assuring them he'd been blessed with an inspiration directly from the Lord Himself, Alice would sense the mill wheel pounding, she'd almost hear it. She'd feel again the sun on her young legs and the almost graceful figure of a man will wander among that giant and absurd machinery, an odd and melancholy figure, foreshortened by the angle from which she saw him so far away now, so slow and indistinct. "The Lord," he'd say, as if it had never been said before, "helps them what helps themselves. He provides for the wants of His creatures, so I thought it mightn't be out of place to attempt an estimate of the numbers in that mighty flock." His eyes, fierce with age, would isolate his listeners one after the other. "I took the column to be a mile in breadth, don't you see, and I supposed it passing over me without interruption for eight hours in the day for three days, as it did." And he'd appeal to Alice, to Calum. "That's the Lord's truth, is it not, you remember? And there's not a one of them left. They're gone like the forest itself." Glaring at the folded paper, he would grow intense, inarticulate, as if encountering his calculations for the first time with that incredible flight still wheeling and darting over the land.

Or else, it would occur to Alice, there was something in those spidery meticulous figures that her father had never understood. "Allowing two pigeons to the square yard, it follows. . .it follows, sweet Jesus, I had eight billion, nine hundred and twenty-one million, eighty-eight thousand birds, and that's, that's something, oh!" Watching his puffy and unpredictable hands refold and insert the paper in his waistcoat pocket, they would shift clumsily, looking for appropriate expressions while waiting for him to continue, to tell them again how he'd built their house on the profits, how this ponderous dining room, the mahogany sideboard and tables glowing beneath china figures and silver trays, the crystal goblets they drank from, the rugs with sombre contorted patterns brought up from Buffalo, the solarium heavy with rubber plants in translucent light, all this and their land, the almost five hundred acres cleared and workable, was made possible by that great flight of birds. "This house," he would finally say, lifting his ancient face to reveal ropy jowls, rolling his eyes to encompass the room, "but we built this house on the profits, didn't we, Mary?" He wouldn't look at her, even though his voice would rise curiously.

She'd nod mechanically, continuing to eat like a surgeon, her hands holding the knife and fork like precision instruments, as she'd mourn Angus growing wilder, tumbling into madness until he vanished inexplicably, to be seen occasionally by travellers on the road at night, and frequently heard by Mary herself, his keening voice hoarse, but she never understood what he was trying to tell her.

Chapter Five

"That was a strange time in a strange year, my friends. A time when evil was abroad in the land (as when is it not?), a time of miracles, a time of later-day fairy tales. It will be forgotten; everything is."

— Edgar and Damiel

XX

On that unfriendly and tumultuous Saturday afternoon, something occurred in his workshop. Something of real import transpired because when he emerged just after supper, with the pedlar mysteriously vanished, he packed his things and went without notice, and even Casey and his boys had stumbled off home; more elastic with conviction and yet somehow nervous, Robert's gait took him magically over the ground. Gleaming with an eccentric pallor, his face had acquired deep lines of purpose about the eyes and mouth, while his forehead shone with single-minded vision, with the clarity of a saint's or gambler's, one who's convinced faith alone will win the day.

As the din of their display and mating subsided, the pigeons settled into the bush almost silently, urgently, for the males had begun to forage for sticks and twigs. The forest floor would be swept clean for miles in all directions as dozens of ragged dish-like nests began to take shape in every tree. But this domestic fervour no longer filled Robert with anguish. Indeed he appeared delighted. Clapping his hands together, with hair spiking out above his ears, he executed a little jig in the yard and right away, without knowing what form it would take, Mary knew there'd be trouble. She'd seen it all before, the impractical gestures and vague incantations. She recognized the exuberance growing in him, a fantastic tumour over which he'd have no control at all.

That night, when Robert Fraser began his inventory, the setting sun hung fiery in an amaranthine sky. Waving his arms as if driving away persistent flies, he insisted everything they owned, each object of value, had to be itemized and an estimate made of its worth. Erring always on the generous side, he began by noting the weight and condition of last year's hay remaining in the barn, the number of bushels of feed grain, of corn for planting, of seed potatoes (at fifty cents the bushel). Then moving into the house, he counted barrels of flour, of pork and herring, of tea and salt. He set Mary to making a list of kitchen utensils, the pots and kettles, frying pan, teapot, tin plates, vessels, knives, forks and spoons. "Miss nothing!" he cried. "How many sheets, blankets at five dollars the pair?" The smoothing iron and quilts, whiskey barrels and empty bottles. There were trunks and boxes, beds, tables, chairs, the wooden clock, an old bake oven, the iron stove and lengths of rope.

Excited and inclined to argue, Mary protested. She tried to insist he explain himself. But crouching over the giant ledger from his workshop, waving his free hand, smiling extravagantly, Robert remained indifferent. He merely asked how much pails were worth, thirty cents? "Don't worry, don't worry." He waved his hand again, laughing suddenly when the sun cast angry light on their window-panes. As each item was entered, its worth decided, Mary felt it lose substance. All of their possessions were becoming vague, insubstantial, as if lost or already sold. Even the doors, the window frames and glazing, the chair she sat in, their winter boots and wraps, everything! Livestock and implements: pigs at three dollars, cows at forty, they must have thirty-eight hens, there's ducks and geese, the horses and then axes, the grindstone, shovels, hoes, reaping hooks and the scythe, augers and handsaws — all were noted in his precise unreadable script. Fearing she'd scream or strangle him, she couldn't speak, couldn't even bring her-self to mouth his name. She lit the lamp and went to find her children, calling them softly in rooms grown flat and impersonal, somehow ominous, as if perceived by someone else, an auctioneer or bailiff checking the mower at eighty dollars, one plough and one rake, harrows, the fanning mill, a small cart and one wagon. His voice permeated the house, its banausic murmur seeping through the floor-boards and walls like an odour.

Feverish with plans, at some point during the night he heard carriages in the yard, *hush!* the muffled clump of hooves and squeaking wheels. Was that Sloot? Lurching to the door, throwing it open, he expected hunters with already crusted hands, Yankee hunters with money in their pockets. But he found only the empty night and the wind.

Taking the phantom carriages for a sign, a promise the hunters would be in Mad River before him if he didn't move, he was up before dawn to check his inventory for gaps and errors. They found him harnessing the team, coaxing one and then the other into their traces. "I'll tell you, Mary..." Dressed as if for a wedding or funeral, awkward in his best suit and shirt, his boots cleaned and his hat brushed, he'd lost none of the previous night's fervour. "Our time has come, for the Lord," he said, "helps them that helps themselves."

Calum and Helen clung to Mary's thighs; the older children gaped at their father from the yard, at the blood on his neck and below his mouth where he'd cut himself shaving in cold water; while behind him, and now above them in the shape of an inverted funnel, male pigeons leaped from branches and twigs to stream noisily off in search of food. "It's the birds. . ." He had to bellow above their din, "the birds, don't you see?" He laughed suddenly. "You see?" Scarcely able to contain himself, swelling with heresiarchal conviction, he thumped his chest mightily to demonstrate the solidity of his plan. "There'll be hundreds of men here by tomorrow. . ." He stared at them, his wife and five children by the fence on the other side of the wagon. They stared back. He couldn't believe they didn't understand. He rubbed the heels of his hands against his eyes. "They'll need powder and shot, they'll need barrels and salt, ice and salt. . ."

Iridescent columns of birds snaked off to the horizon in every direction. Their plumage shone in the morning sun; and at the sound of their wings, buffeted by their flight, the family trembled. Air convulsed in the clearing, and a dry, palpitant heat enveloped them. Seeming to draw breath from their lungs, tousling their hair, their clothing, it already stank of shit.

Clutching Calum and Helen, Mary recognized the drawstring protruding from his pocket. It was the deerskin pouch containing their full savings, he'd taken the money! She was filled with such bile and terror, such exhaustion, she could only stare as he opened and closed his mouth. Grinning, he appeared to be bowing before springing onto the seat where, adjusting his coat and hat, he cracked the reins and departed without glancing over his shoulder.

Relinquishing the children, who drifted off to play or

quarrel beneath the great tree, Mary strode into the house. Drawing a glass of beer, she decided to brew another batch. And she'd make bread, pies, dozens of molasses or pumpkin cookies. Rattling handfuls of dried peas or beans into bowls, adding pinches of soda, she covered them with water; and while they were soaking, she'd prepare an enormous meal for herself and the children. The beer was cool and sweet, so she took another glass, stuffed birch logs in the firebox and sat at the table.

It would be like the episode of the peas! Acting on information he'd heard somewhere, on one of his demented hunches — the start or end of a distant war, a change in government — he knew it for certain, the price of peas would treble by Christmas, Robert had planted nothing but peas. Acres and acres of peas. In vain did she and the neighbours try to dissuade him. In vain did she threaten, cajole and then cry. She'd even brought her mother, Annie Birdwood, to read the waters, to demonstrate beyond all doubt it was a grotesque and misguided plan altogether. Swaying in his chair like an old bear, impatient to the point of rudeness, he'd dismissed her prophecy. Later, kneading his wife's hands, he'd crooned, "She's been wrong before, Jesus, Mary, lots of times she's wrong!" He'd even tried to borrow money or at least get the Major to invest. "It's a sure thing! It is so. You wait and see." Major Birdwood wasn't a fool, no sir. He'd warned Robert; they all had. But he took the warnings as a goad; and since it was a perfect summer for peas, cool and damp, they'd grown like a disease, like tangling spider-crabs, their voracious tendrils seizing together until the whole farm was enveloped in one mad growth.

Never before had Robert been so much a farmer. Striding among his plants, cultivating, weeding and ploughing waterfurs, constructing elaborate frames for drying peas, even his perpetual motion was forgotten. But he still found time to renovate the driveshed, in preparation for winter storage, and arrange substantial loans to purchase virtually every pea grown that summer within a day's ride in any direction.

His brute single-mindedness finally revealed itself to Mary as dementia. At one stroke her husband had become a stranger, indeed a lunatic who, masquerading as a practical man, might shatter with the random ferocity of lightning. Sometimes, when the shadows fell on his face, catching a glimpse of the other behind his unnatural buoyancy, Mary felt the telluric chill that accompanies the Angel of Death on his rounds. But it wasn't physical violence she feared. It was his radiant poison, the ataxic energy threatening to suck her into its melancholy orbit. It would empty her life. She could feel it as on still nights she felt his mill wheel thrumming in the cavity of her chest.

With the crop safely stored in the improved driveshed, he'd spent almost two weeks collecting the peas he'd contracted from others. Traversing the countryside in a carefully plotted and disciplined fashion, he smiled politely when accepting congratulations, for it had been a bumper year. "Make no mistake, Robert Fraser. If the price holds, your fortune's made!" Initially, however, the price fell. "Of course the price deflates at harvest. It's the nature of the free market. Patience. . ." he insisted all during the last weeks of September and into October. But he was losing weight. Grinding his teeth mercilessly, he woke her night after night with muffled arguments, with unintelligible declarations, and still it didn't rise. In fact, on October the eighteenth they heard it had slipped again. Clearly he had to be closer to the market; and so on a bleak rain-driven Tuesday, with the sky shredding itself among black and twisted branches, he went to Toronto.

When Eddie Shantz arrived on Friday afternoon, the rain was still falling steadily. A deleriant monody, it muffled the sound of his approach and, since by now the dogs accepted him, he was in the house before she knew it. "Eddie!" Wiping her mouth on her apron, embarrassed and startled, her hair cascaded loose over her shoulders. "What are you doing here?" Brushing strands from her face with the back of her arm, she'd nonchalantly covered the bean pot. "What a pleasant surprise!" But he had no time for pleasantries. Perhaps he'd not even noticed the flesh of her arms and bosom flushed with the stove's heat, her loose skirt and blouse. "Look," he cried, "have you seen the driveshed? Dear Jesus, the driveshed's bursting open!" And so it was. Taking on the characteristics of a slime mould, it appeared to be moving, crawling towards them through the half light, through the downpour, while the cattle beasts howled in alarm and the children cowered amongst her skirts. Finally, with its roof alive as the lid on a boiling pot, bulging obscenely, it shuddered, with a sodden wrenching noise, and split open to vomit an endless river of swollen peas. The building subsided in slow motion, disintegrating before their eyes, until there was nothing but shattered beams and planks roiling in a pallid mass that surged in the barnyard like a giant slug.

"Son-of-a-bitch!" Eddie Shantz finally managed to whisper hoarsely. "Would you look at that!" But how in the name of God would they tell Robert? Approaching carefully through the rain, warning the children, especially Angus who danced excitedly around the pulsing mess, forbidding them to get too close because like an ante-mundane tumour with a life of its own, boiling around fence posts, it lifted and absorbed the split rails, indeed everything, on its journey towards the house.

"Watch out!" Mary's cries were suddenly answered by heavy grunts that appeared to be coming from the thing itself, a series of terrible heaving moans. It couldn't be the peas. Surely it wasn't the peas?

It turned out to be Oscar, their great glutton of a bull. He must have got into the peas and gorged himself, the black bastard; and now they were fermenting, swelling inside him, doubling, tripling in size. "He's going to bust!" wailed Angus. "I'll save him," cried Shantz, dashing back to the house for Robert's bugle because he knew just what to do. "We've got to get some of that air out of him or he'll explode like a balloon."

Oscar lay on his side showing the whites of his eyes, his dark tongue poked stiff as a small arm from that rictus studded with teeth; while his belly, expanding like bread dough beneath a dark cloth, his belly threatened to burst at every moment, so when Eddie arrived to stuff the bugle up his arse, it was in the nick of time. Immediately upon insertion, there was a vehement bugle blast, a mighty dithyramb that delighted and startled the watchers. "It's working," they cried, "it's working!" But it scared the hell out of Oscar, those tuneless roars; he'd desperately gathered his legs, scrabbling to his feet with thundering blasts at his arse end. Terrified, he bucked and kicked, thereby forcing air through the horn in a virtuoso combination of notes, of runs and arpeggios. Finally, bursting through a fence, he silenced it by hurling himself into the pond; whereupon, with a terrible sucking noise, water poured in through the offending instrument and drowned the unfortunate creature entirely.

As a result, Robert lost not only Oscar and the peas, but his share of the communal threshing machine and half their stock. He also spent the following two winters logging to repay his crippling debts. Chopping and stripping, cutting the frozen trees into twelve-foot lengths, working with the mute indifference of a machine, he became even harder, more intractable. Whether dragging logs to the road with oxen rented from the lumber company, or strengthening rickety bridges in preparation for great commercial wagons, or slumped by the ledger in which he entered the value of his day's work, Robert was like a hired man, an indentured labourer billeted in their house. His hands grew thick and eccentric as hooves, tough hands in a strange lap; and all the while, relentlessly, his voice deflated until, angry as an old gate yet somehow tentative, he spoke of things meticulous and fierce, but they never knew what he was trying to say.

Finally abandoning Mary's bed, he took to sleeping beside the stove. It was his back; the bed was too soft. It seemed a reasonable thing to do at the time. Curling among his pile of blankets, collapsing into sleep before Mary had finished chores, he grumbled and muttered, frequently twitching like an old dog until the children forgot he'd ever slept upstairs.

Leaning to a frosted window on mornings sharp as glass, Mary watched his shadow recede over the snow, against the snow and empty bush, expecting each time to see him pause at the verge, hesitate and then limp back, retrace the snowshoe path he'd made. So beaten down it was, so wide, it appeared a heavy body had been dragged from their yard into the forest. The prospect filled her with dread. And yet each evening after removing ice that gathered like scar tissue, after polishing the panes, she put a welcome lamp in the north window, for perhaps he'd struck himself with the axe or was lying out there crushed by some frozen giant of a tree.

Beneath night skies unaccountably filled with light, the forest crouched dark as moss or lichen, and thus winter continued as if the earth itself was caught, mechanically repeating the same event again and again until there was nothing left but the wind and snow, daylight and then darkness. Her husband's boots squeaking on the frozen steps, a haggard body inside the door, whereupon she'd discover once more it was somebody else, a trespasser, perhaps a madman, for it had been a year of wolves, fierce yelps and deliriant howls, low-slung bodies, will-o'-the-wisps glimpsed beyond the barn or crossing the pond. . . .

Now when spring came there'd been some improvement after he discharged almost half his debt, but another year passed before he was anything like himself. Even so, it was an uncertain recovery, some thought it an unwilling one. "He's a proud man, Robert Fraser, not the kind, no sir, to live with a thing like that. And anyways, by Jesus, when a fellah's gone that long, you're lucky if there's anything to come back."

"I'll tell you one thing. . ." It was a man said this, one man to the others. "I wouldn't like to be Eddie Shantz, not when Robbie. . ."

"Fancy Eddie," agreed another, "not on your bloody life."

"Not if Robbie sees what's been going on under his nose."

"You don't think she's. . .?" Some couldn't believe it, not of Mary, no! "Do you suppose they've actually. . .?"

Wheewh! by God, given half a chance, after a few drinks they'd run that little fart-sucker out on a rail. Damned right. One guffawed, lock up your daughters, slapping his thighs. "I wish to hell I knew how he does it, though. There's a few, so there are, I wouldn't mind a piece of. . ." Naw, he wouldn't tell them, for it's better not said, eh? Hah! "With all respect to the womenfolk, yours and mine, eh? But a fellah's tempted, it's only human, I mean to say, it's only an arsehole crawler like Shantz that'd. . . Now it's not Mary isn't a handsome woman, she is so, she's a fine-looking woman, you can see why a man'd like to, well, slip the devil into hell, eh? I mean to say, if it's there for asking. . ."

"By Jesus, shut your gob!" It's always like that. A man gets full of drink, goes too far, and if cooler heads don't prevail, you got trouble, nasty trouble. There's plenty of broken heads to prove it.

"You ever seen anyone eat like that?" So in taverns or barns, by the edge of roads, steering the conversation to safer ground, the men agreed she'd an appetite all right, a wolf in her belly. And yet, rolling from one buttock to the other, teasing themselves with the unspoken conviction a woman with that kind of a hunger in her. . . "Well, Jesus, she's the body of a girl half her age. There's got to be some connection, eh?" Considering whether or not it was worms and, if so, what class of treatment might suit her best, you can be sure more than one stirred at the dream of somebody lifting Mary Fraser's skirts, of parting her thighs somewhere in Robbie's house, his barn maybe. Does she close her eyes? Is she a squealer? Then coming full circle, as one exclaimed, by Jesus! they'd shake their heads ruefully. They wouldn't care to be Shantz, no sir, not when her old man finds out, although Godamercy me, they'd give something to be there when it happens. . . .

In truth, by the time Robert recovered enough to notice, there was not much for him to find out, nothing at least he could put his finger on. Eddie Shantz was just there, that's all. He'd become something of a fixture, almost a relative.

Returning early from the fields on an ordinary afternoon in July, Robert heard Shantz inside the house and became aware that his children were struck silent by his appearance. Peering from round eyes, they abandoned Shantz and scampered to their mother on the far side of the table, so that ponderous and uncertain, Robert knew he had to say something, take hold, because the little bugger did card tricks, for Chrissakes. "And so what's this?" He smiled the best he could, poured himself a beer from the jug between them on the table, and asked to see what Eddie could do. "You do tricks?" Grinning slyly while Angus and Alice nestled among his wife's skirts, Robert emptied his glass in one draught. "Don't let me interrupt," he insisted. He tried to recall when last he'd spoken to Shantz.

Concentrating on that ungenerous face with its eyes, nose and mouth all crammed together at the centre, a lecher if Robert ever saw one, stiff and stout they'd said, he wouldn't take no for an answer. He was partial to tricks himself, to sleight of hand, eh? and hocus-pocus. Then drawing off another jug of beer and filling three glasses to the brim, he proposed a toast from the head of his table. To legerdemain! Staring emptily, an actor forgetting his lines, Robert opened and closed his mouth. Then resting the glass of beer against his temple, he smiled craftily and tried again.

Angus with his brown triangular face, and Alice, her eyes sharp, pellucid, the two of them with their mother, his children knew all the tricks, he'd bet on that, but he reckoned they'd like to see them again. "What do you say?" He leaned over the table and quick as a snake seized Alice's cheek between his thumb and forefinger. "You'd like to see Uncle Eddie's card tricks, wouldn't you, sweetie, hmmmn?" In the room's hot dry air, the playful voice and his face glistening with sweat, a curiously naked face, struck them dumb. Of course they would. He wasn't to be denied. And so, with the precision of a man watched by professionals, Eddie Shantz shuffled the deck, cut it, shuffled again, and offered it to his tormentor in a perfect fan. Whispering, "Pick a card," in a flat dangerous voice, "any card, but don't show it to me," he looked into Fraser's eyes for the first time in over a year.

Selecting one — it turned out to be the eight of clubs — Robert showed it to Mary and the children before slipping it back among the others. Strangely contained, Eddie kept his gaze on Robert who watched the cards, the slender white hands resembling those from a church window. Eddie cut and shuffled the deck again and again. There was no evidence of chicanery, at any rate nothing any of them could see. His forearms were bare, his movements deliberate if hypnotic, strangely soothing they were. And then he turned and with a twisting throw dashed the cards against a far wall. They hit like a storm, all of them tumbling to the floor, by Jesus, it was something! The eight of clubs, they all saw it, Robert's card, stuck there on the wall by itself. "How'd you do that? Crikey!" But he wouldn't explain it, even though the children grew animated and pestered him. A true magician keeps mysteries to himself, yes! He'd won that round all right and, as a result, expanding in his chair, Eddie Shantz accepted more beer, succumbed to Mary's blandishments, and stayed for supper. He'd show them other tricks, yes he would, heugh-heugh. Did he ever tell them how he got wounded then captured at Fredericksburg in '62? At that, bright-eyed, the two children ventured from Mary's thighs. "Show us your scar!" they squealed like small animals. "Uncle Eddie, your scar, can we see it?"

Emptying his glass, Robert fled to do chores, to prepare himself. It's true, he'd lost the first round, but he'd other strings to his bow; there's more than one way to skin a cat. Dust from the baked earth puffed about his feet when he burst into the yard. He paused and then, with the insistent ringing of a cicada high in the great tree, he went to split wood that didn't need it. Working coldly, driving his axe into the dead centre of each piece, he enjoyed the prospect of giving the little bastard a mouthful of fist meat, of sending him home by weeping cross. He could break his neck, so he could; or maybe a duel, an affair of honour? Finally leaving the woodpile to enter his workshop, unexpectedly troubled by the dull and heavy urgency of sex, he didn't even glance towards his house.

Sometimes evil comes upon him the moment he throws open the double doors and steps inside, but more often it sneaks up on him so that even if he's aware of it he doesn't know. Wild and shameful echoes thread beneath the surface; and his hands, puffy and weak, are lighter than air. The waterwheel churns and thumps above him; the machinery sprawls everywhere into shadow as lewd and familiar spirits enter his body.

At first the pressure in his chest wasn't lust but shame, the blood at his temples, anger. Climbing and threading among the machinery, he resisted, stalking the open spaces surrounding his worktable as if the doors were locked, almost as if he were a prisoner. Then arched in his chair with overalls collapsed below white ropy thighs, spread-eagled on the pallet, he surrenders to limbs and torsos, the private flesh of women, their mouths open and sharp as hawks, to a slim and pretty woman, neat in her brilliant costume, an urgent tension in her arching back and loins, her arms beckon like wings. . . .

"The poor man had to cut his own hand off." Mary said this during a late supper that night, with the children in bed, because of Eddie's scar and the fact that Robert had split a good half cord of wood, but mostly because Casey had just beaten two snakes to a bloody pulp on the road. As a result, it seemed only natural the conversation come round to Joshua Willow and his hook.

"Got bit by a snake," confirmed Robert. "Must be fifteen years ago. Splitting firewood, he reached for a log without looking. And it bit his hand, a terrible big rattler, thick as your neck. It got him right here in the vein, and he laid his arm on the chopping block," *slam!* Robert hit the table with the edge of his hand. "He took it off clean as a whistle."

"I'll tell you what," said Eddie Shantz, his mouth full of rhubarb pie. "It's the serpents I don't like. No sir. I don't like the idea of serpents."

"Well, he packed the stump up in moss, then in clay." Mary chewed delicately, scraping at some crust sticking to the edge of the pie pan, popping little bits into her mouth. "Wet clay, to stop the bleeding, and he walked back to his own people without saying a word."

"Oh yes!" Casey grinned at Shantz. "If it's snakes you want, you've come to the right piece of country. There was a plague of milk snakes, well, uhm, when was that?"

"The Indian feels pain less than people like us." Mary lit a lamp against the gathering dusk. "Even the breeds, they must do, and they've got ways of healing we'd never dream of." Sitting down between Casey and Shantz, she closed her eyes knowingly and opened them again.

"Then there's hoop snakes, you ever seen a hoop snake?" Casey laughed eagerly, his chin almost resting on his plate. "You know, they bite hold of their tails and roll off faster than a decent horse can run." Shantz grew exceedingly pale, the colour of a toadstool. They'd found his underbelly. Hah! Casey snorted. "You get a pack of them after you, that's something to see all right, but none of them match the rattler for trouble."

How true. With a conviction bordering on delight, Robert winked at Shantz who'd broken into a sweat and stopped eating. "And I've a story to tell you about rattlers, oh yes." Lighting a pipe, he poured whiskey all round without meeting his wife's reproving gaze. "This was back in the fifties, you understand. I tried my hand at trapping there for a spell, to tide me over, and one day I chanced on this shanty." They agreed that's a sight for sore eyes when you've been on the trail for weeks maybe, sleeping in the snow and all, never really warm, never warm right through the night. So he'd set to and had a fire going in no time, the place heated up and he'd a right good supper inside him before it got dark.

Robert twirled the whiskey in his glass as if trying to remember something. "I, well, I just piled up the fire so it'd burn a good long spell and went straight to sleep. Well, sir. . ." Shaking his head, he rubbed his jaw vigorously. "I woke to find something crawling over my chest. It was still dark, darker than the inside of a goat, but I knew what it was all right. And then I felt another. This is the God's truth, Eddie Shantz! There was eight or ten snakes crawling into the blankets with me, twisted all round me they were, and one of them sort of began to coil itself right there." He leaned to thump Shantz lightly on the chest. "Just as close to my face as that. So I froze, I'll tell you, the thing is. . ."

"My oh my!" Wriggling his fingers like serpents under Shantz's nose, Casey showed his thick teeth in a grin.

"They were rattlers, Eddie. He shook his tail, don't you see?" Making a whistling sigh, Robert nodded heavily and sank back in his chair. "I couldn't have moved if I wanted to."

"By God, that's a terrible story." Speaking in a hushed sepulchral voice, Shantz spilled whiskey while pouring himself a hasty drink.

"You see, they must of been sleeping beneath the floor and what happened was the fire warmed them. They came slithering out, the whole nest of them, and when the fire died they got cold and I was the only warm spot, eh?" Leering at Shantz, he slapped his thigh with delight. "I can tell you, I just lay there getting colder pretty quick until one after another they slipped away. But as soon as the last one got free of me, well, I jumped for my axe and killed every blasted one of the evil creatures, chopped them into little bits."

"In the dark?" Mary stared at her hands, persisting. "You said it was dark."

"Och, well." Robert rolled his eyes. "There must of been a moon, that's it, the moon came out."

Outside, the night was full of harsh whistles and explosive grunts, of chittering croaks, sighs and rapid clicks, so Mary reminded them of the time a hungry bear broke into the house. She'd shot it right there by the stove. And in turning to look, Shantz saw it first — a sinuous shape in the corner, eight feet long if it was an inch, and thick as his arm. It seemed to be staring at him as he leapt to his feet. "Look out, it's a bloody rattler!" He attacked it with his chair before it had the chance to coil upon itself and strike, while Robert sprang for his gun above the door and Mary, scrambling onto the table in the deafening noise of Shantz's assault, Mary upset the lamp, so the room was plunged into complete darkness. "Oh my God!" wailed Shantz, for the chair had disintegrated in his hands.

"Where is it?"

"A light, for pity's sake," he whimpered. Standing absolutely still, Eddie waited for the lunging strike, the piercing fangs. "I can't see, I can't see."

"Shush." Because she was on the table, Mary sounded assured. "Maybe we can hear it."

As their eyes became accustomed to the dark, they began to perceive large shapes in the room, but none of them dared move for fear of stepping on the serpent.

"I think it's over here." Casey spoke so low and in such strangled tones they scarcely heard him. "By the door. . ."

"No. No, it's near the stairs."

"Did you hear it, Mary?"

"I think so. It's over there."

"Are you sure?" Straining to hear some telltale sound, Robert sidled to the stove.

"There it is!" cried Mary, as Fraser raised a small flame above his head. "In the corner, there. What a mercy! You must have killed it, Eddie."

"Well, don't that beat everything." Casey cleared his throat appreciatively, but Shantz didn't respond. Bending forward, frozen in an awkward position, he appeared smaller, somehow diminished, with part of the chair still clutched in his hand.

Huge broken shadows dashed against the wall when Robert lit another lamp. Curious to view the reptilian corpse beneath the shattered chair, they clustered together. "Oh. . ." Mary's voice failed with embarrassment. "Oh. . ."

"That's not a snake," complained Casey. "Where's the snake?"

"Why, it's just that old piece of rope." Robert started to laugh. In fact, viewing the length of rope, the broken chair and Eddie Shantz trembling with shame, suddenly unable to breathe, he lurched for the wall, hooting, "It's a bloody rattler, *kill it, kill!*"

Hesitantly at first but with increasing gusto, Casey was soon reduced to idiocy. While Mary, pressing hands over her mouth, tried to suppress rumbling chuckles and snorts, but it was no use, they broke in her throat. The three of them were shaking the room with their howls and screams, with cries of *kill!* "You should of seen your face. Oh, oh, I'm dying. . ."

Finally Mary went to Shantz who was on his knees gathering up bits of the chair, trying to insert a leg back into the seat. Biting her lip, she crouched beside him, whispering, "Never mind, but it is kind of funny, don't you think?" But his face resembled a piece of bad fruit. He couldn't even look at her.

Robert collapsed into his rocker, shouting, "Oh my God! . . . Leave it, leave the damned chair." He slapped his thighs weakly. "That was wonderful. I haven't enjoyed myself so much since. . ." Catching sight of Casey's squat body shaking by the stairs, tumbling into another choking round of laughter, his face turning an apoplectic red, Robert gasped, "That beats card tricks!" He wiped tears from his eyes. "It certainly does beat card tricks, hah!"

It wasn't so much that Shantz took control of himself,

for he didn't seem to do that at all. Rather, he became someone else. No longer resembling an angry prune, his face grew thin and mean as a razor, and he approached the table as if watched by a thousand eyes.

They'd talk about it for the rest of their lives. By Jesus, it was something to see! Even Robert would speak of it. Why would a man do such a thing?

Smooth as molasses, certain as an actor sure of his lines, Shantz glided to the table and seated himself opposite Robert Fraser and, laying his hand palm upwards, he pulled out his belt knife and drove it through his own flesh, for Chrissakes, so the blade stuck a good two inches into the wood. Then he told some story about his uncle, an uncle of his, how he'd interfered with his own daughter, carried her with him down the slope of sensual slime, and his brothers found out — he had three or four brothers — so they removed his trousers and wired his privates to a stump. The amazing thing is that Eddie never flinched once, and his voice was so cool you'd have thought he was collecting money while the blood gathered there in his palm. And he never took his eyes off Robert; he watched him like a cat. They built a wall of brush around him, good and dry it was, stuff they'd slashed out the previous year. They set it afire, and Eddie's own father gave him a razor and they left him to roast. "He could roast, you see, he could take his own life or he could escape, well, by cleaning out his crotch, eh? And that's what he did." Shantz stared with uncommonly pale eyes at Fraser who began to rock unhappily, wishing the man would stop. His palm was full of blood now; more seeped between the fingers, while his voice was a precision instrument, a scalpel. "He cleaned out his own crotch, my uncle, my father's brother, so don't tell me about tricks, eh? about pain or Joshua Willow. . ."

In brittle silence, trying not to look at this waxen hand,

they heard the clock's idiot heart, spent logs collapsing in the firebox, the noise of insects, the half-hearted sound of wind machines, and from far off the mournful yodel of a loon.

The knife resisted, but with a jerk he pulled it free, wiped it clean and rose to his feet. "Ladies and gentlemen. . ." He bowed ironically, blood dripping from his fingertips. "Goodnight." Whereupon he left without closing the door.

"Jesus!" Will Casey poured himself a drink. Someone had to close the door, but that meant walking on the blood-stained floorboards. Someone had to scrub them and although Mary would do that later while Robert fed the smashed chair bit by bit into the stove, someone had to close the door and take vinegar and a stone to the table, but no one did anything. They just sat there for the longest time, as if waiting for another shoe to fall. Creaking the door on its hinges, a passing wind had pushed like the sea among beech and poplar. The wooden clock ticked and tocked until Casey stopped cracking his knuckles and rose to his feet. Lifting his glass, he insisted Robert was worth any two or three like Shantz. "You should get him to pay for the chair, a perfectly good chair. . . Jesus, Robbie, why do you suppose he stuck himself like that?"

She sees him on the road from time to time, always at a distance. Occasionally in Mad River she finds herself in the same room with him. His name comes up whenever men talk of politics or ambition, strength and failure. Mary Fraser and Eddie Shantz would never speak again and so she can't guess what he keeps from those elusive afternoons any more than she knew what he wanted from her then, from her children playing in the kitchen or on the porch. . . .

All that happened nine years ago, so distant it seemed another life. And yet Robert took their money. He'll borrow against the house and farm, mortgage everything for powder and shot, for salt and barrels and ice. He'll return with hired wagons and someone like Joshua Willow, perhaps Tom Sanderson, that mountebank and wretched man who'll fumble in his pockets, staring at her while showing the tip of his tongue like a cat.

Swallowing the rest of her beer, Mary Fraser stared through bars of sunlight full of dust at black-bottomed pots and pans on the far wall. And later, standing at the window, she saw the great oak towering with ragged nests above dying trees, some of them felled, others half-cut, abandoned while his machine grew like cancer. Shoots burst into saplings inside his fences, the porch step decayed, and each year burdock gathered stronger behind the barn. By this time in earlier years she'd have been at the garden, gathering debris, the rotting stalks of last year's growth, attacking the lumped and thawing earth with glee, with faith.

Light failed as she brooded. The afternoon sky filled with the clamour of returning pigeons, she could smell them. Not slackening in their precipitous flight until the last possible moment, they descended upon the forest like the plague, like death itself; while Mary, her glass full, smoked one of Robert's pipes. In a moment she'd light the fire for supper. There'd be pigeon stew with dumplings and left-over cornbread, there'd be turnips, greens and then pie. For even though she'd been piecing all day, she was ravenous.

Appearing on the porch, she raised her hand in a curious gesture as if shading her eyes against the non-existent sun. Her children, hurrying from beyond the mill, their faces glistening in a false dusk, what did she see? Clustering together in that wonderful roaring, they turned just as a limb of the great tree split from its trunk and a mass of birds leaped, swirling, crying into the air as it slowly fell, crushing birds and nests beneath it, while more and more pigeons darted and swooped like enraged wasps.

XXI

Feeling his bowels loosen, he lit his first pipe of the day and chuckled while tamping curls of tobacco back into the fire. You can have your blondes and brunettes, he leered at a spider crawling beside him on the seat, but give me my morning's morning every time, hah! Content because he was passing good healthy stool, because its languorous movement from his body filled him with ease and satisfaction, Robert regarded a large wild pigeon through smoke drifting in the open door. Not twenty feet along the path, twisting on absurd red legs, with its grey-blue head beneath a wing, preening in such a way its mantle flashed golden then bronze and purple, with the iridescence of small insects, it was a full-sized male. A handsome bird, he thought; a lovely creature.

Robert's eyes glistened triumphantly while he puffed at his pipe. His gamble had paid off, and tomorrow, for the first time, they'd attack the roost itself. So shrewd he'd been, so astute and daring, that already he'd made more than enough to pay his costs, and the best was yet to come. Even the most seasoned, men who'd followed the birds long before the price went up, even these fellows couldn't recall a bigger, richer nesting, and so they fought for the privilege of buying everything Robert managed to supply. And if prices were high, what matter? They'd make so much themselves, there's enough for all, lots to go around. They'd fork out whatever he demanded.

And so he sent Joshua with the wagons for more supplies, whiskey and sugar, as well as additional barrels and salt, hard cider for pickling. He arranged for as many willow cages as the Indians by Smokey Falls could weave, and they were snapped up for live birds being shipped to markets far as Buffalo and Detroit, to gun clubs in Toronto and London, in Upper New York and even Chicago, to

Kingston and Montreal. Money for jam, it was, and on seeing the crowd of hunters — there must be five hundred by now — he kept on the wagons, immediately hiring all he could find, arranging for more. And, by Jesus, they'd be working night and day, hard as he could drive them. . . .

The bird on red legs had vanished. At one moment it was there, its colours caught like a stray rainbow, the next it wasn't. With only the dappled branch to support his memory, he wiped sour juice from the bit of his pipe and leaned to spit out the door. And for no good reason he remembered a shallow cave beneath the upturned roots of a fallen pine; a turtle shell, knick-knacks and feathers, beads and clam shells caught in the wild man's rutting odour like raisins in a duff. His spittle bubbled and dissolved among brown leaves, poplar and birch. Somewhere above him a woodpecker hammered. In the distance a voice called again. Robert didn't move. Pressing forearms across his knees, he stared at the shadows of branches moving on dead leaves beyond his feet, at the red needles, chips of wood, at exquisite moss clustered on a swelling breast of rock like the forest viewed from an impossible height, as an eagle, some bird of prey, as the Lord Himself, might see it.

Hunters had begun to arrive during the first days in May. At first there was a carnival air, a wild expectancy as crews staked out prime acreage for themselves. Shouting and laughing, greeting friends and avoiding old quarrels, marvelling at such good fortune, they hooted one to another. "Look! Would you look at the size of it?" They established camps and set to repairing spring and purse nets. Methodically they oiled their guns, checked out the lay of the land, and only killed birds to eat them. On those nights the forest resounded with singing, with drunken laughter around fires that roared in every clearing, along every road, as if a jubilant army had descended upon the land.

When it became apparent that Robert had guessed right this time, people forgot about the peas; or if they spoke of them, it was to affirm the man's tenacity. It wasn't Robbie's fault; it was an act of God. Could have happened to anyone. "The point is, he dares, eh? That's what's needed if a fellah wants to get ahead."

Even Mary took on an authoritative air. Neither recalled who's idea it was but she assumed the chore of baking sugar pies, molasses bread and such-like for Robert to sell on his rounds. They went so well that pretty soon the other women, Barbara Casey and Agatha Bullock, joined in with jam tarts and beer. Robert had to drag the stove into the yard, and he set Angus and Calum to keeping the woodboxes full. It fell to Alice and Rose to handle sales while their father negotiated with the hunters. Already he'd persuaded many smaller operators to sell directly to him. He had the barrels and could absorb the cost of transportation, don't you see? He had the wagons. Anyway, a fellah didn't want to be leaving grounds as rich as these, not any more than he had to, hah "Time is money."

Once the women got to helping Mary, their husbands and others, folk Robert scarcely saw from one year to the next, they'd drift round of an evening to see how to cash in on the bonanza. They didn't put it that way right off. They'd maybe ask if anyone had seen their dog, the yellow bitch with a gimpy leg. Or did Robbie reckon maybe they'd push the railroad through to Mad River now this flight's put them all on the map. Then after a bit, after a smoke and some random talk, they might ask how it was going. "By God, there's money to burn here! They're like drunken sailors, them hunters. They make a lot, they spend it too. But, Robbie, now, you're making money by money you don't even have."

Dressed in black these days with a vest, a turnip that didn't work and chain looped over his belly, his boots polished the best he could against the mud and gathering slime, Robert demurred. He'd money enough now and it was his all right.

"Supply," he had said to Will Casey one night, "supply and demand: there's stuff they need for the work, eh? And I've got it, so they buy from me. There's more they want, but money comes harder for that, for pies and tarts, for whiskey, eh? a bit of a drink. So I buy their birds but with their money, it's still their money, they gave it for powder and shot. . ."

Rubbing his hands, he laughed and refilled their glasses. "Come along!" Waving the bottle, he urged Mary and Barbara Casey to join them. "Come along," he cried, "this is the life!" Leaning to Casey, trying not to gloat, he insisted, "You know what happens next? They give it back to me, Will, they give me their money back for the pies and tarts, the donuts, the beer our women make, for a bit of this now and then." When he raised his glass, baring his teeth at the amber liquid, his face glowed like an angel's. "So I end up with their money *and* their birds, more money and more birds, that's the way it should be, eh? Hah!"

He would urge the ambitious among them to collect and dry the innards. He'd buy dried guts, so he would, and the dung, he'd pay good money for that.

"What's this?" they laughed. "You want the shit?"

He nodded, for the guano too meant cash. Rich in saltpeter, he'd sell it to them that make explosives in Toronto.

"Fertilizer, that's more like it, but medicines?"

"Powdered and mixed with molasses," he explained, "it's a certain cure for ague and the belly-ache." They knew that, of course they did; even cancer, for headache, the fever, a sovereign remedy. "But you lads bring me a good dried product, mind, a first-rate product for a first-rate price!"

It seemed better than carrying the stuff into Mad River themselves, all the way to Toronto, maybe find the bottom had dropped out, like Fraser and his bloody peas. What's more, they'd miss spring ploughing, the seeding, for Chrissakes. Better leave him gamble. They'd take the cash in hand. But they didn't like it.

Tom Bullock, calling to his wife there in Fraser's yard with other men watching, Gawd she's still a lovely woman, and strong willed, poor Tom had his hands full, with Agatha shaking her head when he tried to get her to leave with him. She'd a batch to finish. "Donuts," she laughed, "the hunters love them!" Like Will Casey, he should have kept his mouth shut. Robert paid well, so the other husbands knew better than to speak out, at least in public. The Lord knows what they said at home. Anyway, it wouldn't last, just a few more weeks, and they welcomed the cash. Just the same, it caused hard feelings, for it was Robert himself walked Agatha home the night she worked late. Barbara Casey saw them. There was no mistaking who it was sauntering down the middle of the road like that.

Fraser's days passed in the building of drying racks, in the organization and supervision of local squaws to filet and salt the carcasses brought to him each night by the thousands. After supper he moved from camp to camp, offering a drink from his own bottle, chatting with tired but exultant men, negotiating, always scheming. He began to understand the subtle logic of the hunt and how it fit the natural habits of the pigeons, the behaviour of its species. He discovered how by a long-standing convention no hunter would venture into the roost until a full week after the squabs were hatched because before then, if sufficiently disturbed, the adults might desert their nests *en masse*. The whole kit-and-kaboodle might fly off never to return and a fortune would be lost.

There were older hunters, those who'd been in the game

a lifetime, hard little men with sad eyes who told him how it was before things got organized, how millions upon millions were lost from greed when folk charged right in, killing as fast as they could before the flight rose up in disarray and vanished.

"Well, you see, sir," Silas Wilder explained, "once the nestling's a week old the parents are stuck, you see. You can grab 'em smooth as silk right off the flaming nest. They don't even blink."

Dark as thunderclouds, each morning a roar of wings filled the sky as the males returned to the eggs, to the females who sprang hungrily into the air, so that spiralling funnels rose and fell on every hand. It remained magnificent and terrifying; a marvel they never collided; a mystery that in those roiling millions, each found its own nest, its own mate, that the female seemed to recognize the sound of his wingbeat. Before the male arrived, she sprang wildly into the air and was gone even as he touched down.

And so they alternated, brooding and eating, eating and brooding, while hunters slaughtered them on the feeding grounds. And Robert Fraser, hot with success, his unexpected laughter preceding him from the house and signalling his return, Robert tallied the barrels already salted down, the whiskey and baked goods sold, salt by the hundredweight, cages by the score — he missed nothing and lusted for more.

Convinced the birds would return like this each year, that there was some key that would make him a fortune, Robert searched out men like Silas Wilder. He demanded to know how many eggs, how many in the hatch, how long the incubation and what the birds ate, how long they lived and where they went in summer, in winter, the best baits and traps. He watched men stringing seine nets over rivers where low-flying birds would strike them and become hopelessly entangled or tumble into the water to be collected downstream by the men in boats or on rafts. He helped set up a purse net thirty paces wide at the opening and four times the height of a man, which narrowed to the size of a sock, so that great flocks, entering at full flight, were tumbled together, a terrified mass of birds the men could set upon and dispatch with ease.

"I tell you, sir, I had to work and work hard." With a face like old leather, his head completely bald but the rest of his body covered with hair, Silas Wilder imprisoned a male bird under his belly and between his thighs. "If I had my memory, I could tell you of lots like me, ordinary men who knew what work meant." Crippled by running an ox team in winter, as he'd tell anyone, in water like as not, pulling timber for the Baron (a bastard right enough, he wouldn't drag a soldier off his mother), Silas must have been eighty-five if he was a day. "Like what's-his-name," blinking vacantly, "a mate of mine, gunner for the government in '37, he had his leg shot off." Taking the bird's head between thumb and curled forefinger, he clamped his good leg against the lame one. "Easy, you bastard, easy!" He held the bird steady, sewing one eyelid shut and then the other. "He called to see the mangled limb. What *was* his name? Gave three cheers for the Queen and died."

Silas wiped the blood from the bird's face with the heel of his hand, then strapped both red legs to a willow stick. Raising it aloft, he dropped his arm once, twice; and each time the bird, a fine-looking creature over a foot and a half long, beat its wings in alarm. "There," said the old man, "that'll fool them." Laying bird and stick on the ground, he belched happily. "Aubrey! His name was Aubrey Wilson! Once we carried a spoiled bitch of a lady from Whitby to York, it was called then, in a crate, by Jesus!" He laughed a scrawny laugh. "There she lay, stuffed in with blankets and pillows, eau-de-vie, laudanum and the Christ knows what, groaning like death was in her throat, and us labouring beneath like niggers, while all the while these gentlemen. . ." He gestured as if there were offenders, toffs among his gang casting salt over the debris used to conceal their butterfly net. "These gentlemen, they just brought out their money, and knew it was there — until both it and the land was gone."

With bulging eyes, his mouth pursed like a small red button, he stared at Robert. Behind him several men propped dead pigeons to look as if they were dozing in the sun. "Tell me, sir. . ." Retrieving his stick, so the pigeon exploded in a blind flurry of wings, of grunting chirps, he struggled to his feet. Robert expected him to fall at every instant, so brittle were his knees, so intractable his spine. "Tell me," he wheedled, shaking one leg and then the other, grinning at Fraser with an odd expression, while at his side the stool pigeon fluttered disconsolately and then with its head full of blood like a rooster held upside down for the axe, it fell still. "Do you believe. . ."

There was a chorus of whispers. "Silas, for Chrissakes!" The men darted for cover because a dark cloud was rising in the north. "They're coming. . ." The old man scuttled to the anchor stick, secured the stool with its captive bird and then a cord to its other end.

Robert Fraser settled himself so he could view the edge of the bog, the open space ringed by spectral paper birch and poplar, moon trees reflecting light where others absorbed it — and above them now a good-sized flight of several thousand males. They swooped towards the clearing and over the eight men crouched unmoving, breathless, until Silas Wilder placed a reed contraption to his lips and blew a raspy drawn-out note, the enticing call of a feeding pigeon. Jerking the cord, he caused the willow to drop suddenly beneath the decoy male, so that leaping to maintain balance, with blindly flapping wings, he seemed to be calling to his fellows in the air. With suspicions now allayed, they descended to feed upon the salt.

When most of the birds had settled, a wee Frenchman at the end sprang the trap. There was a fierce collective cry of alarm, but too late. Huge wings enclosed them like a mouth, and while a few stragglers escaped, the men sprang quickly to their feet with loaded shotguns. "Huzzah, you bastards. . ." Of the two thousand males enticed into the clearing, not more than a hundred and fifty escaped. "G'wan and tell your mates about Silas Wilder and his crew," cried the hunters. "G'wan, g'wan!" Still waving their arms, stamping and bellowing, they approached the net which resembled a pudding about to burst. Grabbing the shrieking heads poking through the mesh, they silenced each skull between thumb and forefinger or severed it with tinsmiths' pincers.

Thus in every clearing and along each stream, by rivers, on the cleared land of farms and in tangled moose pasture, in beaver meadows and forest tracks — wherever pigeons settled to feed and drink, hunters came from as far away as Dayton, from Utica, Rochester, even Cincinnati and New York, from Des Moines or Columbus. And Canadians too, men out of Toronto, Oshawa, Port Credit and Barrie — they set upon them with spring traps, purse and seine nets, guns and dead falls. They filled thousands of barrels with salted breasts, and almost as many were shipped in ice (most of it supplied by Robert Fraser); and since they'd run out of crates, his woven cages sold like hot cakes. What's more, this was only the beginning, a kick-off. Sorting through silent carcasses, wringing the necks of those they'd missed, stuffing them into grain sacks piled in the bush, they speculated on the Big Money and knock-me-down work to come, the hard-horse grind next day when they'd enter the roost.

Silas Wilder's men swore there'd be no time for jollity after tomorrow, no sir, not until the flock's dead or gone.

Dead *and* gone! "You want to know how to be certain of a fox?" Smearing a crusted hand across his forehead, Silas arched his back. He grinned with teeth so long you could see the roots, and spat on the muck between his feet. "There's some get a fox anytime they want, but the most of us never get a clear shot, that's the truth. Isn't that true?" His fine nervous fingers were smeared with blood; they twisted, writhing mischievously. "You want to know their secret? A fellah told me once, you don't just thunder out after the fox, taking the first shot you can get, no sir, that doesn't work at all. When you see him, you've got to call out real quick, in a good clear voice. You say 'Good morning, sir!' politely, and then you blast him. I don't know why but it works every time."

Sitting against a tree, his torso and head pressed to rough bark, while some scattered fresh debris, concealing the reset trap, and others freshened the salt from a barrel hidden in their blind, Robert watched the old man re-arrange his lifeless decoys, plumping the scruffiest, supporting the head of one with a stick. Then standing back, rising on tiptoe as if to view them as a descending flock might, he kept a weather eye out for the next bunch. While behind him, at some point tearing the stitches from his bloodied eyes, the stool pigeon trembled violently, its powder-blue throat vibrating with an abject clicking sound. From somewhere far away came a low rumbling as of thunder, although the sky remained clear and untrammelled as fresh snow. The forest leaped with variegated greens and yellows, with spangled shadows, the urgency of wood warbler song and their dashing flight. The pigeon too seemed to be waiting, listening for a rush of wings that would signal the new arrivals; but the distant moan had ceased. Young leaves and branches danced lightly, swaying about the clearing, and Robert felt the breeze upon his cheek, in his hair; it ruffled breast feathers on the dead birds, crackled in last year's marsh grass and was gone.

"Tell me, I meant to ask you..." The pigeon was screaming on its stick as Silas Wilder limped to squat beside the tree. Shaking the bird angrily, he glared at Fraser. "Do you reckon that machine of yours, you reckon it will work?" Because there was still thread in the needle; he only had to knot the ends, clamp the bird between his knees and once more sew the torn eyelids shut. "So they say..." Scarcely interrupting his work, the old man smiled cautiously in order to suggest it was none of his business, he didn't care that much one way or the other. "But they say it pretty damn near succeeded the last time you run it, eh?"

Blinking affirmatively, Robert pressed his back against the tree and tried to appear responsive. "It's been a couple of years now." He stared into the bowl of his pipe.

"Why's that?" Robert shrugged, pushing into the ash with his finger, and Silas continued. "That would be something, eh? If it worked I mean..." Finished with the bird, he offered to share his bottle. "I only seen it from the outside but I reckon, from what I hear, you got some work in it."

"I've done it easy enough." It was good whiskey. Robert had probably sold it to the man, which made it the more sweet. He took a second mouthful and after easing it down, he said almost as an afterthought: "But it was all I could do..."

Wilder nodded, for he knew the nature of work all right. Since none of the flocks seemed about to land, he lit a black cigar.

"Some people," grimacing against the smoke, "some people feel..." Drawing, his leathery face appeared to lose its strength, the bright eyes shrank like raisins, while his snub nose became a pair of holes filled with curly hair. "It's sort of, they say, it's like trying to teach iron to swim." Retrieving his bottle, swallowing energetically, he assured Fraser he wasn't one of those, no sir. Somebody would come up with the answer some day, and it might as well be Robert Fraser, eh? "Why not?"

They smoked in silence and, who knows, perhaps they drank a private toast, each of them to some banausic future, to method and discipline in human affairs, to progress as the result of rational design, the vast increase in wealth it must bring and the abundance, the joy in plenty that must result. For what are machines, after all, but a concentration of power? Power entrapped, enslaved, to simplify and enrich the labours of man.

After several minutes Silas wondered if Robert supposed some day there might be a mechanical device to aid in the pigeon hunt. Blinking happily, he guessed it might be possible if a clever fellah designed some class of machine to pluck birds right off the nest. It might be useful for the apple harvest as well. Imagine the commercial prospect in that now, the free time it would engender. Marvelling at the prospect, he shook his head then confessed that for a long time he'd been trying to figure a way of adapting the patented apple corer. "There are problems in it, but all you'd have to do is insert the carcass, turn the handle just so, give it a couple of cranks, and the breasts would pop off easy as kiss-me-arse, easy as pissing the bed, and without losing a sippet!" Abruptly abandoning his cigar, he cleared his throat and the flesh convulsed until it seemed he'd throw up on Robert's boots. "I'd, ah. . ." He managed an artful smile. "The boys and me, we'd be proud to see it, you understand?"

Fraser felt the others — a mixed crew, some French and an Indian — they'd turned their faces and were staring; they could hear every word. When Robert closed his eyes he could still feel them waiting in the sudden heat, for in a sky so pale it was almost white, the sun had situated itself dead centre above them. Just as Robert was getting to his feet, a beating murmur drifted over the clearing, a distant thrumming of wings. . . . Finally, brushing at the arse of his pants, he held out Wilder's bottle until the old man took it. "We'd be more than grateful if you'd show us, sir, what you got in there." Fraser shook his head. He tried to smile. "Maybe even. . ." He couldn't; it wasn't ready. He told them he was sorry; but by the way he stood gazing at the burning sky, they saw he didn't mean it. He stood between Silas and his crew, all of them caught in a fragile stasis, eccentric as dream. They needed someone to speak or move, but no one did. Figures crouched as if waiting for the pigeons, a sign that would release them so the Frenchman with a large black hat might start his hand jerkily, reach up to take it off, whereupon they'd breathe again and shuffle their feet. Was it time? "Look at the sun," they'd cry, "it must be time for eats. . ."

Because it was the last easy day, they'd party tonight and Robert would roast a pig. A small sacrifice, he thought, more like an investment, a ritual meal to bring hunters into his yard. And so with shadows from jolly fires leaping against the forest, against his house and outbuildings, after a fine porker, by Jesus, he'd saunter among campfires from which they'd call, "Mr. Fraser, I've been thinking over your offer. Will you have a wee dram with us?"

Smiling modestly, patting his serge waistcoat almost bashfully, he's glad they've come round. He agrees it's a straight deal all right, fair and square, and how was the pig? His neighbours gathering close to see how it's done are torn between envy and pride; gesticulating hungrily, they knew all along he could do it, or else whoever would have thought?

Agatha Bullock is among them. She observes him with shrewd bright eyes. The kaleidoscopic talk and laughter, that elusive fragrance of salt water, of the sea, the smell of her filling his nostrils, he takes the drink. And later there is music, Will Casey's fiddle among others, and a space beyond the bonfire where people surge and stamp their feet beneath huge sparks like dying stars. Figures whirl, shouting in unison, so he can't hear what she says when she takes his arm, leading him to the dance.

The room is alive with voices in chorus; or one after another, each with a song, having made it her own she's expected to sing it, and whether waulking songs, ballads or hymns, even their laments have such warmth, it seems there's only the singing women clustered around Mary by her stove. They've forgotten what's beyond this room, before or after this moment. And the men, perhaps Tom Bullock and Donald Ramsay, maybe some youngsters, and Angus more than likely squatting with slush-coloured eyes, his hair tight as moss on a fragile skull, even when one of them seizes an instant, stepping forth like Donald holding his lapels, his neck long and lean like a cat's elbow, serenading the ceiling, he snaps off words with his teeth. Outside there are wild and muscular fiddles. There's bursting laughter and sometimes angry shouts. Yet, if the women resent him, they give no sign; their indifference is a wall.

Then inexplicably, even before Ramsay is quite finished, Angus interrupts with a drawn-out note, a phrase that becomes the song, a lament for the Erebus and Terror, for Lord Franklin, beloved Franklin in the Frozen Ocean, for gallant seamen drifting like flowers beneath mountains of ice. He has a beautiful voice. He could have been a singer, they think, maybe an actor. They're enchanted, although none of them know the song or where he might have learned it. There's something shocking in it, something bizarre. His eyes are squeezed so tight they've drawn the skin expressionless as a drum over his features, while the voice, tough and private, it doesn't sound like his voice, it doesn't issue from his mouth or throat but from somewhere just beyond his head. It's a stranger then and not Angus, wild Angus. His lips are moving right enough but he trembles too, listening, only mouthing the words. Nevertheless, they prevail upon him for another, and another, songs he could only have learned from his father, Robert's certain of that, although he can't recall when last he sang them. When he closes his eyes, the lyrics return like forgotten gestures, like the patterns of some childlike game, a dance once learned; but it's Angus now with a reedy wildness of the chanter in his voice. Caught in the centre of an hourglass where sand pours through from the lost rooms of his own childhood, where past rushes to become future, Robert knows the boy doesn't sing for his parents but for the others, for his own children as yet unimagined.

Led by Mary, the women join in, swelling the chorus. Even Robert feels its melancholy grace, a ritual voice like bees, and its promise of how things were, how they might have been. He wipes his lips with the back of his hand, his forehead with its palm because, instead of leaving on one of those fruitless journeys, his father, old Calum Fraser, hanged himself that Sunday after tea, his long body rotating in the public stairwell. . . By Jesus, he will not speak or think on it! And yet, fastening the rope to the floor above, he lowered himself over the railings in such a way as to fill his own doorway, making certain his children would remember him.

The past being aggressive, the present a palimpsest where everything appears in fragments, Robert Fraser has wanted all his life to be older, to partake of more, to share in the sidereal precision of his planets, fierce yet cool as numbers, the accelerating rush when his great wheel finally moves of itself. . . .

They're all singing now, possibly even the men outside. A fiddle explores its thin and private descant; a wavering, ghastly sound, it seems all the dead voices want to speak.

A crazy fiddle that bedevils even the birds. They click and grunt in their sleep. His son's feral tenor, the women's diapason and Mary's gaze. Why does she stare so? Her eyes are bullet holes, her mouth a wound.

Once it had been the skeleton's telluric promise, his *Mammuthus Primigenius*, but where is it now? He hasn't heard anything for more than a year. It must be three. And so despite having already realized a tidy profit from the pigeons, with the hunt about to begin in earnest, the certainty, dear Jesus, of real money, lots of money and its power, he can't fail now because they'll grab them smooth as silk right off the nest and one way or another Robert stands to make a profit on three or four out of every dozen. . . .

At the beginning, it had been easy: her voice murmuring in the dark, just the two of them, the warmth of their bodies and her sudden laughter, so that sometimes opening her knees she'd guide him, receive him with those arms. She'd soothe him in a distant voice and afterwards, with fingertips playing on his face, she'd sometimes croon. . . .

Did that ever happen? Because now he can scarcely remember, it seems unlikely; he must doubt that it did.

XXII

At every moment Angus expected a giant bird to blot out the sun, a falcon, possibly a gigantic sparrow kicking amongst the trees with both feet, devouring men like grubs, like so many seeds, or maybe swooping upon them unawares, a hawk among the chickens, a great owl descending, noiseless as a cloud, to snatch them screaming from sleep.

From dawn until after dark, agile as a squirrel he shadowed teams of hunters as they scoured the forest. Consuming, gluttonous, unable to conjure up abundance, they wore themselves out in destruction, with Angus materializing, staring until men began to report his simultaneous presence in impossibly far-flung locations. Goddamn right, for who could mistake that quick and wiry body, his startled expression? Despite all sense, they swore up and down he'd been with each of them just after noon or before supper. They'd teased him, eh? shouting, "Hey, boy, you come with us, lots of money!" But he only stared like a corpse. It was enough to give a man the creeps. Like a goddamn spook, and so for sport they took to shying sticks at him, clods of earth or carcasses. And while some called him Peter Grievous and others Jack Tragedy, they all agreed, "No wonder his old man don't use him, he's soft in the bloody head. But quick on the feet, he must be, the way he gets around."

"He's blessed by the wild," Will Casey insisted, as he often did, a statement that led to talk of the time he went missing and the bear. "He spent, it must of been a week. It kept him from freezing. You heard him sing?" Most of them had. "It's in his voice." And no one argued with that, for even those who'd never heard him were already insisting they had. "Make no mistake, he's a great gift for the music. Mary will tell you. Barbara too. When he picked this up. . ." Tapping the body of his fiddle so it thrummed, Casey arranged his face, filling it with melancholy pleasure. "Right off he managed a little tune, some tune or other, the first time." Surely they'd heard tell of kids like that? "Born with all the tunes in their head, they've only got to find the words."

A small dark man, a disconsolate fellow with evil skin, blinked violently. He couldn't agree more. "They know things the rest of us don't." But some weren't quite so sure.

"What class of things?"

"Can they make a living, eh?"

They started talking all at once, shouting. A stout blond man persisted, "Can they make a living? What'll this Angus ever do but be a burden, you tell me, eh? You get fellahs like that, pissing more than they drink, and someone's got to pay."

Even though the man with nasty buboes tried to maintain Angus could look after himself, he'd be all right, the others wouldn't have it because they'd all seen him darting through the bushes. He's a loony, that's what he is; he'll end up in gaol or kicking the wind.

"Do you suppose," said one that had not yet spoken, "do you suppose he still sees it?"

"What? Sees what?"

"The bear, you reckon. I mean, he's lurking out there and all, sometimes gone for hours. . ." By golly, they'd never considered that. It might be so, for they knew other cases, wolf-boys and such-like; and once bitten, they were confident of this. "Once it gets into your blood, why, you're never free of it, are you?"

"Jesus!" Casey was incredulous. "What are you blethering about?" For reasons he didn't begin to understand, he loved the boy, he did so, his music, that quicksilver grace. He'd never say it, maybe better than if he was his own, if necessary he'd look after Angus himself.

"Bully for you." The blond man, fresh as a newborn turd, he smiled, then laughed softly. "Not me." Nor many of the others, it seemed, so Casey could only point out the damned bear would be dead by now, what were they thinking of?

"Well, Duggie says he's been down by the Sinclair line with them tinkers."

"Do they got a bear? I'm telling you. . ." But he had to give it up. He didn't want to fight, and besides, they'd settled on bears, chained bears dancing in the road to a drum and whistle, or even better, a spectacle. Many of the Yankees had seen it. They'd fitted bears out to look like engineers and conductors. There was a model steam-driven train too with the beasts hanging on, waving their paws like they were going somewhere, like they were running the goddamn thing, even though they'd no more control of it than children on a carousel.

Every night for sixteen nights it had been the same. Finishing their evening meal after dark, the men began to curse, muttering angrily as they struggled back into their raingear, their slimy boots and slickers. Bone weary, even the prospect of the money they were making was little solace, they beat their large hats against trees, out-cropping rocks, against their leggings. They fumbled for lanterns or lamps, and as lights flared in every campsite, the forest came to resemble a stage set, a brooding panorama against which the bundled figures seemed dwarfed and cruel.

Following the skirts of their coats, Angus had the advantage, for although they might suspect he was there, they'd never know for sure. Grinning like an otter or marten, some creature caught in a trap, he pursued and evaded the hunters. Briefly caught in a stray beam of light, they appeared misshapen, scarcely recognizable as men. Like figures from a troubled sleep, they transported the day's kill, piling it sack by sack near towering bonfires, while somewhere the Bird of Death, a brutal rush of wings, its talons. . .

With darkness came a damp cold that did little to mask the terrible stench of guano, of curdled crop milk. The forest floor was smeared everywhere with shit, with fragile heads and their trailing mess of crops, and the men crunched greasily, stumbling, sliding, so the lights danced, swooping in such a way it appeared the bush teemed with will-o'-the-wisps.

And all the while, as on each of the past sixteen nights,

a mournful peeping chorus grew in strength, in desperation, as the evening progressed. The sound had become so familiar that most accepted it as part of the work — as the roar of furnaces, the scuttling engines, whistles and gongs, that harmony of mills and factories is eventually submerged in the mind. So this dying lament from orphaned squabs — there must have been a hundred thousand by now — this pitiable noise had become familiar as the sounds of their own bodies. What else can a man do? Scarcely big enough for market, they're useless and besides, gorged to bursting, the plump bodies come apart in your hands; and so, for as long as there's adult birds, the hunters will ignore them.

Caught among ragged branches, the moon cast little light on the forest. Soon the men would collapse into bedrolls, into a dreamless sleep; and come the dawn, when they awoke, the chorus will have subsided.

With daylight the slaughter resumed with an urgent sense that time was running out, they must get what they could right now, for the good Christ knows when they'd see another flock like this.

Harangued from sleep then marshalled by section bosses, the men strung out into lines and blanketed designated areas so as not to miss a bird. Seizing each female right off the nest, separating the carcass from its head and crop with a wrenching twist, they quickly filled sacks fastened to their waist. Tying them with an identifying tag, they left them for collection that night and started right away on a second or third, then soon a fourth.

During the first week or so it had been easier, for there were nests within reach, the ground was relatively clean and dry and the men were fresh. But as time passed, they had to go higher and higher, until now with ten-foot poles, heavily knobbed at one end, or with rocks tied to long ropes, they bashed adults from the nest while the more agile scrambled among branches sometimes forty feet above the ground. Wringing necks or breaking wings, dropping the catch to their fellows beneath, these were the monkey-men, quick and wiry; they'd sometimes leap from tree to tree.

Long before noon, maybe after a quick smoke amidst the carnage, with lumpy sacks everywhere filled with dead birds, maybe after a sandwich and endless complaints about the back-breaking work, the sickening smell, the crews were ready to go back over the same ground, and they'd get as many again because the males had returned. Feeding their young without pause, they too would accept the hunter's hand.

"It's like picking apples."

"They're stupid bloody creatures, make no mistake. . ."

"Like shucking corn."

"But it's a good thing for us, so it is."

"Goddamn right."

Angus had tried scaring them, driving them from the nest with sharp cries, but the dumb faith that kept them staring from orange eyes as their heads were torn off, this unavailing calm made it impossible to save a one of them. When he removed individuals to another part of the forest, they sprang from his hands and darted off, returning in zigzag flights as if to welcome the hunters.

Dancing with what resembled wild frivolity, Angus had taken to hurling clam shells and small stones back at the men. He shook his fists until his chest and belly heaved, his mouth contorted. They thought he'd speak but, the loony bastard, if they went to catch him, he was gone. And strange things began to happen. Charging after him with sticks, half a dozen Yankees rounded a thicket beyond the lake and damn near ran into a bear, a great black bitch with cubs, and not a sign of Angus, by Jesus. To hear them tell it, they didn't tarry but somehow, the boy. . . Where'd he got to?

And Will Casey, he'd set out early to see if he couldn't catch a few fish round about dawn; and he swore on his life it happened just this way: there was a mist that morning, heavier than usual. It muffled the sound of his feet as he approached the lake. It was as if his boots were wrapped in wet cloths. With only the plash of water dripping from leaf to leaf and the occasional flute-like song of birds, it was hard to believe in that slaughterhouse half a mile to the east. Here pine needles carpeted the path, dead leaves beneath his feet glistened russet brown, and the phosphorescent mist enclosed him like a pool. On arriving, he startled several ducks feeding by the shore. The colour of gun metal and just as still, the lake appeared to rise into the mist. Imbedded in it, as in a wall, were a pair of loons with sharp serpentine heads and necks.

As he clambered into the canoe, the ducks landed with a splash somewhere to his left. For reasons he didn't understand, perhaps because the sky crouched so low over the earth, he found himself moving in secret, paddling without removing his blade from the water. Dipping their heads beneath the surface, the loons pretended he wasn't there. The mist was burning off now and he could see farther, but still he drifted in the centre of a vaguely prophetic circle.

As he explained it later to Barbara, he'd a most curious sense of apprehension. Even before it happened, before Angus appeared, Will Casey knew he wasn't going to fish that morning. Behind him a large animal surged in the underbrush without revealing itself, and then there was a tremor on the surface about twenty or thirty yards ahead. A bulge appeared as the water rose. It broke and he thought of beaver; but with that extraordinary rush of panic that overtakes men in the forest, he saw it was a human head, a swimmer with one naked arm reaching for shore, then the other, so wan they were, so effortless, that Casey knew it was a drowned man. Screaming like lost souls, the loons rushed across the lake with a pattering slap of wings.

Crouching in his canoe, Casey watched Angus Fraser pull himself naked onto a rock. The two loons, circling now, beat so close overhead he felt their wings striving on the still air. The boy was shocking white. An Indian Pipe, stripping water from his body with both palms, he crouched to retrieve his clothing from a hollow stump by the beaver house. Dressing himself with disturbing grace, it made Casey feel as if he were spying on a woman. Flushed as a mountebank, praying for escape, he began back-paddling into the mist, so Angus wouldn't see him; but the sun was burning it off faster than he could retreat. The kid must of come out of the beaver house, for Chrissakes. There was no other way unless he was amphibian, unless he could breathe under water.

Poised with his mouth open, Angus observed the canoe and its occupant mirrored in the oily lake. Raising the paddle in greeting, Will Casey was tempted to call out because the morning was clear now, the sun stronger, but what could he say? Departing shadows were stained with red, an ominous blood tone trembling behind the leaves. A heron rounded the point and, seeing men, it let out a rasping croak and veered on heavy wings; and with that, Angus too was gone.

"There's real trouble, dangerous trouble in that boy," the hunters agreed, "so keep your eyes peeled." But he's too fast, a proper weasel. They scarcely ever saw him, but they heard him, they knew he was there.

By noon one day the adult birds will have gone, leaving the forest silent, desolate. The guns remain still. Mucking half-heartedly, occasional figures might collect fresher corpses. Most will rest in preparation for the end, the finale so dreaded by old hands, because you never get to straighten up from dawn until supper, it's shitty work right enough, and in a pest house too. How much better it was at the beginning when all a man had to do was set the traps and wait.

Lounging nostalgically, with whiskey supplied by Robert Fraser, contemplating their money and how to spend it in Des Moines, in Buffalo or Toronto, Chicago or Cleveland, each in his imagination has returned to a wife or sweetheart. If they stir themselves to poke up the fire, to rummage for bread and cheese, when they wander from one group to another for companionship, perhaps a game of chance, their bodies appear servile, abstracted and lonely. After six or seven weeks on the grind, with bad food and no women, sleeping like as not where they lay, after the cruelty of their toil, the strain and boredom of it, their thoughts have drifted elsewhere like rounders or gypsies, like the minds of men too long at war.

Emboldened by the silent, empty woods, all manner of predators will converge to feed upon the carnage: slender, long-legged weasels, the graceful marten; there'll be raccoon and bear, elusive panthers, the bobcat and lynx, wolves, foxes, hawks and eagles, the crows, buzzards and owls. They'll all descend with what appears like rage. And while most will feed on the ground, others will set upon squabs in their nests, for they know, as men do, it's here they'll find the choicest meat.

At some point soon, succumbing to euphoria, the fledglings will launch into the air, hurl themselves free with startled cries — at first just the strongest and most venturesome, but their example will infect the others until everywhere a generation of pigeons will be scrambling frantically, fluttering from branch to branch to the ground, or falling like small pillows. While from taverns in distant towns, from the company of women with soft arms and bellies, hunters will return to their own bodies, to the hunt's attenuated lust and wonder.

They'll discover new faces among those crowding into the forest, whole families with children and soldiers from the garrison. There'll be preachers, men off the lakes, gangs of women from Toronto, merchants, even toffs. And because there's a festive mood abroad, a comic urgency will return with the newcomers. Ashamed of their languor, for it suggests itself as faint-heartedness, and being too long on the job without a break, the hunters will stare boldly at the women, openly appraising this one's full breasts, the accentuated shape of another's hips and flank. Gesturing among themselves and sniggering, they'll charge into the forest to show them all how it's done, how money is made.

With crops that are grossly swollen, stuffed in a last parental act, each squab emits a wailing cry: constant and raucous, a communal lament punctuated by screams when predators, driven back by approaching men, they now attack from the opposite flank. Congregating as their nature dictates, beating with impotent wings, the fledglings scuttle. Surging like overwound toys, they collide and tumble, converging in torrents, until the forest floor boils. And wheeling and darting above, buzzards and falcons, raptors of every kind, plunge among them with screeing cries.

Knowing they've a day and a half before the young begin to fly, maybe two if they're lucky, urged on by squad bosses, the hunters soon forget both newcomers and their own homes. Lost in the present, with the earth seething before them, they become dizzy automatons. Seizing each bird by the back so as to imprison the wings, mechanically turning it breast up, catching the head and bursting crop, they tear it in one piece from the body, and grab another, then another. They might as well be machines. When the bag at their waist is full, there's another, the exploding mess from each crop is identical and all birds look the same; draped in regulations sacks, stumbling in leggings and boots, even the men will come to resemble one man.

Grunting softly as the day progresses, empty except for pain in their backs and shoulders, occasionally one or another will straighten. Wiping sweat from his brow, he stands as if listening. Then, sure enough, he'll hear it — a rising shout, fantastic, unfocussed, it will sound as if from every direction at once; and because they all hear it at the same time, a singular drawn-out bellow that rises then fractures like yelping barks from a horde of savages, it fills them with terror.

It is Angus Fraser, completely wild now, his hair matted, his clothing torn, covered with blood and guano. The voice soars, screaming with prophetic fury, until it breaks in another series of barking coughs from the ridge where he capers and leaps. And the men, like cattle beasts, they'll mill together for comfort, watching as Mary Fraser reaches with both hands. "Angus," she'll say, leading her husband up the slope. . . .

PART FOUR: 1878-9

Chapter Six

> "... between the alarm of a world without
> end and a world without point, there is
> no middle way."
>
> —V. S. Naipul

XXIII

Knowing she'd never accustom herself to the new house,
that because the sets had changed somehow the players
had too and her life was a different story, Mary sneaked
from room to room without recognizing corners or vistas.

Each morning for months now she wakes as if approaching a mirror, only to discover a stranger within, somebody
else, perhaps a twin that died at birth or herself in another
time. Filled with disgust and fright, she's taken to affixing
labels to ordinary objects, lists to cupboards and their
shelves inside. It's impossible to tell if she does it for
others — so they'd replace jellies, wash cloths or brooms
where they belonged — or for herself, so she might identify
known objects by their names. Meticulous but spidery,
words like Flour and Salt in brown ink, Tea, Bread,

Flannels (guernseys and drawers), Calico Prints and Winceys. Words like Cups, Teapot, Dishes, Candles and Rugs, they bloomed everywhere like immortelles. And yet, as winter progressed, with the shrieking and snapping of invading frost, an emptiness resounded more violently within.

From that moment three years ago, in the summer of the wild pigeons, when Robert set himself to organize the construction of a brick house — *her* house he insisted, as if that might take her mind off Angus — Mary knew it wouldn't be the refuge he promised, but a monument, a tower of silence. And so it was. No matter how she and the girls dusted and scrubbed, a grey film descended over the rooms, the furniture and curtains. Cobwebs appeared in every window and corner. She could almost see them grow. And no matter how she searched among the furniture and walls, rearranging or labelling objects, tiptoeing up and down the stairs, she could find nothing but a silence like bread dough swollen beyond the point of collapse; formless and undifferentiated, it filled even the space between her and the children's voices.

Sometimes retreating to the original house, where hoarfrost glistened in empty rooms, where fine snow hid the tracks and patterns of their life, Mary wandered from one room to the next. Outside, the forest crouched still and dark. Beneath a sky trembling with an alien light, the snow burned with its reflection. Time stretched empty and static as the bush itself, unobserved, unremarked, as if she were no longer there, until starting up, staring uncomprehendingly, she'd discover herself shuddering violently with the cold. It was dark; another day had passed. Her family would want their supper. . . .

It was a cruel winter, with an endless series of storms arriving like waves on northwesterly gales. No sooner did one subside, leaving enormous snowbanks about the yard, wind-sculpted drifts a dozen feet high, when another followed; so that without his machine and the animals, Robert mightn't have left the house at all.

Many mornings revealed the tracks of wolves about the yard, and at those times the cattle beasts greeted humans anxiously. Leaning against them, turning their ponderous heads to stare from rolling eyes, they'd bellow with hunger and relief when Robert or Calum, sometimes Mary or Alice, shook the dried sweet grasses into their mangers. And on these mornings too the milch cows' udders would hang like empty gloves with no milk at all.

On still cold nights she dreaded the accusing song. "Where is he? Robert. . .where has he gone?" She knew it was useless; she had to stop talking like this. Nevertheless, a soaring melancholy howl would begin, sometimes as close as the pond, its solitary voice brittle as moonlight. Alive or dead, gone back to his bear like as not. It kept him warm. Sometimes Robert tried to comfort her, but since she invariably wept he was afraid. Shaking his head as if to adjust his thoughts he'd pat her shoulder or arm, he'd stroke her back as if she were a horse. And still the storms continued as if the earth itself was caught, mechanically repeating the same event again and again, until finally even the wolves left and there was nothing but the wind and hissing snow.

Oblivious to the circle of hunters, begrimed strangers, the stink of the bush, she'd reached for him on the hill. "Angus. . ." But he didn't recognize anything. Stripped of all particulars, his face burned like a guttering candle until his eyes turned dead as snow. Then, with a mighty shout, freezing them in their tracks, he darted quick as a weasel, bounding on stick legs he'd vanished. Oh, they looked for him all right. Everything was done that could be done. After the squabs were finally killed or terrified into flight, even some hunters joined the search, but none believed they'd find him. "He don't want to be found. That's the truth of it, eh?"

After a decent interval and as if to reassert his purpose, the significance of his vision, Robert tackled the Great Tree himself because he was determined a house would replace it on that bloody knoll, no matter what. Besides, as he'd promised for years, "It's mighty straight in the grain and will split like a ribbon." Sure, now he could fence the entire farm with the rails it contained; they couldn't deny that.

There was no use Mary protesting, nor anyone else, for that matter — not even Will Casey. "I don't know what you mean by a Goth, Will, but I do know a house will stand right here. You understand my meaning? Here!" Stamping his foot on a protruding root while spitting on his hands, he could have hired others, God knows he had the money now, but waving his axe in circles because of their opposition, he struck the first blow with such fury the head all but vanished into the bark. "My house, this house. . ." Grunting so they scarcely understood him, jerking violently in an attempt to free his axe, he shouted, "There'll be a brand-new house on this spot, goddamn right, and it'll grow just as strong and last six times as long as any goddamn tree. . ." With his face contorted, so close to tears everybody sidled away in embarrassment, he had in the end to loosen it with a sledge. "There'll be Frasers here," he bellowed, waving his hat in the air as if they doubted it. "There'll be Frasers when this goddamn forest and all these trees are gone!"

Sheltering in the noise of his mill wheel, they watched him, a dwarfed and furious figure tip-tapping away, causing the chips to fly like a woodpecker, a demented beaver. Settling into a fatalistic rhythm, he swung from the waist, driving with his arms and grunting, withdrawing, shifting his weight to swing again, hewing into the closed and yellow wood with such ease now, such regularity, it seemed he might run forever. Shining in its regular arc, the metal hesitated each time before descending, the chips flew one after another, and still he worked, with anger throbbing like blood, swinging and chopping, excavating a torn rictus in its ancient side.

Perhaps because it seemed a quixotic adventure, and certainly because Will Casey, whose offer of help had been rebuffed, was with Mary on the porch while children gathered along the fence like swallows, Robert, now almost forty-seven, worked harder and longer than he might otherwise have done. When he finally gave up, his hands were numb and his fingers white. He'd have fallen over if he kept on much longer, or chopped himself in the foot. Anyway, his back was seized like a rusty hinge. Trying to flex himself, to straighten his spine, he nodded when Casey again offered assistance. Fraser swung the axe nonchalantly beside his leg and grimaced. For God's sake! From his hour's work, there was only an accusing grin, an abrasion scarcely breaking into the sapwood. He hadn't begun to touch its power, the life in its time and growth. . . .

Even with the two of them hacking away until their teeth ached and they saw double, they still had a long way to go when night fell. Towering above its wound (a terrible excavation now), the tree gave no sign, revealed nothing. Sharply etched, graceful as roots in a darkening sky, its dome swayed with young growth. "She must be, how old do you say?" Somewhere close by a thrush called as they prepared to leave. Bell-like and lonely, the notes fell like water in a crystal pool. Resting his hand on the heavily ridged and corrugated bark, staring up the trunk, Casey waited to see if the bird would sing again. "Anyway, she must be three hundred years. . ." But Fraser reckoned it was more like four, even five. "That's something all right."

Slowly returning to the house, limping painfully, they

tried to imagine five hundred years. "That's. . ." But they couldn't. Will suggested the Great Plague, the Black Death. Robert considered then rejected the idea of his mammoth because the mere thought of it troubled his mind, and besides. . . From far off, resonant and assured, came the voice of a barred owl. Wood smoke curled about the house and a figure moved back and forth inside the glowing window. Hawking above the two men, bats fluttered and swooped, as if thrown in the air by children. Casey was maundering on about the wars with France when Robert, slapping his leg with delight, cried, "Albertus Magnus! For God's sake, that's five hundred years, it's got to be!"

They were passing beneath the wall of his machine as Robert described with urgent gestures how it was Magnus that fashioned a human machine. "Imagine it! The mechanical man capable of opening doors. By Christ, it could talk, Will!" Brimming with that conviction usually associated with madness or terminal faith, gesticulating dangerously with his axe, Robert implored his friend to cast his mind back, to imagine. it. "A drudge, only three foot tall it was, and square as a box with a head and eyes, but ready all the time, no question of that. He never slept and was powerful strong." Crouching so his arms dangled, resembling some creature, he growled in demonstration, and baring his teeth, laughing suddenly, he capered like an old bear. "You get a menial like that. . ." Robert had to raise his voice against the forest, for it heaved and cracked now in the rising wind. "A menial like that, you fix an axe to him, for example, or better, you get a crew of them wound up, you understand what. . . Hey, Will! You listening to me at all?"

Rolling his eyes, Casey seemed lost in other thoughts. He jerked his head, and just as they got within earshot of the house, just when Fraser began to persist (laughing because they wouldn't have to eat, for God's sake, you don't have to pay or feed the suckers), he seized him by the elbow. "Robbie," he whispered, squeezing urgently and repeating the name. Then there was lightning and after a long time the growl of thunder. "How's Mary?" In the shining window, her soft body hovering by the stove, she appeared to be listening.

"Well. . ." Trapped by the hand, he couldn't leave, that insistent claw, for Chrissakes, what could he say? Except maybe, "She's taking it hard enough, I reckon. She's taking it hard."

"Jesus, Robbie." Casey's face was white. He let go of Fraser's arm. "You got to be gentle. You got to understand, eh? what she's going through."

It was Barbara, that bitch, put him up to it. She fashioned the words. He wouldn't have spoke, not Will Casey.

"Now listen!" Modulating his voice because of its edge, trying to soothe as he might a spooked horse, a cross dog in the road, stepping back from his friend, he tried to sound reasonable. "For Chrissakes, Will, that boy was wild from the start, you know it. You mind the day he was born?" But Casey merely stared, so maybe he hadn't spoken. . . .

Suddenly unable to breathe, stumbling to his knees in the north central field, surrounded by a mediocre catch of barley, Robert once found himself wracked by coughing sobs. God help him! His son, such a lovely child. . . You should be pleased, Robert Fraser, you should be proud. . .

His mouth tasted of bile. "What would he ever have done, Will?" Ignoring the first drops of rain, the two men gazed at one another in silence. Urgently clearing his throat, spitting because of nausea, Robert didn't know what to do.

As carrion melted into the earth and its stink subsided, their neighbours, people like the Fletchers, childless

Agatha and Tom Bullock, even Eddie Shantz, those new folk past them along the line and others towards Mad River -- they all soon forgot the hunt and, for a time at least, Angus Fraser. Poor crazy boy. While bluejays fell silent, secretive as the earth, while the young grew old, Mary and Robert Fraser could only pretend. If he touched her, she wept, at first in silence as if it was his fault, as if he'd failed at something, then helplessly until it seemed she'd never stop. Perhaps if they found a body, if he was dead, perhaps it would be better.

"Annie. . ." Robert spoke suddenly, "Annie knew right away. She read the waters. I told you, she read the waters." Fraser took Will Casey's hands in his. "That's true, isn't it? She saw right away he was trouble, eh? That he'd never learn to live with people." But true or not, Mary couldn't forgive him. Why not?

Robert was in danger of confessing hurt and anger, his terrible premonitions. Clinging to Casey's hands as he might to Mary's, he just managed to catch himself in time. "There's worse things." Brushing at his sleeves and trousers, he then spoke of some child in France, a boy child born with another face, a second face on the back of his head.

"For God's sake, Robbie!" Unable to believe this, unwilling even to listen, almost convinced Fraser had fallen over the edge (It runs in families, it does so, the sins of the fathers. . .), Casey tried unsuccessfully to manoeuvre his way onto the porch.

"When he got older," Robert continued, "they discovered it was a girl's face, then a woman's. She couldn't eat or talk. They didn't know who she was." He paused for effect — or maybe he was making it up? Clearing his throat he grinned wearily. "Imagine that, eh? Another person, a twin, inside your head. It's true. . ."

Observing massive thunderclouds beyond the barn, Casey wracked his brains for a comparable story, some shocker, even a pithy anecdote to re-restablish his position;

but memory failed him. Besides, Fraser was wound up, under a full head of steam. "She could roll her eyes, Will. I read it somewhere, she could laugh. By Jesus!" Robert frowned at the thought of it, but also with satisfaction, that relief which comes after a narrow escape — for he'd almost revealed himself. "She could laugh and cry, but she couldn't talk." Hissing between his teeth and grunting, he kept Will Casey from the steps. "Hold on!" Staring dramatically, he almost had to push the man. "The fact is, I reckon she must of been able to think, what do you say?"

"Holy shit!" Hearing his voice with a flash of rage, Casey didn't want to say that. Close to tears, listening to the porch shaking in the wind, he heard how the storm circled closer upon them. Why was Robbie telling him this? And what did the story have to do with them? Even if it were true (which Casey would doubt until he retold it), what does it matter if she thinks or not?

Perhaps sensing he'd gone too far, Robert leaned, until Casey could smell his sour breath, and smiled. "Too rich to be a freak, he tried to live a normal life, but there was no escape, eh? Not for either of them. Not for the young man or the girl. . ." Shifting so the two of them faced the porch, he motioned Casey on ahead, in fact he thrust his friend towards the door, while rounding off his morbid tale. "They both were trapped, don't you see? And as a result, well, he shot himself. In the head, Will, right through his own head, and hers too, on his twenty-second birth-day. The honeyed freedom. . ." Laying an arm across the other's shoulders as if he were drunk, as if he had trouble with the stairs, whispering, "The honeyed freedom they have not in their lives," he opened the door and propelled Casey into the room. *"Hah!"* he declared, as a politician might on encountering an unexpected crowd, but it was his wife and children in explosive shadows as the lamps flared.

At that moment a rain shower charged through the

forest towards them like an object, something urgent and alive, fleeing the thunder, as creatures do a forest fire. So what could he do but shut the door and offer Casey a drink? What else could a man do?

Her face a badly set pudding, Mary glared such injury, such affront, as if he'd. . .what? For Chrissakes, he'd done nothing! Fetching the bottle and cups, searching for a scathing expression, rehearsing it while Casey tried to decide whether or not to greet her, Robert Fraser still couldn't meet his wife's gaze.

"Evening, Mary." Having said that, Casey was uncertain if he should sit down.

"You should be home, Will Casey."

"The storm," he began, then stopped. "Anyway, I'll be gone in a minute.

"Missus, leave him be," Robert said, "the man's been. . . Mary!" But before he'd a chance to finish, to tell her how they'd worked their arses off, the tree was halfway down and her house (it was *her* goddamn house, after all!), her house would be ready by spring, without saying goodnight, there wasn't a bloody word out of her, not a how-dee-doo, she bustled the children up the stairs. So all he could do was grin weakly and gulp his drink. Hoping to convey a man-of-the-world's injured concern, a dignified sort of resignation at the foolishness of women (she'd be weeping, they both knew that), he smiled a ghastly smile and rolled his eyes at the noise of her footsteps overhead. He remarked how good it was after a spell of work like that to sit down with a dram, to rest the old bones. But his words had little effect and, as a result, after listening to the storm for a bit, Casey went home.

He was back in the morning with his best axe, his own bottle and a rhubarb pie from Barbara. "It's for Mary," he said, "in case she don't feel like cooking."

Although the two of them were stiff as boots, they

quickly set to because Mary wouldn't make an appearance. Robert said she'd taken the children for a walk, so the pie would sit there on the table until dinner, maybe longer.

Alternating strokes, neither willing to pause before the other, they maintained an easy tempo, as of walking or using a scythe. Each cut of the axe loosened, gouged out a single chip, until their boots were covered and their shirts, even their trousers, were plastered with sweat.

They worked in silence, chipping and slicing, pausing only for dinner. Finally, late in the day the tree began to receive the axe with an imperceptible shudder. Redoubling their efforts with a grunting rendition of My Grandfather's Clock, their faces contorted so it appeared they suffered pain rather than elation, they drove to the finish in the heartwood now. The bitch is coming down! Forgetting the house and every other reason, they might have been children at play or dreamers, they might have been dreaming.

She came down a treat like the Merryweather Oak. The great branches pulled her clockwise, ever so slowly. With a terrible rending at the hinge, she corkscrewed, gathered momentum, until ripping into the forest she gave a savage leap. She exploded from the stump as if all the years of her life and growth, the primal force of twigs and branches, of blind roots and tendrils, the generation of new wood and bark, was released in that instant when she bounded and crashed.

Almost delirious, as if inheritors of her power, the men capered excitedly, scampering like squirrels along its length. If only Mary had seen it, or the children. If only Barbara was there! Tossing their hats in the air and shouting, drinking numerous toasts to the present, to the future. "Especially the house," whispered Fraser, leaning against the stump and closing his eyes. "You know how long I been here, Will? Twenty-goddamn-five years. That's what. . ."

"Yeah," said Casey, "we're here almost twenty. . ."

"Mary and me, we've been together for, how long? eighteen, more than eighteen years. So it's about time, eh?"

"Poor as rats," agreed Casey. "We all been poor as rats."

"But not anymore, not anymore."

He'd have a gang in before the weekend, as many as he could get, some to clean up the tree and others to pick stones. "There's no goddamn shortage of rocks!" He imagined men dragging them in from his fields on stoneboats for the cellar walls. Hired men, he thought with satisfaction. Employees. Then with the tree cut up and the site cleared, they'd dig the foundation. He'd have them start here, right here. Digging his heels into the earth, leaning back with a fresh pipe, his head filled with visions. Sharing Casey's bottle beneath a sky so blue it seemed black, drinking and smoking, he succumbed with his arse sinking into a cushion of humus the colour of rust. He lost himself in a patch of sunlight. An orange butterfly, an exquisite wee thing, settled to take salt from his hand. He couldn't feel it on his skin. He felt only the sun.

In the distance, a dog barked. Somewhere in a forest stretching as far as night, perhaps in a shallow cave or prowling the edge of a pond where herons hunt on stick legs, where small birds hawk for insects, Angus is there somewhere. And where is Mary? "C'mon," he said, "let's eat that pie." His friend was getting old; he must be fifty. Beneath his beard the flesh of his face was puffy. It would be soft to the touch, as mushrooms, and as white, staining purple beneath the thumb.

"I saw him, Robbie." Uncertain whether to speak, he managed to continue. "He came for his whistle." Trilling from a thornbush a wild canary leaped into flight as they descended towards the house. "And then by the lake," he said as if Fraser didn't care. Perhaps the same bird, with Angus stealing through waving grass, does he tear out handfuls? Inhaling the moist sweetness of it, as his father has done, perhaps he rubs it vigorously against his throat and the back of his neck before throwing it away and seizing more. "Do you suppose Mary visits him? Barbara reckons. . ."

"Stop it!" Calling his name breathlessly, maybe Alice or Calum, do they congregate, hidden beneath the roots of a giant windfall, do they all fear him? "Enough!" Thrusting his hands deep in his pockets, Robert Fraser refused to discuss it further.

The work would soon take on heroic dimensions. Even as Robert argued, insisting upon eccentric plans against all objections, as the hillock of raw earth and clay grew from the hole they dug, square timbers arrived for the frame, cherry wood and maple for detail, white pine and red, spruce, cedar and walnut — all of it well-seasoned in his father-in-law's mill. There came wagon-loads of red bricks, of orange for variety, bundles of slate for the roof and glass for the windows. Labourers came and as the rough work got done, so did craftsmen, and with them the merchants, the hucksters, a representative from Foy's Furniture and Carpeting, a piano manufacturer with only one eye (a *piano* within the reach of all!). There were men in checked suits, others in worn serge, touting "the Burgess," a Low-Pressure, Steam Heating, Patented Wrought Iron Boiler to ensure a Warm House Day and Night; or the Dry Earth Closet (with Cameron's patent automatic Cinder Sifter); the Eagle Steam Washer or Wringing Machines. Interior decorators trotted into the yard with wallpaper samples, with tiles and stained glass, knick-knacks and flufferies. Others promised the finest of stoves or Insurance at Cost (as there are no *stockholders*, there can be no *profits*). And one, a limping buffoon of a man, drunk as a fiddler's bitch, he insisted his Anti-Friction washing machine was a marvel. "The clothes," he shouted, "the clothes are stuffed into this frame, see?" And then, submitted to the action of *two hundred floating balls*, "They're clean in a jiffy. Even the filthiest come out perfectly clean. . . ."

Towards the end of the first week, while digging out a particularly stubborn nest of roots in the cellar's northeast corner, an oddly mismatched pair of brothers unearthed a solitary bone. Dirty yellow, big as a man's arm, with one end rotted away, perhaps a shin bone, it caused all work to stop. "A mastodon!" exclaimed Robert when he saw it. The nipple-tooth. But search as they might, there was no further sign of a beast. "It must have washed here maybe, or the rest has disintegrated. . ."

He had to explain, to describe the animal, which led to talk of the other, how he'd turned it up with his plough over there, in that field right there. Pointing past Mary ascending from the yard, pointing beyond his buildings to a mature field now, Robert discovered he had total recall. How piece by piece he'd laid it out on virgin ground, assembled it himself, then Carruthers, his journey with Tom Sanderson to Toronto, by Jesus! Telling them of Owen, "You can't imagine!"

Casey remembered, sure he did. And Dr. Tom? Loping back and forth, waving his arms for space and attention until the workmen drew back, pausing astride the bone, Robert recounted in a high voice how this Richard Owen, well-placed he was, with a name for himself, he had this Great Exhibition of antedeluvian monsters in the Crystal Palace, in Sydenham, in 1851. What a spectacle that must of been! He was talking about London, so princes came, eh? And lords. There were ladies and men with shiny boots. Common folk too, the ordinary folk, they came in their thousands. And Owen, he told them how Richard Owen had thirty people to a sit-down dinner inside the belly of an *Iguanodon*. "They were all there, it was that

big — princes, landgraves, famous professors and the lot."
Then winding up, peering from face to face, Robert tapped
a forefinger against his nose and insisted famous men had
fought like cats and dogs for a seat at that table — some
even, well, they offered access to their mistresses!

"No!" muttered some, while others sniggered.

"Yes!" cried Fraser, with the growing assurance of a
politician or preacher. "They did so. Heugh-heugh. Even
their wives. . ."

Snorting at the prospect, despite Mary's presence, the
men hit each other with elbows, doubling up with "Ha!"

"Wheesh," hissed another.

"Heh-heh." They rolled their eyes, chuckling as one
brother suggested they could have his for nothing, for the
asking. "Haw!" They laughed out loud, for who'd want
her? But a barge-arsed and clownish fellow, one whose
vacant grin suggested he wasn't a month away from mid-
summer, he cried, "Where is she?" Stabbing the earth with
his shovel. "I'll take her."

"Haw-haw." But really they wanted to know more.
"There's not much good news." They wanted stories. "Go
on," they said, "tell us more. What else?" And since there
were some who remembered Fraser's beast, they pressed
closer, but that was years ago, Robert couldn't tell them
where it was, he wasn't sure. There'd been some hanky-
panky business, something to do with unpaid bills of
freight in Omaha, and he hadn't the money, not then. He
wouldn't have told them anyway. It wasn't their business.
It was gone, vanished into the railway, into the system.
There's nothing a man can do about that.

Carrying the bone to his workshop after eighteen years
— the boy's age, he was born that summer — cradling it to
his belly, Robert tried to ignore Mary's hand trembling on
his arm. First the tree, she seemed to say, and now this
bone. "Robert. . ." What were they laughing at, those men

243

returning to work behind him? Two figures beneath a white-blue sky, Robert Fraser and his wife, descending in this clearing he'd cut from the forest with his own hands. She said it again. "Robert!" And then passionately, "We don't need a new house, not now. Not in that place." There was nothing for him to say. "What if he comes back?" Pulling at him, shaking to make him stop, to make him listen, she began to weep. "He won't recognize his home. When he comes back, he won't recognize his home."

Glaring at her, this woman. "That's foolishness," he said, "and you know it." She held his stare, returned it in kind. Their eyes locked, so it seemed like hatred. Because one of them had to speak, he tried to soothe her. "He's gone, Mary. He's not going to come back. You got to understand. . ."

"He's out there." Over her shoulder and beyond his fence the maze of branches, twigs and young leaves, filled with shadows, they leapt into focus, and somewhere in the distance he heard a man's voice. "Barbara saw him," she said, but Robert scarcely heard her. "She did so, Robert!"

As he turned away, she screamed, "Haven't you done enough?" And then with her face contorted, as if prey to madness, Mary hit him. "Haven't you done enough?" Again and again in a wild flurry, grunting "Haven't-you-done-enough?" in time with the blows, she had to leap up to strike him above his arms folded around the bone. "Haven't you. . ." But she couldn't get at him, couldn't hit him hard enough, and she became aware of the futility of it.

Staring like a man suffused by a cockfight, a hanging, with the welts from her hands on his face, he waited until she stopped before he moved. Although he'd done nothing, Robert breathed as heavily as she and his face was beet red.

Meanwhile, through all of this, men on the site held their breath while pretending to work, for what would he do? Caught in clumsy poses, peering from the corners of their eyes, somehow ashamed to have witnessed that hopeless scene, they nevertheless strained not to miss a gesture.

"We've visitors," he said, but he spoke so quietly none of the others heard him. "You best go inside and compose yourself."

Teetering for an instant, abandoned by fury and left with panic, with unspeakable regret, they contemplated each other so it appeared they might embrace. Then clutching the bone as if it were an infant or a corpse, Robert turned on his heel. "He hated you," sighed Mary before he'd taken a step. "Did you know that, Robert? Your son always hated you."

Inevitably the building progressed as summer ripened into fall, then into winter with storms and driving rain out of the north. Square timbers were set upon a stone foundation. The frame went up as his bricklayers arrived. And while there was some trouble with the tower (they couldn't manage to start the round one just right so they made it square), on the whole Robert had little cause for complaint, except it was turning out to be slower and a more expensive proposition than he'd intended. The fan transom, for example, it was twice the cost of what they'd told him. And the elaborate three-coloured slate roof took time. So did the patterned brickwork, the staring pilasters and voussoirs, the keystones moulded with scotch thistles, not to mention lintels with neo-classical enrichment, verge boards cut to resemble tiny pairs of cherub wings and, best of all, his mullioned oriel window under the eaves. But, Jesus, the money! He'd no idea. . .

Stalking the site and haggling with suppliers, battling ferociously to maintain his design but on a more sensible scale, Fraser somehow managed to hide from Mary, indeed from everyone, that his house, remarkable as he conceived it to be, with exquisite turned work in its posts and spindles, with cast-iron treillage, corn-ear moulding in plaster, six-panel doors, semi-eliptical vaults, with a brick privy enclosed in its own rose arbour, and perhaps a barrel vaulted porch with classical columns, would devour most of what he'd won in the Great Hunt.

At all costs Mary mustn't know because, well, with the uncertain state of her health, it wasn't fair. Besides, he might as well reveal his belly like a thrashed dog as tell her the house was. . . Unngh! The prospect revolted him and, as a result, spending less time with the crew and more in his workshop, Fraser found himself thinking obsessively of what he must do with his blasted machine, his life work, after all, his *magnum opus*. Yet each day he approached it with a gathering sense of nausea, of failure. Crouched and staring at his orrery, at the planets poised around his sun, knowing there was a flaw, he'd find himself skittering over the surface of thought. As if enclosed in its shell like an egg, his machine remained caged and silent, an accusation and a mystery. Its struts, wheels, weights and counter-weights, its gears and pendulums, push-and-pull rods, the whole of it oiled and waiting, he knew the answer lay somewhere here.

Perhaps if the sun was hot! Maybe that was his problem. And so he constructed a mighty brazier on stilt legs. He heated the sucker with charcoal until the sun glowed like a madman's eye. He boiled vats of water, filling the room with steam, with clouds and mist. He rattled sheets of tin for thunder; while from a pair of Vernoy's Family Batteries near the ceiling, sparks leaped and showered to the floor.

Finally, when all else failed, swallowing his pride, ignoring his fear, he went to Annie Birdwood. "It's the machine," he blurted even before sitting, before she'd understood he was there. "What can you tell me about the Perpetual Motion?"

She remained at her table as if he hadn't spoken. Her goitre, that ghastly collar of flesh, had twisted her head, forcing her to stare like an owl from under her brows. "Can you. . ." Shuffling unhappily in her silence, Robert tried again, but with vigour, with a matter-of-fact confidence, as if the two of them did this all the time. "What might the waters say? About my machine, eh?"

He'd begun to wonder if she knew he was there when she drifted to her back door and led him to the spring that rose from a broken rock in her garden of hollyhock and aster, of grapes and wild roses along the fence. Dashing water into a cracked basin, the old woman knelt, swirling the water counter-clockwise, and stared while a breeze rattled thick leaves of rhubarb at his feet.

"Do they tell me what I must do to succeed?" Robert Fraser was beginning to feel like a fool when she proferred the basin with both hands. "No," she said, "don't touch!" She tipped it for him to drink, to finish it all, and she smelled of herbs and spices, perhaps of cloves. "There are thunderheads," she finally whispered, her eyes rich as cream, "and fire. . . They speak of a storm, Robert Fraser, of storm." Closing her eyes as if about to cry, she murmured, "Oh, Robert. . ." Then her eyes popped open. "There's nothing more." She was insistent. "Nothing. They speak of storm, that's all."

Maybe it was the early frost or folk had more time on their hands after harvest. In any case, they began to encounter Angus at crossroads after dark. Or setting out for chores before breakfast, they saw him drift behind the barn, and some who never saw him swore they heard him, like an animal, a beast in rut. Others said he looked fine. "Sure, he did. A little wild, his hair's not been cut. He never spoke a word or made a sign." Did he smile? "Not so you'd notice." And then sometimes they spoke of savages, of wildmen and hermits, "them that's touched by the bush." Recalling the time he went missing, how long was it? four days in the bitter cold, maybe a week, speculating that's what did it. "That week with the bear, he was touched by the wild, he was so. It got into him like ice."

"Froze his soul," they nodded soberly. "And once that's done. . ."

"But, look, he'd of made a fine trapper," said Will Casey, not knowing if he was faithful to the parents or just to Angus, the elusive child who came to him like a stray. He'd never revealed the boy's stormy birth, those teeth, his mantle of fur. "He'd of made a fine. . ."

"Savage," they laughed. "There's nothing you can do with an Indian. There's some that's suited where others aren't. Can you ever imagine him doing a decent job of work?" Still, they had to agree with Casey there was no one better in the woods, and most had stories to prove it. The way he covered ground, eh? even as a child. You'd think maybe his mother was frightened by a wolf, a moose, for with hands in his pockets, smooth as silk, he'd show even the best man his heels.

Then at some point they retold and embellished Casey's story of Angus coming up out of the lake, bare-arsed as the day he was born. Or maybe they'd recall that fantastic yelping scream, the way it sounded from every direction at once. And several reported seeing him in a clearing, his face black with silent laughter, his arms outstretched like branches, and fluttering all over him there were pigeons, wild pigeons. . . .

Still they had to marvel at the way he sang, like a changeling, he'd the gift all right. Casey would gain some ground here. "The fiddle," he cried with relief, "the fiddle as well. He could play such tunes as you've never heard." And seizing a man's arm, searching for words, Will Casey rolled his eyes. "As soon as he picked it up, the fiddle, right away he. . ."

"Hold on now!" Dr. Tom, with his predator's smile and yellow teeth, hunching inside oversize clothes, he wouldn't mind not bumping into the boy on some dark night or other. They all agreed. They'd appreciate a glimpse of him in daylight, yes sir. In fact, there were some went out of their way to find him.

Unbeknownst to each other, Mary and even Robert prowled the woods in search of their boy, the paths and streams, but they never saw hide nor hair of him until one morning in the new house Mary heard his voice. Pulling down the covers after their second or third night, shaking them as if to release the imprint of tussling bodies, she will remember a smell of burning garden rubbish at the window, the ripening death of autumn, dust swirling in sunlight. The children were outside and Robert with his machine. Her back to the corner, she was stripping the soiled bottom sheet when a sighing moan came fierce as breath, such a dolorous sound! Just once that first time, but unmistakably his voice, as if he'd slipped into the room, as if he was behind her. Unable to turn, she spoke his name. "Angus?" She said it again, listening to the mill wheel lumber and thump outside. Crows called to one another. A bluejay screamed twice and was still. Torn and haunted, his clothes in rags, her son had come, but there wasn't a mark on the floorboards, nothing to reveal his passage. Scurrying into the hall and down the empty stairs, flying through strange rooms, she was too slow for him. She discovered the back door ajar but the yard empty. She stared at the barns and paddock, the pond, the sluice and great wheel connected by the noise of rushing water. She gazed beyond the white picket fence to the old house, and behind it the forest like a bronze and russet tapestry shot through with scarlet ribbons.

Searching the house, she encountered it as Angus must have seen it. After the cabin's enclosed rooms, log walls and pine planking, after textured shadows, elusive figures and distant voices, the substance, the coherence of memory, after all this the brick house. Brand-spanking-new as it was, it seemed an empty pail, an unused china bowl, but at least the corner from which he spoke was no longer hollow. Even in the morning's full light, it had acquired a sombre texture, a reassuring substance from which she'd derive much pain and comfort.

Contemplating it from her bed, Mary thought of mourning, a life of mourning which condemned her. It wasn't just Angus, because that had come to seem inevitable. Very clearly, precise as her hands, each individual finger on the coverlet, she understood how in his poor life, its vulnerability and confusion, the hurt he bestowed and received, Angus was a mirror. Nor was it merely the old house, although remnants of what might have been, the voice and hopeful figure of a bride, remained there in the doorway. She mourns that too, herself as a girl with all the expectations she'd brought from childhood, that spectre, its feverish excitement draining away like blood. The noise her body made in love and childbirth, the inconsolable crying of children, their fear and sorrow, and other voices, hers and Robert's in so many guises and so many years, Angus sleeping before he fell and Robert's grateful body in her arms. . . .

While many would accept his appearance as proof the boy had died, perished in the wild, that his shade had come to bid his mother farewell, Mary took it as a sign of his love. He'd come to tell her something, that's it, he's fine, and because she didn't understand, Angus would return that night and from then on.

Lulled then irritated by her husband's breathing, staring into the gloom, Mary lay awake until Angus came. But why didn't he speak to her with words? What was he trying to say? She began to doubt herself, for he always began with that drifting sigh as if breath escaping the body. He sometimes whistled and once he shrieked until writing and filled with despair she tried to block her ears, to shut him out. But still he wailed and moaned in the wall sometimes, in the room, outside the window, a mournful groan until she could stand it no longer. "Robert! Wake up, Robert, wake up. . ."

Returning from wherever he was, from whatever escape he fashioned in dream, finding her weeping, Robert tried to soothe his wife. "It's the wind," he explained, but there wasn't any wind. "Yes, there is," he insisted, "listen. . ." Scrambling from the bed, throwing open the window, he struck a pose so she could hear, and there might have been a breeze perhaps. In any case, Angus was gone. "Look," he smiled to divert her, but it was dark so she barely heard him. "There's northern lights, lights off the Frozen Ocean. . ." And so there was, an eerie pattern like worms convulsing from the horizon. However, it didn't help, and later his hands wouldn't either, his voice in her ear.

In situations like this, he became such a child that neither would remember what he tried to say. What could he do, how could he know what she wanted? To move, they must leave the room. And gathering a quilt about her shoulders, wild-eyed and insistent, she declared they must immediately move into the spare room. "Are you coming or not?"

If he'd gone with her, things might have been different, but how could they have known? Perhaps they didn't care anymore. Robert and Mary Fraser, husband and wife for almost twenty years, Mary with a candle in the doorway and Robert back in bed; the two of them certain now as death and still she went. He let her go without a word, without another chance. He might have joined her if she hadn't spoken with such force, if she hadn't shuffled off like that with the candle, leaving him in darkness. It's not Angus, it couldn't be, it's the wind. There's a fault, Mary, in the design — there's a wind trap where the tower joins the house, or maybe it's the window, there's a space by the corbels. . . But she wouldn't be persuaded.

Feeling his way in the dark, is it possible he followed without knowing what he would say to her? In the hallway, by the glow of her candle, the distorted rectangle of brown light leading into Angus' room where she lay, he could have seen the newel post, the top of the stairs. What was she doing? He wouldn't know if she heard him before she doused the light as he approached. Had she done it to make it easier for them? In any case, Robert lost his nerve and returned to his bed, and as a result, possibly without meaning it, they took to the separate rooms each would die in. . . .

So they awoke this mid-February morning one after the other in separate beds, as they'd done for more than five months. Mary's room (the one she'd set aside for Angus) contained a single bed and dresser, into which she'd gradually moved her clothing, a commode and a hooked rug in bright colours that Annie had made when the boy was six. Feeling neither a stranger nor at home, she'd grown accustomed to objects appearing one after another as they did in wan light; to the empty severity of its walls and her breath like smoke above the coverlet. She also noted the wind had died, so perhaps the storm had finally passed.

It was Mary who found Will Casey. Dressing beneath her nightgown after warming her underclothes within the covers, she was always the first to rise. There was water on the boil and porridge in the pot before Robert and the children appeared in their rumpled and disconsolate parade. She was alone and grateful for these moments before full light. Absorbing warmth as the fire crackled then roared in the grate, she was able to pretend she inhabited a world comfortable as the teapot she poured, a world her childhood might have recognized, an expanding but hopeful place where mystery came not as fear but excitement.

Cupping her hands around a mug of tea, warming them as she drank, Mary Fraser gazed through a frosted pane at the forest black and white with snow. There was a stirring upstairs, her children complaining and Robert's boots on the floor. As she leaned closer to the window, she became conscious of something odd, a blob of unexpected darkness imbedded like a shadow in submerged light. Polishing the glass, she tried to focus on the twisted line of a shoulder and arm, a wool cap, but she couldn't make out what it was. It looked like a man emerging out of that snowdrift. He was leaning on the fence, staring back at her through the window. As it turned out, it was Will Casey, frozen solid, dead as mutton, his face blackened by fire and then by frost.

Dressing hastily, grabbing a heel of bread, Robert wouldn't try to dig him out, not yet, that would come after he'd confirmed what they both knew. "You best come with me." It was to Alice he spoke, not Calum or Mary. "If it's bad and it probably is. . ." He was matter-of-fact, as if a neighbour had merely asked for help with wandered cattle, a horse stuck in a bog. "We won't go too close, eh?" Excited and appalled, trembling like a bobcat, Alice bundled into her clothing.

"Robert. . ." Mary's belly churned like a sackful of eels when she gave him the worn quilt. "His face. . . Would you at least cover his face." Watching them leave, father and daughter with an identical rolling snowshoe gait, hearing them struggle past the window, she turned her attention to the young children, to Helen and Rose, to Calum at the window. There was nothing else she could do.

A flock of snowbirds sprang chittering from the ground, and circling above them, flew in a close-packed bunch to settle among seeds and dead grasses along the far edge of the clearing. Snowshoes hissed and crunched as they strode in pale sunlight. Except for their noise and a light breeze rattling dry branches, the forest remained silent. "If he makes it over the fence... Still and all. Burned like that, it's a miracle he got so far as he did." Neither wanted to think of what they'd find at the end of this familiar path.

"Daddy... Would he of hurt badly?"

"Not the cold. Fire hurts, but not the cold. He soon wouldn't know he was burned anymore."

They encountered his tracks from time to time, untouched, mute in a hollow or beside some frozen rock face, and once they stopped. "In the storm, in the dark and cold," she said, "he must of been so cold. Maybe he didn't know where he was. Maybe he didn't see the house." After the first time they trudged by them as if they didn't see.

After some struggle they arrived at the crest of an enormous frozen wave completely filling the road. As they scrambled stiff-legged down the face of the drift, they startled a band of raucous grosbeaks that darted from tree to tree. It should have been jolly, she thought; how many times had she tumbled and slid like this with Angus, with her friends Katie and Sam. A sudden movement caught her eye, a bounding creature into the bush. By the time she checked her sliding descent, it was gone. Approaching, they found the tracks of a large cat, a panther. The prints were bigger than her father's open hand, and between them was the brushing mark of its tail. "By God, eh?" Robert stared uneasily where the spoor disappeared into the bush. "You know, I never seen one of them before."

It had lain watching after they appeared at the lip with birds exploding about their heads. Maybe it saw them now, its yellow eyes unwavering. Alice shrugged as if trying to convey disinterest to someone other than her father, who in any case wasn't paying attention. Leaving her he'd gone to where the panther had apparently found something. The snow was dark with blood, and as she got closer she recognized the haunch of a horse, Casey's piebald mare. Digging with one of his snowshoes, hacking at blood-frozen snow, red globs of ice, scraping finally with his hands, Robert Fraser uncovered the animal's carved belly and reached inside. "By Jesus Christ!" For they both heard it, a faint mewling. "It's alive. . ."

Since the carcass was pretty well frozen, he had to pry it apart by pressing down with his knee and up with both arms inside. "Can you get her?" Lying flat on the snow, wriggling, Alice manoeuvred carefully, seizing the viscous covers, they were like liver, hauling a bundled infant out the black mouth. She discovered her father too was weeping, his big face made ugly. "Poor little bugger," he whispered over and over again, "poor little bugger."

Undoing his coat, his undercoat and shirt, pulling up his vest, he unwrapped wee Harriet Casey and nestled her against his naked belly (blue with cold she was, and wrinkled as an old sausage). Refastening his clothing, with the child sucking weakly, he set off home so fast it was everything Alice could do to keep him in sight.

All business-like and efficient, Mary took charge. She immersed the tyke in a tepid bath, which turned red with the mare's blood, adding warm water while feeding her sweetened milk and later gruel, all the while soothing in a voice none of them recalled hearing before. Alternately she soaked and towelled, fed and crooned, until Harriet began to cry lustily with pain instead of death, with hunger. "She'll be all right, praise God. I don't like the look of those fingers but she'll be all right."

"His mare must have foundered, you see, in that drift. There was signs, plenty of signs, you mind that, Alice?" Drinking black tea by the stove, Robert struggled with his friend. How desperate it must have been. . . in the storm, with blackened hands, the frantic horse, his terrible face. "And when he couldn't get her free. . ." Killing his mare with a belt knife, carving her open, he'd scooped out a space in her belly.

"Well, he had his head screwed on all right." Chafing

one small arm and then the other. "It kept her warm, didn't it? You can say that for Will Casey. He had his head screwed on." Sunlight on the table and floorboards; a blade of it, sharp and clear across the stove.

"And he almost got here, eh? Poor old. . ."

Calum was back by the window, staring out at Casey beneath the quilt. And the two women, his wife and daughter, they dried the infant, dressing her in the oversize clothing Helen last wore.

Emptying his cup, Robert would go out to where the house was still smoking like as not, the charred timbers of a giant campfire with only the chimney standing, and all of them dead after these years, the whole blessed family. Leaving the remains until they'd frozen, what was left of them, a charnel house of encrusted bones, leaving them until they were hard as anvils, he'd feed the stock and milk the cow. He'd have to do that every day until the drifts packed hard and the road was sure, then he'd drive them back to his own barns.

But first he dug out Casey. By leaving the blanket on and working from behind, he managed to avoid that burned but oddly peaceful face. Maybe Alice was right, maybe he hadn't known? With the look of a man who'd done what he could, so calm, there was nowhere else he wanted to go.

Eventually dragging him on a sledge, his body was frozen almost into the shape of a chair and had to be propped on either side with logs, Robert set off along the track he'd made with Alice. It had been decided they'd keep the kid. Mary was right, she had no kinfolk, not that any of them knew, and he'd work the farm, keep it good for her, a dowry when she came of age.

It was tough going because the sledge, not balanced properly, it dug in hard to the left, but he persisted. He could use the land all right. It was a first-rate farm and all that stock because Casey had some of the best pigs and the machinery. . . .

Descending the drift in such a way as to avoid the piebald mare, he hit a patch of crusted snow, it was almost ice, and the sledge scooted ahead so that Casey almost got away from him. Losing the guide rope, Robert had to lunge, throw himself full length so he caught hold of his friend's booted foot just in time. How had he gotten out, for Chrissakes? How had he got his boots on, and the child? Sweating inside his clothes and cursing, he'd have to pick a grave, more than one, out of the rock-hard earth. But he'd call on others for that, neighbours, maybe even Shantz. Bent as he was, twisted like that, he wouldn't fit a coffin. They'd bury him in a sack without ever knowing what happened, why the others were lost, all of them lost, and yet Casey was fully dressed. . . .

XXIV

Even with the extravagant cost of his mansion, perhaps as a result of its grandeur, its conviction, and despite time lost on the perpetual motion, on futile attempts to track down his mastodon in the States, Robert Fraser prospered. In fact, he'd never been so busy or so inventive. While spring produced several pigeon flocks, it was no windfall. They must have gone elsewhere. But he forgot his disappointment when the watchmaker, Victor Burnel, wrote to explain he'd been advised by a man well-placed in government, an entrepreneur, "a fellah who'd make a bit for himself, to be sure," that Cabinet had decided on a northern route for the Great Trunk Line, so Mad River would get the railway after all.

As a result, with invisible money, cash raised on his farm and Casey's, on his noble house and reputation for wealth — beginning with the Globe Hotel and a fine stone warehouse — Robert went into real estate. At the same time, he found a hard-working simpleton, a Swiss, to work both farms, thus freeing himself to pursue his affairs. Installing him in the old house despite Mary's objections, he set the man's wife, a pudgy and energetic woman the colour and texture of a partially cooked turkey, to making cheese which he sold with great success from the hotel where he began to spend more and more time.

Through his growing friendship with Victor Burnel and the governing party, by the time they announced the railroad and offered tenders, Fraser had already sewn up contracts to supply bridge timbers and track ties for the thirty-eight-mile stretch between Ardvassar and Mad River; while the Globe Hotel, better situated and larger than Jacob Brodie's Queen's Hotel, became *the* railway hotel, and Robert Fraser's future was secure.

At home, apart from an uncommon dryness, and Mary who'd begun to see strange children skipping in the empty yard, things went just as well. The Swiss, whose name was Herman Belcher, was so earnest, so reliable, you'd have thought he owned the farms. And Alice, smart as a whip, took hold of responsibility, recognizing the value of their second farm, as it was now called. It was she who proposed joining the two by hiring a gang to clear a corridor south of the road. Bright-eyed and critical, she employed local girls for the expanding cheese works. Because her father was away so much, she knew he needed an agent, a bookkeeper, and so she became his eyes and ears, his voice and memory too.

Each Monday before he set off for his office in Mad River, she marshalled his employees in the cheese factory. Standing on a chair, his voice ringing, Robert listed his demands and expectations for the week, the orders to be filled — so many rounds of cheese, wagon-loads of timber, of ties. There were fields to be seeded down, others to be weeded, ploughed, stumps to be burned (they'd have to put that off until it rained, would it never rain?), and maybe a shipment of turkeys was expected or a breeding milch cow. There might be a temporary crew coming to clear another half a dozen acres by the road, pigs to be slaughtered or sick beasts that needed tending. And all the while, as he counted off the chores on his fingers, poking his fist in the air to inspire enthusiasm, slapping his thighs and stamping his feet, he kept an eye on Alice who crouched beside him. Smiling at her father, she checked each item from the list she'd prepared and discussed with him the night before.

Swelling with the sombre pleasure of authority, Robert Fraser decided one morning it was time to pay his daughter a salary. Alice accepted the money as her due, knowing that without her all work would grind to a halt. Her father was away until Wednesday supper, and increasingly he'd not return to his family and farms but to the perpetual motion. As his various enterprises fell into place, each with a healthy life of its own, he was possessed by the old hunger, with scarcely time to eat or inquire how their days had gone. On one occasion he mentioned a major contract. "A plum, by crikey! Firewood. We'll have to double the crew, treble it. And do you know why? It'll be Fraser wood. . ." slamming his hand on the table, "Fraser wood that fires the engines, do you hear that, Mary? It'll be *us* that produces steam." Grinning as if he hadn't meant to, as if he were among strangers, leaping to his feet, he retreated through the door and away to his machine.

"I had a dream. . ." Brushing tangles from her mother's fine hair while Mary fed meticulously on leftover bits of carrot, Alice said, "I dreamed we were on the piebald mare, Casey's mare." The two of them, her mother riding backwards, her arms clutching Alice, holding on for the dear life, the mare surging between their thighs while her mother, eyes cavernous, frenzied, her mother's small body pressed against her like a child as they careened down a long brilliant slope, like glass or sand. "The mare must of taken the bit in her teeth, nor could we dismount."

"When Angus was a baby, just a little boy. . ." Delicately chewing, Mary considered the sound of her own voice. "I used to dream that he could speak, even before he opened his eyes. He had teeth, did you know that, dear? Did I tell you that? He was born with teeth?"

"What would he say?"

"I have them still." She gazed towards the window as if to see children skipping, singing in the yard, but it was night and the panes were black. Alice released her mother's hair. "Don't stop, dear. . ."

"Can you remember what he said?"

"Oh yes, it's as if I still hear him." Closing her eyes when the brushing resumed, leaning back, she sighed happily. "Would you like me to get them?"

"I've seen them, Mother."

"I still have them, you know."

"You've shown them to me."

"He didn't like your father," she said because Alice had stopped brushing again. "Even then, even when he was born, he didn't like your father. He told me." For the moment forgetting to eat, Mary appeared quite pleased with herself. "You know," she said, her voice languorous with sleep, "he hated him, he always hated him."

There was a second dream, one she'd not tell her mother, indeed she'd forget it herself if she could: Barbara Casey with her children in no room Alice had seen before. Sam and Katie, young Tom, all the others, even Harriet — they were aging as she fed them, cruelly insisting, although they weren't hungry. Nobody was hungry, yet her red hands continued chopping and cutting. Alice couldn't make it out. What was it she apportioned and served? Then, as if Barbara was her own mother, Alice was eating something appalling, stuffing in something gristly, clammy as old porridge. Yet it wasn't her body protesting, joining in with the groaning sighs, the weeping; and then Missus Casey had another bruise. "Will done it. It was Will!" On her left cheekbone this time, and ugly it was, brutal like bad meat. And as Alice watched, there came another; it blossomed on her forehead with blood like flames from her nose and mouth.

Young as she was, standing no hanky-panky from her men, she got rid of one young set-me-up just for blowing her a kiss. "That's it," she said without a second look, "you're finished!" And he was, limping off with Fanny Belcher's gargling laughter, a delighted conspirator. "You run into trouble with any one of that lot, just anything at all, and you come to Fanny, you hear? To my old man and me. We'll soon have his trousers hanging on the line."

Her mother drifted like fly ash through days and nights, while her father was either in Mad River or his workshop, no longer pretending, the two of them useless. And so Alice took it upon herself to see that Rose and Helen (both of whom tiptoed in the shadow of their mother's gentle madness as if Robert was the sun), that her sisters and Calum pulled together, taking turns preparing meals and doing chores, with wee Harriet (who never slept), and working in the fields, with the geese and turkeys. . . . By God, she did take hold! There wasn't a one that knew them didn't remark on it. "A jewel all right. Poor thing."

Through all of this, young Calum, clear as a pool, he showed every sign of a bright young man who'd go far. A crackerjack at sums but abstracted, he'd argue the leg off an iron pot if he wasn't stuck into some book or other. A doctor perhaps, a lawyer. And so in a lucid moment Robert Fraser decided to move him in with the Birdwoods, his grandparents, so the boy could attend the Mad River School.

Soon after that, in one of his weekly letters to Victor Burnel, written to explore the progress of some deal or other — the shipment of meat or skins, the feasibility of mangle-wurzles in this neck of the woods, or the present market for ironwood staves, for woven baskets (fashioned by natives!) — towards the end of his letter, after assuring his friend he would indeed consider standing for the Parliament, he permitted himself to ask where Calum might board the next year in Toronto. A decent house, so he could attend a decent school — Jarvis, for example, maybe Upper Canada College. Did Victor have any ideas on that? Of course he did. The reply came by return mail. The boy was welcome to stay with him, yes, he was. They had a small room off the kitchen, and Missus Burnel, not having children of her own, she'd be delighted. Writing at great length, Burnel insisted a boy would do better at Jarvis, that Upper Canada College might be all right for snivelly-nosed toffs and bed-wetters, but a country boy like Fraser's Calum, a young man of the people, he'd have to earn his profession by hard work, by patience. "There's no better place than Jarvis for a young fellah that knows the value of work and loathes privilege. You must believe me, dear friend, I know what I'm saying. The world is changing, and withal, a child's brain is a complicated bit of biological machinery that needs precise and enlightened attention." The Burnels would be honoured to keep an eye on Calum as they would have on one of their own. Indeed Robert and his missus could remain confident the boy's character, intellect, his sense of decency and manners would all be attended to in a thoroughly rational and modern fashion.

Shutting up like a clam, his face dark and elusive, the boy was filled with rage. He was not yet accustomed to his grandparents' house, to the distant life that had brought him there, and he began to feel like a filly trained for the races, a prize hen or pig being fed for show.

After constructing his most persuasive case and making numerous drafts, Robert answered Burnel, describing not only his own delight but his conversations with Calum — how the boy's face had glowed, his young spirit leaping at the opportunity afforded him by Victor's astonishing kindness. The boy not only welcomed this golden chance, but the responsibility, the sense of dedication he must maintain and nurture if he wasn't to betray Victor Burnel's generosity. There were good people willing to put themselves out for the boy, and the Burnels were good people, none better. The mister was a brilliant man, that's what Fraser had said, and he made certain Calum understood it. He made him swear he'd dedicate his best efforts to be the rational young man one had to be to get ahead in the world of progress through education.

And then immediately, almost as a reward, he described each detail of his experiments with Perpetual Motion. He had much to report, nothing less than a breakthrough, and Victor was first to get the news — he'd found the key! Yes, he had. Given the appropriate astronomical configurations, his machine would almost certainly work.

But first he had to set the stage, reveal the nature of his rejuvenating centre, his orrery. Directing Burnel's mind back to that evening thirteen years before when the two of them, with Rochefoucault Hackett in the Frozen Ocean, with Prof. Carruthers and Dr. Tom, they'd all discussed the sublime machinery of the heavens (as Victor himself had described it, did he recall?), the precision of planets, the relentless probity of constellations, the sun, our moon, in their constant scrupulous workings. He reminded his friend how he'd revealed to Robert Fraser the simple yet essential truth that scientific exactness and mechanical time are inseparable. For every tick, a tock. God the Great Watchmaker, the banausic heavens, Hevelius and Galileo, Orffyreus and Huygens! Opening a whole world as it did, this discovery made his creation possible. For what, after all, is Perpetual Motion but that seen in our own solar system, the planets themselves, our moon, our earth, its tides and currents? That's the key, the redemptive centre. It came to him all in a rush, don't you see, an inspiration. Did that ever happen to Victor?

As if the Demiurge had breathed on his forehead, as if a door somewhere had opened to him, Fraser knew he must construct a giant orrery, an inspired model of the solar system with the eight planets exact in their relative sizes and weights, positioned around the sun in such a way that when set in motion by him everything would move in miniature grandeur, their orbits mirrors of the originals.

In letter after letter, craftily inserting questions about the nature and timing of Calum's removal to Toronto, the procedures for enrolment at Jarvis, for example, the conditions under which the boy would move into Burnel's house, bravely listing the books and pamphlets he'd read, the libraries he'd visited (some as far as Detroit, even Chicago), the experts he'd consulted, he celebrated his machine, its organization of elemental powers, its hunger made manifest in a consuming motion that must race through all the ages. But more than that, he cheerfully confessed to almost fifteen years of failure, culminating in the crushing discovery, in '74 it was, almost five years ago, that his orrery — and it was a beautiful piece of work, make no mistake! — even *his* orrery had failed to do the trick. "Ah, my friend, it hadn't come easily, not a bit of it."

Introducing frustration and despair, as if they were old friends, he revealed his wife was no help while his neighbours thought him mad. Indeed it must have been the Lord Himself who sustained him because he'd rededicated his efforts, he'd persisted, yes he had. Hard work may have bitter roots but its fruits are sweet. There's no substitute for faith. Wasn't it Hannibal who said, "I'll find a way or make one?" And yet. . .

As if dreamed by someone else, his face shining with a strange yellowness or hard as bone, sometimes belligerent with hope but most often empty, desolate, a figure distant now as his father, and strange, a stranger with his own blood, how could Robert possibly convey to Victor Burnel what he hardly remembered?

And yet, causing that great brass sun to tremble, the planets to shimmer in eerie light, the waterwheel thumps and clacks as it has for more than fifteen years. If in failure it has sustained him in the kind of illness that's been his life, what will it do in triumph? Sometimes, usually at night, with his heart pounding as if it might escape its cage of bones, he encounters his father, old Calum. Like drifting snow or sand, he sighs in Robert's throat and whispers.

Try as he might, proferring his success at business, the increasing potential of Alice and Calum, the fine brick house — "Look at my house!" — the land cleared and productive, his employees, and his perpetual motion. . . still he must battle this ruinous spook.

Is it any wonder he grew more and more remote? If anyone chanced upon him at these moments, his children maybe, or Belcher, they'd quickly withdraw, to peer through chinks in the wall, through dirty windowpanes, even down at him from among the rafters high above his head. Observing him stalk the rooms filled with machinery, hunkering down as they might at a spectacle, a camp meeting, they'd keep an eye out for Alice. Lean and dark, always on the verge of outrage, she'd harangue them back to work in a flash.

None of them could know Robert was struggling through to a particular Lord's Day in October, that season of bolides, harsh winds and aphelions, of apogees and clustering darkness, a unique and compelling Sunday, a time of meteorological tensions when the Heavens — according to his calculations and the Farmer's Almanac — the Heavens themselves would fall into an appropriate configuration whereby his machine would most certainly triumph so that man's life and labour on earth would be utterly transformed.

Eventually, in his last letter to Victor Burnel, written on the seventh of September with a terrible fire burning off to the north, he invited him to attend the Great Moment, the Demonstration, and came round to describe that astonishing day in April when after thirty-six or forty months of vacuity and helplessness in the face of his orrery's failure, the growing conviction his goddamn machine was a fraud anyway, a poisoned chalice, on that morning of April eleven, Robert Fraser on an impulse sprang up from the corner where he'd been sitting. The ancient bone, lying on a table beneath his hovering planets, he would insert that bone into his solar system. Feverishly correcting the balance and timing, he discovered there was only one place it could go, a swooping elliptical path that carried it between Saturn and Jupiter, then far out to the extremes of the room. Its yellow-grey form dryly spinning as it paused before drifting back, its sinuous egg-shaped flight imparted such a harmony to his vision, a wholeness, a certainty he hadn't even imagined, that Robert Fraser was reduced to tears.

Alice, who had been inspecting milk cans in the dairy when her father engaged the main gear to the waterwheel, recognized its caterwauling scream. Startled and thrilled, she darted into the yard. While Mary, searching through cupboards on the third floor, when she heard the shuddering groan as brutal cogs bit one into another, she closed her eyes, rested her face on her arms, and waited without hope or expectation.

The great wheel seized in cascading water as the workshop heaved, wrenching against itself. Countless smaller wheels joined in the din. Levers and shuttlecocks, weights and counterweights protested as energy tore through the system, breaking in a violent sequence as the immense and beautiful machinery settled into driving motion. Even those who'd never heard it before or those too young to remember — Helen and Rose, dragging wee Harriet like a rag doll — they joined Alice and the Belchers, men loping in through the woods and others from the fields. "By God, the old man's machine! He's started her up!" The word spread like wildfire. He'd disengaged as soon as she accelerated to that point where her internal motion matched the external, that of the wheel in water, so that most of them only got to see her winding down; but still and all, is that it then? "By Jesus, she's off and running. Look!" But it wasn't, he wasn't ready; its rumbling thunder collapsed to a hum, then to a clatter.

Alice, standing ready by the door, she forgot about the work at hand. Right away she detected a new, authoritative sound in the machine's workings.

With water surging in the race, she longed to creep once more among the slopes and risers, to slither in and see her father running from gear to plunger, from wheel to wheel, crouching, listening, then darting moth-like to repeat the process.

With hair spiking out above his ears, he made automatic measurements and lightning adjustments in response to the warnings, the signals. "You see, you see," it cried, "here is the key. No, here!" As if wakened from a long sleep, resisting lifelessness, in vain did it strive to divert him from his plan, in vain did it protest; and so inevitably returned to stillness, once more entrapped, it could only brood accusingly, threaten him with sullen purpose.

Convinced he wouldn't soon set the beast in motion again, Mary approached the window, peeking between the frame and velvet curtains to watch Alice whose hands were claws, her gestures peevish. Waving the others back to work, sure as a weasel, she vanished behind the workshop. Whereupon Mary spat angrily on her hands. Who are these people? she brooded. Sadly neglected, with only a hint of their original force, the wind machines stirred below her in the empty yard.

It scarcely rained but twice or three times that summer, and while spring had been good and wet after the giant snows of February and March, the dryness of summer, the sun's dead heat, soon baked the earth hard as bone. With tempers flaring, nobody could remember a year like it. Simple disputes became litigation. Men fought brutally over fencelines, uncertain debts and promises. There was one slaughtered his whole family, then hanged himself in his barn beyond Mad River. And desolate women methodically beat their children as huge dry storms with wind and thunderclouds swept over them from the south — storms with little rain but lightning, and with the lightning came fire.

On a dozen occasions Alice had to release her crews, deploy them with others. Tom Bullock and Eddie Shantz, friends and strangers from town, old man Fletcher and his boys — they were all out because a blaze threatened the road and bridges or maybe the Bullock place, a homestead here or an inn there. And once for several days it seemed Mad River itself would be consumed. Cutting and slashing, no sooner did they turn one blaze in upon itself than another sprang up, and another, until it seemed all work must cease while crops withered on stalk and vine, and the parched fields turning silver blew away like mist.

Robert Fraser worried himself sick over the descending

water level in his pond. Whether driving his buckboard through screens of smoke so thick he sometimes had to hold a wet kerchief to his nose and mouth, or staring into the vast night sky as if to memorize its magic tapestry, imagine how it would arrange itself for the Great Event, and what esoteric signals and meteors must appear in a night grown even more labyrinthine, luminous with the destruction of distant suns, he became increasingly obsessed by that stagnant shrinking pool, by the weakening flow in his sluice. Reduced to a trickle that scarcely budged the great wheel, it would soon cease altogether.

"Forget the fires!" As if it were his daughter's fault, insisting they wouldn't burn this year, he tried to keep the crews at home. Jeering and cursing at the old man, shying imaginary clods of earth at his back — as many among them had done to Angus in that year of the wild pigeons — scornful of his decline, the failure of his dream, they limped out of the yard to fight some fire or other. Glaring after the men with sweat on his bulging forehead, Robert opened his mouth as if to speak. Prodding her father, tickling the poor creature, Alice promised him a conduit, anything! they'd bring water in from a spring. . . .

Capering excitedly in the doorway he cried, "That's it! The very thing." He slapped his palms against his chest until she said it again, a conduit, but he must stop this fuss, get back inside where he belongs. Anyway, surely it would rain?

Once, slipping from the house after supper to poke along a circuitous path to the lake until silence enveloped her, no longer hearing men's voices, almost skipping at last, breathless and exuberant, impudent as a rabbit, Alice darted from the track. An enormous boulder, its surface scabbed with lichen and moss, its reflection trembled in a brown pool where the forest grew tangled and dense. Crawling the last little way on her belly, Alice expected to see, what? Forest birds gathered by the spring, a wood thrush, perhaps something larger, a fox or deer maybe, for she came upwind and it was cooler here, already dim with secretive light. A red squirrel chittered angrily as she passed. Small creatures spread out from her like ripples on the surface of disturbed water.

She might have been eight or nine again, with Angus somewhere, the two of them dark as otters and just as quick. Was it Angus she'd find? So cautious now she scarcely seemed to move, she inched towards the last veil, the tangled curtain behind which the pool and its boulder had been waiting. Even here the forest floor was shrivelled and dry to her touch, the shadows warped and menacing.

At the verge of the clearing, she parted dry foliage like a curtain and smelled the unmistakable odour of tomcat or mink, that dangerous musk. It caught in her throat and at that instant there came an explosive leaping crash that blinded her. Convinced it was someone, some stranger or even worse, Alice stared wildly at the forest. Impenetrable, it clustered on every side about the pool, the boulder scaled with lichen and its reflection. "Who is it?" she called and from somewhere far off an empty breeze shivered the leaves and branches about her head.

XXV

Towards the end of September with cattle beasts panting in the fields, with fish rotting in blighted streams, the air was so thick with dust and soot, with the burned smell of charcoal, that on blowing their noses folk discovered black smudges in their kerchiefs and their phlegm was grey. No longer distracted by the wanton glow beyond the forest at night, nor the swift and violent storms bursting over them with mocking thunder, prey now to strange fevers and ague, the workmen bickered among themselves, every man jack of them ready for trouble. They'd not signed on for this! The blasted fires and some wee girl as a boss.

Alice bombarded them with questions, with contradictory observations, in the hope of diverting them, of forestalling violence. She promised a cask of whiskey when the work was done, and set them to cutting basswood logs for her father's conduit. Brusque yet appealing, her authoritative manner tempered by cunning, she feared they'd lose all they had gained in the three years since the Great Pigeon Hunt. Going among them where they loitered in the yard early one morning (already hot as noon in August), she saw how strange they'd grown, strangers with red eyes and sooty faces. Instructing Herman Belcher to slaughter a plump and tender ewe, she clasped her arms over her breasts as they approached, grown men like that, drawing so close about her, and most would give her a bit of hard for a bit of soft; and she'd treat them different after that, she would so. Clasping her breasts, explaining they'd roast the ewe, and if the work went well, what with the whiskey they'd have something of a ceilidh, a party with the dairy girls. And while she might suspect as much, she'd never know they'd crawled all over her in their beds at night. Or seeing her stoop, the heft of her thigh, her flank beneath that cotton skirt, they'd touched her, some of them here and others there, to open her body. By Jesus, they'd give it to her good!

But there must have been one, surely there was one that thought he loved her? Certainly not Herb Spilker or lupine Henry Munn, not the Negro, Sam White, not Gibby Bowes with his famous sneeze. None of the foreigners either. Deferential, even flattering, tipping their hats or looking the other way, whether afraid of Fanny Belcher or that crazy father, perhaps confused by the girl's desperate resolve and hunter's eyes, the fact is if they thought of her at all, any of them except Tom Gilpin, if once they got her over the garter or into a hot corner, that would be the end of it. But not Tom. A scrawny boy who'd end up teaching school, he knew how they talked among themselves after supper, stretching as they did and smoking, feeling the day's work ponderous in their bodies. Greedy, they'd try to figure if any of them had got into her, if Herb Spilker, sneaking off like that with his hair slicked back, was he after his greens with the boss, eh? But he wouldn't tell. "Hah!" he chuckled in a contented fashion while hitching up his trousers, "I'll never tell." And even though they knew it wasn't him, it wasn't Spilker, it had to be someone.

"Big conk, big cunt," wheezed Gibby Bowes, causing the men to nod wisely, for that was true all right, you could be sure of that. It was certain as death with a beak like hers, by Jesus, she'd a nose on her. He better take care, though, whoever he is. He'll find himself married to the devil's daughter and living with the old folks. "Heugh," they laughed, "heugh-heugh."

But it was Tom Gilpin that acted. He shadowed her and not a one of them knew it. Night after night, sometimes just after dawn, well-scrubbed in a clean shirt, he was a prig, saving it all for some Lisa, so they never suspected it was young Gilpin. On the pretext of checking his snares and deadfalls — more often than not he brought back rabbits too — he didn't seem the type, not at all, to harbour dangerous thoughts like that and cruel ambitions.

Pausing by the shed, pretending not to see her cross the yard, he knows each tree, from which particular limb he can stare right into her bedroom at night. And close on her trail — is it this that keeps him going? Early one morning, tiptoeing to the far edge of the lake where nobody goes, he's missed her slipping into the water, but there she is! Her hair collected in a red kerchief, with shoulders whiter than her forearms, white and so smooth, she swims with the languid motion of a frog. And a pair of loons, their sharp, their serpentine necks; one, then the other, dipping their heads beneath the surface. He's manoeuvred into the best position to see her emerge, to feast upon her stripping the water from her body, and her breasts so full, with small pink nipples, her belly, that wispy bush between her legs. . . . Flushed and staring, it's all he can do not to groan aloud. She's drifting out of sight, just her head now and its reflection drifting beyond the beaver lodge. Where's she going?

Sometimes when he appeared with an armful of rabbits, their peeled and muscular bodies, Alice wondered what it was made him tremble so, and why, among them all, it was only Gilpin never met her eyes. Did he fancy her? If he did, she'd get rid of him double-quick, she wouldn't stand for that. There were lots, God knows, who needed his job.

Week by week, becoming more precise and demanding, as if to spite the men, Alice Fraser took to concealing her body. Even in that great heat, the dead heat of a blast furnace, she was wrapped in cotton shawls with skirts like bedspreads and her hair drawn tight beneath a red kerchief. Sweating like a pig and angry, she longed to get her hands on the warehouse, the Globe Hotel, to make them work as well as the farms, to take control. She had other plans, glorious and impossible dreams, lots of them! And more than that, gloomy and menacing as it sometimes seemed, she had Time. Time was her ally and her goad.

Too much was happening in that year of spectres. Measuring each gesture and expression, she protected herself as best she could with her youth, gathering from small but avaricious victories an authority and wisdom, an indifference to the molten sky and dun-coloured earth. Even so, her administration of that complex and fatal enterprise had begun to sap her strength.

"Do you believe the end of the world is coming?" Soft as down, her mother's voice had taken on that pellucid colour of air in unused rooms, of water in a vase. "Angus says. . ." Opening her purple scarf to reveal the fresh carcass of a bird, its grey-blue head and absurd red legs. "He brought me this," she marvelled. "It's only one eye, you see? Would you look at that?" And sure enough, the other was puckered up like a dried clam. "It's dead." She didn't seem concerned, but still and all, smoothing the feathers like a rainbow fading at its throat, adjusting the wings, she asked in a puzzled but encouraging tone; "Where are the others?" She smiled gently. "I haven't seen so many this year."

"It's the heat, Mother. There's no water."

"He says they've all gone away to South America." Blinking slowly, she was still a pretty woman and not old, not more than forty-one or two, but subject to visions, a translucent woman and so soft now, like a slender mushroom sprouting in that inexpressible moment when dusk becomes black night. "You can scarcely blame them." Enfolding the corpse, she said it again. "You can scarcely blame them, can you?"

Robert contemplated the panorama of cleared land from its highest point, the knoll behind his house, his land. It resembled a sea frozen with the memory of storms, an abandoned and violent bed, a boulder scabbed with lichen. Marking off each week, reckoning each hour that fell before the Event, he was lost in contemplation of an increasingly desperate future, of menace and collapse unfolding in the Void like a tapestry. Waking sometimes in tears, Robert Fraser in his own body, in the texture of his flesh and spirit, where spirit inhabits flesh he's encountered death, old Mr. Grim himself. Still, he tinkered, doing whatever he must to clear his mind and focus his powers, imagining his machine in full flight, imperfect as it was.

Almost cherishing this insistent mortality in which there's nothing but dread, approaching young Harriet Casey perhaps, a toddler now, she flees screaming from the noise of his feet, as if he's been somewhere and taken something. And then soothing her as he has his own children, Angus and Calum, Alice — who treats him now like an amiable fool, a simpleton — crooning into the child's accusing silence, he sees again they're on their way to death, like Angus, the Caseys, all of them in a raggle-taggle procession. But what storms there will be. Oh Jesus! What murderous storms.

As the Day approached, during those baked twilight evenings of September and then October, with lightning and thunder beyond the trees, wearing his best suit every day, Robert might be seen through the windows of his workshop, checking and re-checking each component of his machine. Or else he'd retreat to an unlikely corner where, resembling some creature in a zoo, he'd perch on a strut beneath the eaves or curl himself up and scarcely ever come out at all.

And so it was by the time the third week in October arrived, most of them — the lumbermen and dairy girls, the Belchers, even his own family — had pretty well forgotten Fraser and his dream. It was as if he wasn't there.

In the last week of October, on a Saturday before the dark of the moon, there came a distant, metallic thrumming, a huzzah-hurrah, singing, whistling, drumming and shouting — a parade announcing its arrival from at least a mile and a half away.

They gathered there in the yard, the whole kit-and-kaboodle, to walk about dizzy with heat, rubbing their eyes to clear them of smoke and soot, and there wasn't a one — not Alice, not Mary, certainly not poor stupid Herman Belcher — not a one of them guessed it was Robert Fraser and his perpetual motion that brought them all the way from Mad River, from Ardvassar, and some from Toronto. They'd come from everywhere, a raucous and festive crowd, pilgrims to some holy place.

As soon as he identified the whistles, the fifes and drums, Robert knew it was an audience on the march, an unwelcome one at that. Didn't he have enough? Groaning "Enough!" and bursting from his sheds like a bull from its chute, he'd send them back. "No!" Bellowing in the road, he waved his arms at Jacob Brodie leading the procession with a partially roasted ox. "Go back, go back. . ."

But his voice was lost in a great shout celebrating his appearance; whereupon, like a drunk falling downstairs, the band rattled off an enthusiastic, if almost unrecognizable Yankee Doodle. Men fired guns into the air, thus causing a team to bolt in terror, then the whole terrible crew surged past Robert Fraser and into his yard.

"By Jesus, Robbie, I tried to keep them away." It was Victor Burnel, leaving the mob, his wan saturnine body. "I truly did, but you understand my meaning? It's too big a thing you've got here, too big a thing entirely." His face earnest, appealing, because he knew it was a private invitation, of course he did. There was only supposed to be a small group, dedicated men, the elite, for Chrissakes, mechanicians all. "But somehow the word got out," he later tried to explain, with the hullabaloo outside, the rich aroma of roasting ox and music, the wild noise of fiddles and laughter bursting in upon them, the select few who stood in the shadow of his machine.

"It was Hackett maybe, was it?"

"Not at all, not at all." Furiously rubbing the extravagant lump beneath his skull cap, peering from small wet eyes, Rochefoucault Hackett turned his plump face from one to the other. It wasn't him. "Good Lord, no! It could have been anyone. The Frozen Ocean, it was full of it, don't you know, of drunken talk, of enthusiasm. I'm telling you, Robbie. . ."

"But couldn't you. . ." Confounded, clenching his fists, Robert asked why they didn't forbid it. "Couldn't you have stopped them?"

"If my aunt," snorted Burnel, "if my aunt had been my uncle, she'd of had a pair of balls under her arse, eh?" And they all agreed there was no dissuading men that had sniffed the smell of progress, the elixir of growth. "And that's what brought them here today, my friend."

Gesticulating with long arms, soothing his host for fear the man might do something rash, Victor Burnel didn't want to see Fraser run amok as he did after the hanging, and so he asked to see the machine. "It looks like a fine piece of work all right. Will you show it to us?"

"You should be pleased," whispered Rochefoucault Hackett. "You should be proud."

"And the centre, your rejuvenating core. . ." Shuffling slightly, his child's body perhaps more stooped and his voice like cigar ash, Prof. Carruthers spoke for the first time. Gazing enviously, reaching to touch this component or that, he wanted to know about the orrery. "Does it really work?" Pointing, he wanted to see it, raising his little hand, imperious so they all stared at Robert, at the bolted doors. "Is it there?"

He expected an answer, an invitation to enter, to view that giant orrery they'd heard so much about, but Robert wasn't listening. With his head hung low, he cracked and pulled each knuckle vigorously, then reversed his grip and began again. If he'd been a smaller man or less inclined to violence, if he'd not been on his own turf, the three men — Carruthers, Burnel and Hackett — they might have insisted.

But as it was, revolving about him in a slow dance, they meandered together as Robert limped around his machinery in silent thought.

Beyond the forest, day began to depart, subside in a welter of clouds, so that it was only in a certain dun-coloured tinge, a jaundiced glow, that sunset briefly appeared. And then it was gone.

Lounging in the reflection of cooking fires outside, smoking listlessly, they knew Robert, despite his fear and hatred of that crowd, had to proceed with his experiment or lose a year. It might be two or three before the Heavens aligned themselves like this, trembled with such astronomical tensions, such wild and harmonic configurations. "Besides," as Burnel gently wheedled, "it's only natural. Once they see, ordinary folk like that, once they've seen it works. . . What strange intoxications befall us as we rush with unprecedented speed into our restless and striving future? The masses applaud. They must applaud the victory of our dynamics, the triumph of Mind. . ."

"Yes, yes," cried Hackett from a pile of empty grain sacks near the abandoned Wheel of Orffyreus, "many mysteries are being solved, and will be solved, through the magic of science." The Intelligence of Man. That was the point all right.

It was finally dark and they'd begun to repeat themselves. Shadows rustled crazily as if filled with insects or small animals. Slapping hands against their thighs and grunting, they rose because the matter was settled. Anyway, not a one of them yet had got a drink.

Soothing and reassuring Fraser the best they could, they propelled him into the yard. "Hurrah!" They led the crowd in another roar of welcome. "Hurrah! Hurrah!" And what a festive scene it was.

Robert Fraser refused all offers of food and drink, casting off those who pummelled him on the shoulders. And yet as the hours passed, he became strangely animated.

Light shone in his eyes with a rare brilliance, with a kind of cunning, as he watched the dancers and heard the music. Glancing at curious lights in the sky and nodding, sometimes chuckling to himself, smoking pipe after pipe, he seemed content, maybe a bit tense, and why not? It's his big day. Tomorrow's his big day. And if the machine, if his blasted machine don't work with this crowd and all, what an arse-hole crawler he'll look then, eh?

"Hah!" they guffawed. "By Jesus, wouldn't that be something, if the sucker doesn't run?" Throwing themselves back into the festivities, hooting with abandon, wicked with anticipation, some danced with other men's wives and girls such as Alice Fraser, their lithe young bodies wriggling like lizards, arms and shoulders bare. It was something all right, the way they carried on, and some you wouldn't expect it of either. So decent folk withdrew to their own fires where wrapped in indigo coverlets, they turned their backs on the revellers, muttering among themselves. While high above, filled with wheeling constellations, with showers of Bengal fire, gracefully arranging itself, the black night settled upon them. Overcome with drowsiness, the dancers withdrew. The fires subsided and one by one folk succumbed to the dead matter of darkness among the stars, to a restless sleep filled with eccentric dreams.

Up and out before dawn, with a band of ochre light to the east, Robert had to pick his way among bodies still caught by sleep in the yard. Men and women snored with the half-open mouths of idiots, grinding their teeth, protesting, most of them strangers reliving some miserable and private detail or drained by the wilted fury of that endless summer, with their eyes rolled back as in death. Self-mocking yet vicious, they'd come not to marvel or celebrate but to gloat at his wanton, his failed ambition. Even his friends. . . .

Rising bright and clear, the sun promised a perfect day. The storms that had been charging upon them all summer had withdrawn, leaving the air limpid, almost tactile; so the first clunk of machinery, the straining whine as cogs engaged, as wheels and levers, weights, plungers and pulleys groaned into motion, these first sounds were muffled, as if originating underwater, scarcely troubling the sleepers. But then, almost immediately, there was a caterwauling scream, a stuttering howl that had them all on their feet and shouting, such pandemonium! Briefly caught in surging water, the Great Wheel seized, trembling violently, causing the whole ramshackle building to heave, to writhe upon its foundation.

Half awake, barging through the crowd, came Victor Burnel, barefoot, with nightgown flapping over his trousers. "Robert!" But the door was barricaded and the windows sealed with feed sacks from within. "Robert," he roared against that terrible noise, "for God's sake, man. . ."

As countless smaller wheels, levers and shuttlecocks, weights and counterweights, joined in the din, as power from the mill stream charged through the system, a violent and primal sequence took hold, so the shuddering clatter, the wrenching tremor, flared up with such fury that folk stumbled back in alarm. "Look out!" By Jesus, "Will it hold?"

Apocalyptic, the whole blasted thing looked ready to explode. Convulsing like a sackful of drowning cats, throwing stray boards off its roof, it chased most of them from the yard in clouds of dust from the parched and quaking earth. "Holy shit," wailed Rochefoucault Hackett. There were shouts of glee. Could it be true? It seemed about to leap right off the bloody ground, maybe scream away like a sky rocket. But no. Weathering its crisis, apparently bursting beyond entropy, it subsided. The terrible clatter faded to a roar, then a smooth and comfortable hum. . . .

Still, there was no sign of Robert Fraser. Victor Burnel, Rochefoucault Hackett, Alice, even Agatha Bullock — they all tried to bring him out with ratta-tatta-tat, with flattery and discreet requests. "Robbie?" He's got to be in there, eh? Calling his name louder, bellowing "Robbie," with complete strangers joining in chorus. Had something gone wrong? Should they break a window? Some were all for it, but Dr. Tom intercepted. "I'm telling you, boys. . ." Baring his yellow teeth, he appeared even smaller with age inside his suit. "It's not me that'll stick my head in there if he doesn't want it. He'll rip the face off anyone comes after him, I'm telling you. . ."

"Yes," they agreed, "there's that to it. Hmmn." And since there was nothing to be done, they collected in groups, smoking, skittish as ponies as they waited for the next instalment. For Prof. Carruthers had explained, "He's got to disengage from the waterwheel, don't you see? That's the crux of it."

Without hesitation or variety, methodical and disciplined, it went on and on. As a result, by mid-morning some in the crowd were getting impatient. Practical fellows, they muttered "What next?" and "Is that all, for Chrissakes?" Surly buggers, they infected their fellows.

Just before noon there was a group preparing to leave when Tom Sanderson declared the wheel was going faster. "Is it going faster?" Sure it was. And true enough, apparently gaining speed, they could *see* it accelerating. "That's it, dear blessed Jesus!" Incredulous, surging forward, cheek by jowl they shouted as the wheel turned, *driving* the water now, forcing it faster and faster through the sluice in an awesome surge, a torrent. "It's like to empty the goddamn pond!" And then, disengaged by Fraser, it was spinning free, the Great Wheel revolving like a propeller winding down, dethroned at last. But, not the machine itself. "Would you listen to. . . Oh! Oh!" The perpetual motion, that immense and beautiful machinery, they couldn't stand it, how could they stand it?

Just when their frenzy reached its peak, just when it appeared there was to be no release, no fulfilment, they'd stand in awe until it was finally time to drag themselves away, re-enter a world forever changed, just at this moment, Robert Fraser appeared in his doorway. Begrimed, covered with dust, he was welcomed by a mighty roar. Dazed, burning in ecstasy, he tottered into the arms of a weeping Alice as the band struck up and the whole forest resounded with cheers, with whistling shouts and the bark of guns.

Victor Burnel, Carruthers, Ches Hackett and Robert's neighbours, even complete strangers, they all struggled to get at him, to shake his hand and shout their names in his ear. So deafened were they by their own voices, by the prospect of fame and the mechanism's banausic roar, there wasn't a one heard deep in its bowels the rending crack, its primal fury, as the machine, appearing for an instant to gather in upon itself, exploded in every direction. Shards and pieces, cogs and shattered metal, the brass sun, the earth, its moon and all the planets — everything burst free, tearing through the walls and roof, carrying great chunks of the building as it flew among screaming people. Retreating in panic, some were struck down. And the Great Wheel, finally cast from its axle like an enormous and brutal hoop, it crushed fences and carommed through the barnyard like a whirlwind. Bounding once, springing into the air, it struck the driveshed a devastating blow, then crashing into the forest it vanished from sight.

Returning as if after a long illness, wrapped in a coverlet despite the heat, Robert Fraser sipped at a mug of broth while surveying his smouldering ruin. Such desolation! Like the embers of a giant campfire, with even the old red willow shattered, scorched as if struck by lightning.

Convinced he knew the problem, that he'd do better next time, Robert would have to make it stronger, that was clear enough, but it worked, the damned great lovely thing! Gathering his family about him — or what was left because Alice had gone with Calum to Mad River since the hotel wanted a capable woman's touch — he seized them with his voice and eyes. He explained, "There are ten metal balls out there," gesturing vaguely with his free arm. "And we're going to find them, eh?" He smiled with such resolve they dared not disagree. "And the bone, the ancient bone!" Laughing like a boy again, he lurched to his feet. "Whoever finds the most gets time without chores. Hah. . ." And thus began a desolate search that would last for the rest of his life because, try as he might — and, Jesus, didn't he do the best he could? — all they ever found was the moon.

About the Author

Graeme Gibson was born in London, Ontario, in 1934 and grew up in various Ontario locations as well as spending a year each in Halifax, Fredericton and Australia.

Since leaving the University of Western Ontario, he has lived in England, France, Scotland and Mexico, spent most of the 1970s on a farm in rural Ontario, and now lives in Toronto with writer Margaret Atwood and their daughter Jess.

He has two grown sons, Matthew and Graeme, from a first marriage.

Active in cultural politics since the early 1970s, he was instrumental in the formation of the Writers' Union of Canada and was its chairman in 1974-75. In 1978 he was the first participant in the Scottish/Canadian writers' exchange. He is presently writer-in-residence at the University of Waterloo.